Mabel
the lovelorn
Dwarf

For my parents
Jake & Barb

ACKNOWLEDGEMENTS

When Mabel entered my life nine years ago, I never imagined the journey we would take together and the numerous people who would join us on this adventure.

Jeanne Cavelos, fearless leader of the Odyssey Writing Workshop. If you hadn't mentioned there weren't any good stories about female dwarves, Mabel never would have come to be. And thank you to my Odyssey '05 class, Mike DeLuca, Daniel Akselrod, Brian Hiebert, Jeff Howell, Shara White, Michele Korri, Erin Hoffman, Scott H. Andrews, Jason Ridler, Justin Howe, Cathy Purdue, Jennifer Brinn, Maggie Della Rocca, Susan Sielinski, Susan Abel Sullivan, and Kate Marshall, for encouraging me to pursue this foolishness.

My Seton Hill Triumvirate, Betsy Whitt and Matt Donahue for your support, encouragement, and friendship.

My Seton Hill classmates, in particular Erica

McEachern, Calie Voorhis, Nu Yang, Aubrey Gross, and Traci Castleberry. All the amazing mentors at Seton Hill University, but especially my mentors, Leslie Davis Guccione who taught me how to edit, and to Anne Harris who gave me permission to write a novel about Mabel.

To my family. My parents Jake and Barb, my brother Darrell, my sister-in-law Cheryl, your support means the world to me. My nieces Katarina and Angelica, and my nephew Thomas. You have motivated my writing and this book in too many ways to count.

Neyva and Ryan, my teen beta readers, who saw an earlier version. Your enthusiasm was invaluable in helping me go ahead with this project.

Amanda Fremion, who, because she kept asking me what was happening with this book, got to read an earlier version. It was your persistent interest in Mabel that encouraged me to revisit the novel and take this giant leap with it.

Members of my writing group, Evan Braun and Bev Geddes for your support, and friendship.

My editor, Samantha Beiko. You did an amazing job! Thank you so much for all your hard work on this book, making it the best it can possibly be.

My cover artist, Jordy Lakiere, who agreed to a request from an unknown author from Winnipeg, asking him to create cover art of a female dwarf. Thank you for taking the image I had in my head and making it real.

Alex Hughes, who joined me on this crazy venture as my publicist, coach, and friend. Your support has been invaluable in this process.

And last, but not least, Gerald Brandt, Adria Laycraft, and Robert J. Sawyer. Your friendship has carried me through many good and tough times. We've laughed, skipped, and sashayed through it all. I couldn't have done any of this without you.

It is a truth universally acknowledged that a female dwarf, upon reaching the age of maturity, is in want of a suitable mate.

—Meet Him and Mate Him:
1001 Ways to Meet Your Perfect Dwarf Mate

CHAPTER 1

CAP ON straight, beard brushed and worked into two thin braids, I bounded down the stairs. Da and my twelve brothers all grinned at me from the kitchen table, even the ones who were usually sleeping by now after working the night shift.

"Look at you," Max said, pushing me down onto the bench between him and Bernie.

Kenneth reached over the table and tugged on the twi braids in my beard. "Hoping to attract a mate on your first day?" he asked.

I smacked his hand away. My beard was still on the scraggly side and I couldn't risk losing any of it if he accidentally pulled too hard.

"Taking her duty seriously," Billy said. "That's what I like to see. Well done, Sis."

I beamed as I helped myself to a heaping plate of eggs, sausages, and toast.

"Mabel, we are so proud of you." Da set a soft brown leather bag beside me. Inside were brand new pick-axes, hammers—everything I needed. "A little something in honor of your first day as a miner."

Some might think that this wouldn't be a big deal to me because I come from a family of miners. Certainly, as the youngest I'd seen enough of my brothers receive such a gift on their first day at the mines to know that this was standard. It was part of the rite of passage for those lucky enough to enter the mines and therefore not one to be taken lightly. Especially by me. Not too long ago, it had been a very real possibility that I might not be hired for the mines. As the only female in the family, it was my duty to carry the family name and reputation on my shoulders. The shame would have been unbearable if I hadn't made it to this day.

I would never take being a miner for granted.

"Thank you so much. I can't believe it. I just... thank you," I said.

"You're a Goldenaxe, Mabel," Bernie smiled. "Believe it." He kissed the top of my head and went upstairs.

Danny, Wilbur, Bobby and Billy all patted me on the back, grumbled congratulations, and retreated to their beds. Their staying up for me filled me with pride. They'd done this for each other on the first day at the mines. I would have thought they'd be tired of doing this by the time my turn came along.

I helped myself to a few extra pancakes, and passed a few to Ross and Max. I needed the fortification for strength, but also to make my belly stouter. Strength and stoutness were important for mining. They were also what would make me attractive to potential mates. A thicker beard and a lower voice would help with that too, but I couldn't control those.

"My dearest Mabel," Da said. Were those tears in the corners of his eyes, or was it moisture from the steam in the kitchen? "Your mam—" He stopped himself. He hadn't meant to mention her. I could tell by the way he pressed his lips together. He had relaxed too much, let some part of a secret slip and now he wished he could suck it back in.

I clutched my fork, every muscle in my body tense. Mam died when I was little more than an infant. I used to ask about her, but Da and my brothers would just scowl and change the subject. Eventually I gave up. So why would he mention her now? Unless there was something I needed to know about her before I started work, something that could affect my prospects at finding a mate. I knew the chief foreman had hesitated hiring me because my mam hadn't been a miner. Would her career choice and early death mar my mating prospects? "What about her?"

"Nothing." Da turned back to the griddle.

He had brought her up. I couldn't let him change the subject now. Not if it would affect my future and that of my family. "No, really. What about her?"

He scraped the iron pan. He didn't want to tell me, but he had to, and he knew it. "I'm sorry, pet." He put the spatula down. "You look so much like she did on her first day at the mines. It reminded me of how she and I would hold you in our arms and dream of the future you would have, and here it is. She would have been as proud of you as we all are."

Mam was a miner? But the chief foreman had no record of her. Why had Da lied to me about her? Why was he so dismissive of such big news? Something wasn't right about any of this. I looked to my brothers for help, especially Max, who was closest to me in age, and just as curious about Mam. They all kept their heads down, shoveling food in their mouths, including Max.

"I'm sorry," Da said and pointed to the braids in my beard. "This is your big day. You have more important things to worry about than your still-grieving da."

The message was clear enough: The time had come for me to step up and find a mate to carry on the family line; the duty of female dwarves. And now that I was a miner, I could find a respectable mate; maybe even improve on the family name and reputation.

My oldest brother Frankie tapped me on the shoulder, "Let's go."

Go? In that moment, I forgot all about my conversation with Da. This was it. I was finally going to the mines. I rose slowly and picked up my bag of tools. It felt like sprite wings fluttered in my not-so-stout belly. What if I turned out to be a terrible miner?

Da hugged me. "Have a great first day."

I slung the bag onto my back. The weight of the tools was comfortable, like they belonged with me. I straightened my cap and took a few deep breaths. This was really happening.

Frankie held the door open.

Our stone cottage sat in the thick forest surrounding the base of Gilliam Mountain. The city of Gilliam had outgrown the mountain several generations ago. Only the oldest and wealthiest mining families still had dwellings inside of it. I usually loathed walking through the forest, but today, either my dwarf-blood failed me, or my excitement was too strong.

Though the morning held a chill, a hint of warmth from the waning summer staved off the threatening cold. The wind tickled my cheeks. The scratching of the leaves in the breeze was music to my ears. The gold sunrise pierced the forest, deepening the browns and greens of the trees and bushes lining the path. Gilliam Mountain loomed majestic.

I was used to taking the path to the right, to the toy workshop where I'd worked the last few years training for life as a miner. This morning, we took the path to the left, toward the mines.

My mines.

Pale green and blue crystallized stalactites and stalagmites filled the damp entrance cavern. Frankie pointed out the cleansing pool, a spring burbling from the wall of the mountain into a pond filling the right half of the cavern.

"That's where everyone washes their faces and beards at the end of each shift," he said with a hint of awe at the beauty of it all.

Even after all these years, he still loved the mines. I hoped I would too.

Frankie allowed me to admire it all for a few minutes then pressed me onward. I could have stood there all day.

From his own bag, he took out a lantern, lit it, then led me out of the entrance cavern into one of the dozens of passages that branched off of it. We descended down a long, gentle staircase that took a wide turn to our left before leveling out into another, much smaller cavern with several crosscuts and diverging drifts. Frankie started into the crosscut closest to our right. "This one is yours."

My crosscut.

I followed him through the narrow entrance. The crosscut widened into a stope fifty yards in where teams of miners had explored and excavated over the generations. Frankie lit the lanterns hanging along the wall, warming the ancient air and casting magnificent shadows against the beautiful, craggy stone.

"Before the others—"

Something sparkled at the edge of a lantern beam. I took a step toward it.

Frankie grabbed my arm, holding me back.

"Mabel, your attention for a few minutes."

"Right. Sorry," I said but looked for another moment before turning back to Frankie.

"I realize this is your first day and it can be a bit awe-inspiring, but I assure you, the beauty never fades. You have many, many wonderful years ahead in the mines."

Overhead, a soft rumbling grew louder and closer. Within minutes the roar broke up into clusters of chatter then distinct voices.

Was I going to meet my mining partners today? I hoped they'd like me.

I heard a gasp and turned around to see Emma, my best friend. "Mabel! This is so perfect. I'd hoped you'd be our new partner." She dropped her bag and hugged me. Thank the gods I was with Emma.

I faced the entrance, anxious to see who else I'd get to work with. I broke out in a huge grin when Phillip entered the crosscut. This day could not get any better. I got to mine with two of my best friends.

"Hey. Welcome," Phillip said, all cool and casual.

Hands on my hips, I frowned at him until his demeanor broke and he hugged me too. "This is going to be fantastic working together," he said.

Frankie interrupted us. "You'll have plenty of time for talking later. Emma, Phillip, keep working where you left off yesterday. Mabel, bring your tools and come with me."

He led me to a section of the crosscut a few feet from my friends.

"Don't I get to work with them?"

"After I've trained you. Now, I want you to run your hand over this rock—carefully, slowly. Tell me what you feel."

I did as instructed but wasn't sure what he wanted to hear. It felt like stone should: hard. I looked at him, hoping for some kind of hint of what I should be feeling. He was smiling, not scowling. At least he wasn't disappointed in me.

"Get up close, smell it, press on it," he said.

I did, taking my time, pressing, tapping, sniffing. At first I didn't understand what he expected. But then I pressed my ear to the stone as I tapped and pushed on it. "It's firm, but almost spongy, like there are air bubbles beneath the surface, and a sulfur scent," I said at last.

"Very good. Now take out your axes."

Learning about the textured stone was fascinating. And my brother was pleased with me. I removed my tools from my bag and spread them out on the floor, out of the way of everyone. I looked at my three pick-axes.

"The harder the rock, the bigger the axe you want to use. This rock is fairly soft so you want the smallest one."

Soft? I picked up the axe, hand close to the head.

"Who taught you to hold it like that?" Frankie asked.

"No one. Why? Is it wrong?"

"It's perfect. Good natural instinct, Mabel. With

gentle, small strokes, scratch at the wall."

The rock fell away from the tip of my axe in a fine white dust that soon coated my beard. Now I knew why no one mined before their beards were thick enough. It wasn't just an issue of attractiveness. The thicker the beard, the more it kept the dust from the face. My scraggly beard had been a concern during my interview. But I guess the chief foreman thought it was thick enough. Or my pleading had convinced him of it. The dust worked its way through my beard's almost adequate protection and scratched my skin. I could do without this discomfort.

"Smaller strokes," Frankie said. "Very good."

Frankie's instructions were slow and methodical. He was so patient and encouraging that even though I was scraping rock for hours, it was exhilarating.

The horn sounded, signaling the break for lunch much too soon. I felt like I'd only just started! Frankie gave me leave to join Phillip and Emma.

The cafeteria cavern could easily fit a thousand dwarves. Crystals lined the ceiling, and tables sat among pillars of stalactites and stalagmites. The wild boars roasting on open spits smelled more succulent than anything I'd ever tasted.

Phillip and Emma directed me to a corner of the dining cavern populated with others our age, most of whom we'd worked with or at least known in the toy workshop. Emma tugged at the braids in her beard, reminding me of my duty. Any time I wasn't actually mining, I needed to look for a mate. For my first day, this was the perfect opportunity to see what my mating opportunities might be. We sat near our good friends Jimmy and Zach.

Jimmy put a hand on my back. "How are things going, Mabel?"

"Excellent."

"I hear Frankie's a great teacher."

"The best."

"You've got Frankie?" someone yelled from down the table.

"That's Oliver," Jimmy nodded.

Oliver's skin had a touch too much color; not a nice gray, but he was a miner and had two braids in his beard signaling he was interested in finding a life mate. I supposed I should consider him as a possible mate.

"You're so lucky," Oliver sighed.

"He's our coach and Mabel's brother," Phillip said.

"You're a *Goldenaxe*?" Oliver stood, bumping the table in his hurry to get to me.

A bit clumsy. He grabbed my hand and shook it, his grip too firm. I might wait and see if any better options came along first.

"You must be the youngest. I'm such a fan of your family's work."

Well, *that* made him a more favorable possibility. And a strong grip probably meant he worked hard and had strong mining skills. "Ah, thank you."

Jimmy elbowed Oliver out of the way. "A bunch

of us are going to The Bearded Prospector Tavern after work. You'll join us, won't you?"

"Of course she will," Phillip said.

"I guess I am," I shrugged. "I'll see you there."

In the afternoon, Frankie had me feel more stone and smell it and asked me to point out the differences in the textures of the walls of the crosscut. I ended the day chipping at some solid rock with my biggest axe.

"Good first day," Frankie said when the horn blew to end the shift.

"Thanks. Can you tell Da I'll be home late? I'm going out with my friends to The Bearded Prospector."

"Will do. Stout ale is the best tonic after a day in the mines. Have fun."

"Thanks."

Emma and I walked to the entrance cavern and joined the throngs gathering at the cleansing pool. I took off my cap and thrust my head into the water like everyone else. Glorious cool water rushed around my face and flowed through my hair washing away the dust. When I came up after half a minute, I wrung out the water from my beard. I ran my fingers through it to fluff it up.

Hundreds of us headed out of the mines, down the three-abreast path in the forest, around the base of the mountain, and finally to The Bearded Prospector, the preferred tavern of Gilliam miners. Dozens of dwarves were already drinking outside the Prospector, and there were ten times as many behind me. I didn't see how the tavern could hold all of us if patrons already spilled out its doors. No one else seemed to take notice, so I went in with them.

The powerful yet refreshing scent of stout ale greeted us the moment we stepped through the door. A gray haze of pipe smoke hovered over the room, which was much larger than I had expected. Ancient mining axes hung on the walls, placed there by generations of miners upon their retirement.

We pushed our way through the crowd until we found an empty table in a back corner. Emma squeezed herself in between Zach and Jimmy. Phillip said he would get the first round.

Zach launched into the story of how he'd found his first emerald today. His find reassured me that this was all real, that it would happen for me, too.

I was the last of my friends to get hired on at the mines. I'd worried for so long, believing I wasn't going to be good enough, that I'd never get here. But I'd finally made it. And today proved it had been worth the wait. I couldn't stop grinning.

Phillip returned, arms laden with tankards. I helped distribute the ale. Before anyone could take a sip, Phillip raised his mug. "To Mabel, on her first day at the mines!" We knocked rims.

"And to Zach, on finding his first ever emerald," Jimmy said.

I couldn't wait to find my first emerald. I had so much to look forward to.

"I was thinking of going to the movie theater tomorrow after work," Zach said. "Anyone want to join me? Sevrin's in a movie playing there."

The movie theater was a new arrival in town. I hadn't heard many dwarves talking about it yet. I hoped that was because most dwarves didn't know what to make of movies. We liked our mining and our ale. To do much else wasn't considered respectable, though I didn't see why. There were plays put on all the time and as I understood it, this was the same except the action was somehow captured in a wizard's crystal and projected on a screen, and that I had to see.

SPLITTING OFF from the crowd to walk in the opposite direction from The Bearded Prospector felt wrong yet exciting. I'd only been working at the mines for two days and already I felt like I was breaking tradition.

Frankie had scowled when Emma, Phillip, and I talked about our plans today. Da and my brothers, especially the four oldest, Frankie, Patrick, Mikey, and Danny, had grumbled about the theater opening in town ever since it was announced. "No respectable Dwarf would be seen in one," they'd said.

But we were with Ben and Zach, mountain dwellers from respectable families. And Sevrin was *in* the movie. There was no dwarf more revered than

Sevrin.

Perhaps Da had a point though. We walked in the opposite direction of The Bearded Prospector, away from where most of the Gilliam miners lived. The forest trees crowded in on the path.

Emma walked with Zach and Ben, her arms hooked through theirs, but her attention was clearly on Zach. She was telling him about the time she'd gone to a movie in Mitchum. It looked to me like she was trying to impress him.

Phillip, Jimmy, and I followed. I smiled. The three of us were together again. We'd spent months on our masterworks together in the toy workshop. We were great friends before then, and now we were family. Every now and then, Zach glanced in our direction. He'd done a masterwork with us as well, though he'd left shortly after I was selected for the extra training. Still, there was a special bond between those of us who had been chosen to practice and demonstrate our skilled craftsmanship on a special project. I had the feeling that because of that bond, Zach would have preferred to walk with us.

"I've never been to a movie, have you?" Jimmy asked me.

"Are you kidding?" I scoffed. "My family has been too busy mining to go anywhere there might be a theater. They might have when Mikey was competing in axe throwing, but I was too young to remember. I know my family, though, and I'm quite confident in saying that they wouldn't have gone to one then."

"I don't think movies were around back then," Phillip said.

I had to think about that. He was right. Movies had only been around for a couple of dozen years.

Jimmy nudged me and pointed at Emma who had dropped Ben's arm to walk closer to Zach.

"How long has she been flirting with him?" I asked.

"Since she arrived at the mines." Jimmy said.

"He doesn't seem too interested," Phillip added. "Don't blame him, though. Until you started working with us, she'd been constantly talking about how masterworks are for the slower dwarves, to give them more time to grow into their mining bodies."

If she hadn't said the same thing to me for months, while she'd gone from toy-making to mining, because she wasn't chosen for the masterwork, I'd have been upset. I'd believed her for a long time, until my wonderful brothers set me straight. I shook my head. "She'll have him interested in no time. And when he is, he'll have long forgotten her ideas on masterworks."

The horrid trees thinned and we came to a clearing bordering the neighborhoods of miners, hunters, and shop workers. I supposed it was a strategic location, to try and draw in the biggest crowds. I was just relieved the theater wasn't any farther away from the mines.

I hesitated at the edge of the forest so I could take

in the beauty before me.

I knew the theater was a new construction but I hadn't expected this. To say it was made of stone just wouldn't be adequate; pretty much every building in Gilliam was made of stone. The walls of the theater were large, rough, layered, and built to look like a mountain, with the front of the building looking like a cross-section cut into that mountain. "Wow. Who owns this?"

"Remember our vocational advisor from the toy workshop?" Phillip asked. "His son, Callum."

Even though the vocational advisor generally spoke of mining as the only real true vocation for a dwarf, he must have thought owning a movie theater was a respectable enough vocation for his son to allow him to open and run one in Gilliam. If he didn't, he was crazy, because by the looks of things, Callum must be doing pretty well with the theater business to be able to build something this spectacular.

Inside, the lobby was a smaller version of the entrance cavern of the mines. Callum was certainly doing his best to make mountain dwellers and miners comfortable. If only comfort and appearances were enough to earn the approval of even the most traditional dwarves like my da and brothers.

There were only a handful of other dwarves in the lobby. A lot of expense was put into this building. I hoped it gained more popularity soon. I'd hate to see it close before it really got going.

"Tonight's on me," Ben said.

"What?" Phillip asked.

"Mabel's joined us at the mines, Zach's first emerald yesterday, and my first emerald today. We have a lot to celebrate."

"Congratulations, Ben," I said. "This is very kind of you, but you don't have to pay for all of us."

"We all like to celebrate first emeralds in our own way," Ben said. "Zach bought a few extra rounds of drinks yesterday. I'd like to buy the tickets tonight."

"And a round of drinks tomorrow," Zach said.

"You got it," Ben said with a smile.

Ben bought our tickets and we walked through. On the way into the auditorium was a stand with a stack of movie programs.

"They even have magazines," Emma said, picking up two and handing one of them to me. "Callum knows his business."

The dim, flickering candlelight illuminated the smooth stone walls and the red velvet seats.

Emma marched us all to the third row from the front where we could get a whole row of seats to ourselves. I was happy to see several more dwarves enter behind us.

A theater usher blew out the candles around the room. I turned around and watched the projectionist set the wizard's crystal between two fine metal tines of a fork and tap them. The tines vibrated against the crystal, releasing the images, projecting them onto the white screen.

I settled into my seat and stared at the screen and

the images flashing on it. How were the movie makers able to capture the action like that, in a crystal? The images were so clear and the sound so perfect. At times, I managed to turn around to look at the crystal because it *couldn't* be real, but seeing it certainly convinced me it was.

When Sevrin came on the screen, all of us in the theater cheered. I'd seen pictures of him, I'd heard the legends, but I'd never seen him like this, so real, so close. His voice rumbled and I swore I could feel it vibrate through me as he declared war against the elven army amassing on the other side of the mountains. His speech to the dwarven warriors, rallying them to his cause, it was like he spoke to me, stirring the passion in my heart. I was ready to join his cause. I think all of us in the theater were. We yelled the war cry with the warriors and cheered them as they charged into battle.

The scene changed.

I stopped cheering.

The room dimmed as *his* face filled the screen. I sat up straighter. My heart fluttered like a leaf in a light breeze. My insides felt like mush. I tucked my hair behind my ear and ran my fingers through my beard, tugging on the two braids. I was unable to look away from him: his long, straight blond hair, smooth chin. The spark of mischief in his piercing blue eyes jolted my heart. I licked my lips as I watched his lush mouth form the words, his gentle voice lulling me into a trance. I held my breath, mesmerized by his long, thin fingers, his slender yet powerful arms. Heat rose in my cheeks.

Aramis, leader of the elven army, stared out at me. I leaned forward, sinking into his splendor. He raised his bow, drew back the arrow, his arms sinuously powerful, preparing to release a hail of arrows at the dwarven army.

The dwarves outnumbered the elves. Aramis would be crushed. Sevrin *had* to let him live. They couldn't harm Aramis. They just couldn't. Yet there's no way I could cheer for Aramis.

The war was devastating. The dwarven army lost more than half of its numbers. Sevrin survived, and so, much to my great relief, did Aramis.

I wanted to listen to Aramis speak forever, to revel in the beauty of his being. I wanted to touch him, hold him, kiss him. I wanted… him.

I was in love.

With an elf.

I sank into my seat. How could I be attracted to an elf? An elf, of all beings. A tree-loving, open-air, too-afraid-of-dirt-to-do-any-work, fine delicate-featured pretty-boy elf. Elves were a completely different species from dwarves. Love between us was impossible.

CHAPTER 2

"THIS CROSSCUT was started and abandoned long before Da began his mining career. A year ago—"

"I get it." I said, exasperated by the non-stop history lesson. I just wanted Frankie to be quiet, to let me use the monotony of work to think about what I'd experienced the other night at the movie theater— the wonder of the wizard's crystal and the beauty of Aramis. "I know we're a part of a great mining tradition. Why else would I want to work here?"

I combed my fingers through my beard to remove most of the mine dust matting itself into the hair. I think I only made it worse. Right now that mining tradition and thinking about the movie were the only reason I endured any of this, espeicially the monotony.

"Good then," Frankie said. "As long as you know. Some seem to think this is only a place to meet a mate or gain prestige. It's my job to make sure you are here for the right reasons." Frankie looked sideways at Emma who rolled her eyes.

If Frankie thought Emma's determination to find a mate was a problem, he should talk to her, not lecture me. What he should do is try and see things from the perspective of a female. The mines were the best place to find a respectable mate. Da told me every morning that when I wasn't actually working, I needed to pay attention to the males with two braids in their beard. Any one of them could be my life mate. He said I should make sure the one I choose is respectable enough to carry the reputation of the Goldenaxe name.

But maybe Frankie was right, sort of. I was distracted. Not because I was too busy thinking about the fellows. It was the movie. More specifically, the movie magazine. I'd practically memorized the whole thing in the last couple of days, learning everything there was to know about making movies, and, of course, Aramis.

Before work today, I'd been in the middle of reading an article about how Radier, the Wizard who'd recorded the movie on his crystal, had to ride alongside the dwarves and elves and get between them during the battle sequences, risking great injury. I kept imagining myself in his place, the risks he'd taken as horses thundered past, arrows flew, and axes swung. How many near misses had there been? Had Radier needed to use his magic to protect himself? What if one of the weapons had gone astray? How much time did he get to spend with Aramis, and Sevrin?

I would rather be watching the movie again now that I knew more about how it was made. Actually, I'd prefer being in a movie to scratching at this stubborn rock. I couldn't make a mark in it.

"Frankie, just help me figure out what to do here. The large pick isn't doing anything."

"Really?" Frankie put his ear against the rock where I'd been working and ran his fingers over the area. "Come here. Do what I'm doing."

I patted at it a couple of times then stepped back.

"Do it again. Let your fingers be your eyes. Do you feel it?"

"Feel what?" Did Aramis have to put up with this kind of nonsense when making a movie? I bet he didn't.

"The change in the rock."

There was a change? Interesting. I caressed the stone up and down, side to side, pressing into every dent and crevice, searching for the edge and feeling for a difference until I found it. "Yes. Where I've been working is the same hardness but a different, rougher texture."

"Good. Phillip, Emma, come do the same. Do you feel it?"

They stopped what they were doing and joined

us, imitating our rock exploration.

"Yes," Phillip said.

"I think so," said Emma.

Frankie pushed them away from the wall. "I knew it. I knew when the chief foreman assigned me here to re-explore that the emeralds I'd found weren't a one-off. Mabel, with the medium pick, I want you to gently tap the rougher part."

The rock cracked into thin spidery lines like the shell of a hard-boiled egg. Finally something different from scratching the rock.

"Very good Mabel. Very, very good. You may have found something. Thank the gods I never gave up on this crosscut. Now take out your chisel and with the tip, dig in between the cracks and pull out the pieces. Be very careful. You two, watch what she's doing."

Had I really found an emerald?

I picked at the cracks. The outer part crumbled beneath my touch. Below the surface lay hard packed dirt rather than stone.

"The mines are our cathedrals to the gods of our creation," Frankie said.

"Now what do I do?"

I didn't *really* think mining was boring. I'd just forgotten how fascinating it was; how much I loved it, especially the detailed work.

"Get your brush and with small strokes wipe away the stone the same as when you were scratching it with the pick." Frankie stood beside me, his arms crossed and his fingers twitching. Either he was really happy for me, or dying to get in to work this wall instead of me. "When we mine, we worship our creators. The treasures the mountain holds are gifts from the gods."

I had found an emerald, I knew it, but I didn't want to say anything out loud until I saw it. I imagined I was in a movie with Aramis, working as miners, finding our first emerald bed.

I grabbed my brush and swept at the rock. *Is it real, Aramis? Have I really found my first emerald?* I'd cleared a fairly large area of the outer shell, about the size of my upper body, and the dirt under-layer. There it sat, the most beautiful thing I'd ever seen, glittery, glassy and green. *It's as beautiful as you are,* Aramis said to me.

"Frankie!" My voice shook, *I* shook. It was too exciting to keep inside.

"What do you see?"

"Frankie." *Aramis!* I pointed at my first emerald.

"Sweep a little more around it."

I did and he whispered, "Yes, yes, yes. Congratulations, Mabel. You've found your first bed of emeralds."

I dropped my brush and covered my scream. The gods accepted me and chose to bless me.

Frankie squeezed me, picked me up and spun me around. And as happy as I was to be celebrating with Frankie, I wished it was Aramis who hugged me and gave me a kiss to commemorate my find.

"I am so proud of you." Frankie put me down. "Right. Everyone. Get back to work. Mabel, when you've found the edges of your emerald and taken it out, keep it, a gift from the gods for your devotion." He winked, grinning from ear to ear.

Frankie was so passionate, reverent even, about mining. He nearly convinced me I should never want to leave the mines for anything. I understood then why Frankie, why none of my brothers, were interested in finding a mate. I momentarily considered abandoning my own search and removing my braids so I could join in his full devotion to the mines. Unfortunately, I'd never heard of a female miner so devoted to her craft she declared herself uninterested in mating. That was not an option open to females, to me. Maybe there was less pressure on Emma because she had an older sister. But even she had to fulfill her duty to mate and have dwarflings. As the only girl in my family, that pressure was doubled.

I brushed and blew away the dust, careful not to scratch my emerald. Aramis looked over my shoulder, smiling, his eyes sparkling, his dimple deepening. He whispered to me how much he knew I would find it, how he knew I was meant to be a miner, a skilled miner, how proud he was of me, and how we'd have our own celebration at the end of the day.

The emerald was bigger than my hand. I didn't think anyone could keep a gem that size, but Frankie said I could so I put it in a side pocket on my tool bag for safe keeping.

Frankie helped me excavate more of the site, chatting the whole time. "I knew this would be a productive crosscut. I knew it. 'Give it up,' they said. 'Not even Frankie Goldenaxe can find gems where there are none,' they said. But I persisted. Mabel, I am so proud of you for being the one to find the emeralds. And so early in your career as a miner. You're keeping the tradition in the family. I bet you've got an eye for locating gems."

"I appreciate your vote of confidence, but I just scratched at the rock where you told me to."

"Sure. But you could tell there was a change in the rock. It's the first step. So many crosscuts have been abandoned because miners don't know what to look for. They give up so easily. It's a lot of hard work and often we don't find anything, or it can take years to get to the gems. So many will say the rock is too hard, or there is nothing there. I have the ability to spot places where we should look. If you keep in mind what you learned today about the difference in rock texture, you will go far here, Mabel. You will go far."

If every day was as exciting as this one, finding gems, life would be perfect. But that was only the reward for mining, for endless days of chipping and scratching at rock. And as an explorer, like Frankie, it wouldn't just be days of chipping and scratching, it would be years. I loved his faith in me, but—and I hoped the gods would forgive me for thinking this— I didn't think I wanted to spend my life in such boredom.

We'd barely started on the emerald bed when the horn blew to end the day. I didn't want to stop. Frankie appreciated my enthusiasm but assured me we could be working on this part for many days or weeks to come. "Go on to the Prospector to celebrate. I'll take your tools home for you."

I couldn't move inside the Prospector without people congratulating me on my find and asking for details on how I did it. The first request for a recounting of my tale came with an offer of a drink. Next thing I knew I was surrounded by eager listeners.

"So you've got your brother Frankie's eye for exploration," said Ricky, a friend of my second eldest brother, Patrick. "Let's see if you've got your brother Mikey's talent for axe throwing. A contest?"

Suggesting I had Frankie's skill for mining was a great compliment but a huge exaggeration. And Mikey's axe-throwing skill was out of everyone's reach. Mikey had been Dwarf Games champion in axe throwing.

I was too small to remember much of our family trip to the Games. The only really clear memory was of the *thunk* of the axe sinking into the throwing post in our back yard. The rhythm of it used to lull me to sleep. Soon after he'd won the Games, Mikey stopped throwing. Even so, his prowess was legendary.

"A contest," the room resounded with the unified shout.

I glanced at Emma and Phillip. Maybe they'd come up with a reason why I couldn't compete. They had a smaller group around them to hear their version of the story of my first emerald. Emma straightened her cap and tugged on her beard as she talked and accepted drinks. At the call for a contest, she looked at me, smiled, and said, "I'm in." So did Zach and Jimmy.

Dwarves don't turn down challenges, and I wasn't going to be the first one to do so. "You're on," I said to Ricky. Good gods, this was going to be embarrassing.

We were followed to the back of the Prospector by half of the patrons, including my brothers Patrick and Mikey. Like there wasn't enough pressure on me simply to live up to his reputation. To have him watch? This wasn't going to be just embarrassing. This was going to be mortifying.

Of the six competitors, Emma and I were the only females. We each took a few practice throws to get a feel for the weight of the axes. As Ricky reset the target, Mikey and Patrick edged their way to the front of the crowd. I motioned to Mikey with my axe to ask if he wanted to join us. It might take the pressure off me. He shook his head, raised his mug to me then took a sip, smiling. I hoped that if I couldn't make him proud, at least I wouldn't blow the contest and shame him.

I stepped up to the marker. I held the axe at the base of the handle. Raising my arm, I closed my left eye to improve my focus. I brought the axe back then hurled it forward, releasing it. I didn't hit the exact center of the target as Ricky and another fellow, Curtis, had, but close enough and slightly better than Zach and Jimmy. Emma's throw had hit close to the center too. On my second try, I hit the second ring, still better than Zach and Jimmy. Emma's was well off the mark but Zach stood at her side instructing her on her technique. My third try, I hit dead center. Emma didn't but her throw had improved over her second. I finished third behind Ricky and Curtis. Considering they were a lot older and had more experience, I thought I had done all right. Actually, just hitting the post was a victory for me.

"Not bad at all," Ricky said. "You've got some raw talent. Just remember, I'm the Prospector's champion."

"Ah, don't mind him," Curtis said.

Others soon surrounded me, talking about regular contests held at the Prospector, and the new emerald bed I'd found. I'd established myself as a part of dwarven tradition as a miner. I loved it all, and yet I found myself tiring. I wanted to go home, look at my emerald, and read more of my movie magazine.

"Well, that was fun," I said to Emma an hour later, after I'd managed to break out of a conversation.

"I know." Her eyes glittered. "And several of the fellows talking with me tonight have offered to court me. Don't worry, I only accepted offers from the few mountain dwellers among them."

I hugged her. "Congratulations."

"I hope you've been selective in whom you'll be courting."

Was I supposed to be trying to get offers of courtship out of this? Did *everything* have to be about finding a mate? Couldn't I just enjoy myself? "Oh, yeah. Maybe a little too selective. Anyway, I'm going to head home. I'm exhausted."

"Have a good night. I'm going to try and get a few more dates before the night is up."

Alone on the road home, I thought about my amazing day. "Aramis, I found an emerald," I whispered and told him everything. "Having you here with me, really here, not just in my head, would have made it a perfect day."

"I'm proud of you, Mabel," Mikey said, catching up to me on the way home.

I froze. I had to be more careful. No more talking out loud to Aramis. Wait. If Mikey heard me, he would have said something. He had only given me the biggest compliment of the night. I relaxed a little. "Thanks. I thought my nerves might get the best of me."

"You're a Goldenaxe through and through. I knew you could handle it. I talked with a few of my friends during the contest. We think you've got potential to go all the way with this. If you'll let me, I'd like to coach you."

"All the way? You mean to the Dwarf Games?"

"I do."

I hugged him. Mikey, my third oldest brother, axe-throwing champion, thought *I* had enough talent to get to the Dwarf Games—only the biggest sporting competition among all dwarf nations. They were held every five years and the next one was coming up in just over a year. He believed in me enough to put in the time and effort to return to a sport we all thought he'd abandoned, to train me.

"I take it you'll let me coach you?"

"Yes," I squeaked with excitement as we entered the house.

MIKEY'S OLD throwing post stood at one end of our back garden and on the ground beside it was a small leather bag. The post hadn't been out here in years. I thought it had been destroyed or thrown out. He must have kept it in storage somewhere and brought it out today, which surprised me. He hadn't thrown an axe in decades. He hadn't talked about it, either. I assumed something incredibly horrible or painful had happened to make him give it up, though none of us really knew why. Maybe he hadn't given up on throwing as completely as I'd thought.

The first thing Mikey did was walk me through a series of stretches.

"It's important to have fluid, loose, flexible muscles," he said. "Mining is terrific, but it keeps us stiff, stuck only in a few positions. To be a champion thrower, you need to keep limber. These exercises we're doing now, especially the stretches, do them every morning and night, and of course at the beginning and end of each practice."

I wasn't particularly flexible but the stretches felt pretty good after a long day of mining. Mikey assured me that with time and patience, my muscles would loosen up.

After that, he had me work on building up my strength. "Mining is great for shoulder strength," he said. "But you need it all over to be a champion."

He had me do push-ups, which I was disastrous at, only managing to do five proper ones. Then it was sit-ups, squats, lunges, and arm raises. He said, "Using your own body weight for resistance is best."

Finally, after endless exercises, which I think made my already-pathetic, less-than-stout stomach shrink, I got to throw an axe.

Mikey delved into the bag in front of us and took out one of his hand-held throwing axes and lovingly placed the beautiful piece of craftsmanship in my hand. He'd used this axe to win the Dwarf Games. The jewels were inset into the handle and the handle was varnished so it was smooth in my hand. I wouldn't feel the jewels when I released it. In the Dwarf Games, this axe must have been spectacular to see spinning through the air, the gems flashing in the lantern-light.

"You did well last night, but I want you to forget everything you did. Last night's contest never happened."

What kind of talent did he see in me then, if he wanted me to forget it? "Okay. It never happened." I agreed to it, but I was a little hurt. It wasn't like I was the only one in my family that showed an interest in the sport. My brothers have all bragged on more than one occasion about winning a throwing contest at the Prospector. There had to be something good in what he saw from me. Mikey had quit the sport. He never talked about it. Now, with me, his eyes were shining with such enthusiasm, it was like he'd never stopped throwing. "But, why?" I had to know.

"Throwing at the tavern is fun and you can get away with less than perfect technique," Mikey explained. "To be a champion, I want you to have the best training and use the right technique from the start."

"So should I never throw at the Prospector? What if someone challenges me?"

"Of course you can throw there. You should. Though it hardly resembles true competition standards, it is good practice. The next time you throw there, you will have the best discipline and technique of all of competitors. You'll stomp their asses. Especially Ricky. I know he's a friend of Danny's, and I like him well enough, but he's gotten too big a head over being top thrower at the Prospector. He needs to be dethroned."

"So why don't you do it?"

"I'm too old," he said, a little too quickly, I

thought. "Now. I want you to hold the axe at the lowest end of the handle, like that. Perfect. Hold it firm, but not tight."

He wiggled it in my hand until I had the right kind of grip.

"Excellent."

He helped guide my arm up and back, so I could feel the proper angle it should be at. Then, in slow motion, he moved my arm up and around and stopped it at the exact place I should release the axe. We repeated these motions several times, slow at first, then picking up the pace. He had me continue the repetitions without his help while he watched.

On my first effort, the axe thumped at my feet. I think I was lucky not to lose any toes. Mikey had me repeat the motions several more times before my second attempted throw. The axe wobbled out of my hand and landed only a little closer to the post. After several more pitiful throws, I was getting frustrated.

"Remember your technique," Mikey said. "For now it is more important than hitting the post."

I took a moment to regain my composure before throwing. After a few more tries, I finally hit the post. It was glorious the way the axe slid from my hand, spinning once, end over end, and the iron head piercing the wood with a *thunk*. It was the lower edge of the post, but still, it was a hit. I threw my arms up and cheered. "Mikey, did you see that? I hit it. Did you see how it flew? It was so natural, so fluid."

"Well done," Mikey said, with only a twitch of a

smile. "Keep throwing."

I did, and eventually hit the post again.

"Good. Focus on your technique."

"What's going on here?" Da yelled, thundering out of the house as my axe bounced off the ground in front of the post.

"Mikey's coaching me," I said, retrieving the axe.

"I can see that," Da said. "Mikey, a word with you, please."

"Of course. Don't stop, Mabel."

I continued to throw, but I also listened in on their conversation. They weren't exactly being quiet about it.

"It's great to see you out here, son, but *why* are you coaching Mabel?"

"Da, she's got talent."

"Yes, but why *Mabel?*"

"I just said why."

"Mikey. Mabel just started at the mines. She needs to focus her time and energy on finding a mate. How is she going to be able to do that if she spends all her non-working hours back here, alone, throwing axes? Besides, she's having a hard enough time getting a stout belly and this exercise isn't going to help."

Hey. That was mean.

"She needs to use every asset she has," Da continued.

"It's not my fault she looks like... you know," Mikey said.

Mam? Do I look like her? When Da said it the other day, I thought he was just being sentimental.

"Da. I know how important it is that Mabel find a good, respectable mate. But she has a few years to find one. With the right instruction, she can win the Dwarf Games. We'll have another champion in the family. Think of the honor and respect that will bring our family. This will only work in her favor."

"Fine," Da growled. "Mabel."

I turned to him. "You need to eat more, especially if you're going to be training like this."

Why did it always have to be about looking a certain way to attract a mate? Couldn't I just do what I enjoyed doing, look the way I look, and be loved? "Yes, Da." I threw the axe, another beautiful throw.

CHAPTER 3

"HAD A date last night, with Ben," Emma said on our way to work. Two weeks since the contest at the Prospector and already Emma had gone on six dates, each one with a different fellow. She always beamed as she gave me the latest report on her pursuit of a mate. It was wonderful to see her so happy.

"How was it?"

The shine faded from Emma. "All right, except he talked about you all night."

Why would he do that? "Maybe he was nervous and wanted something to talk about. He probably talked about me because you both know me. I'm sure the next date he will focus all his attention on you."

Emma shrugged it off. "It doesn't matter. I'm not set on him or anything, even though he's a mountain dweller. Zach is more what I'm looking for."

Da would love Emma as his daughter. He'd asked me *again* today about what my courtship prospects were and if anyone had shown any interest. I think next time I'll lie and say I'm just being picky or weighing my options. Maybe that will make him happy and keep him quiet about it for a while. A few days, at least.

We stepped into the cool darkness of the entrance cavern. Several males crowded around Emma, pushing me away from her, including Ben who kept Emma close, holding her arm. He asked her to go on another date.

I didn't get a chance to hear her answer. Ricky sidled up to me and I thought, almost hoped, for a moment, for Da's sake, he might be interested, until I saw his beard, which had never, for as long as I could remember, ever been so much as kinked by a cowlick, never mind a braid. "How about a re-match at the Prospector tonight? Just you and me." he asked.

Ricky, the one Mikey said needed to be dethroned and that I'd be the one to do it. I looked forward to seeing his expression when I showed off my new throwing skills. "Sure. Sounds like fun."

"Excellent." He smirked. I didn't know why he did that, or why he even asked for the re-match. It wasn't like I beat him last time. "I have to warn you, I've been practicing. Be prepared to lose big time." Ricky winked. It was like he took pride in defeating one of Mikey's siblings. I guess if he couldn't compete against Mikey, he thought I was the next best thing.

"We'll see about that," I said as he and his friend, Curtis, walked away. Mikey was right. Ricky did need to be dethroned and I'd be more than happy to "stomp his ass," as Mikey said.

That evening at the Prospector, I was glad Mikey had made me practice throwing into the wind the last several days. I'd complained that all official competitions were indoors so I shouldn't have to suffer like this. Mikey had rebutted that it built my throwing strength and endurance, and that I wouldn't have the advantage of throwing with the wind indoors either. Now I wondered if Mikey set up the throwing post in our back garden to face the same direction as the one at the Prospector so there would be no surprises whenever he entered contests here. At least I assumed he'd entered contests here when he was starting out as a thrower.

With the change of seasons, the wind had turned from a warm southerly to a biting north. Except for the warmth of the sun, the cool air predicted an early onset of winter. Of course it wouldn't matter how great my endurance or strength was if my hands were too frozen to let go of the axe.

Because only Ricky and I competed in the rematch, everyone else watched, including Mikey and Patrick. Mikey's presence last time had made me nervous; now, having my coach with me kept me relaxed.

Ricky flung the axe at the post. If I had thrown that way, Mikey would have yelled at me for my sloppy technique, calling it loose and bendy. I glanced at Mikey who snorted into his ale, confirming my theory. He was probably surprised Ricky actually hit the target. Ricky retrieved his axe and swaggered back to the throwing line.

I rolled my eyes. I didn't remember his form being so bad last time. If he could do it with such horrid technique, I had no excuses.

"I thought you said you practiced." I snickered and flapped my arms, mimicking his hideous throw. Everyone laughed, including Ricky's friends.

I stood at the line, axe in hand, flexing my wrist and closing my eyes. In training, Mikey always told me to visualize myself pitching the perfect throw. When I visualized, I added a little extra to the scene. I imagined myself in a movie, fighting alongside Aramis. I often pictured myself throwing the axe in a perfect tight line right into the heart of Aramis's enemy. Of course, I never told Mikey that part. This time I visualized myself throwing to win a competition. Losing the competition meant Aramis's execution. If I won, Aramis would be freed and I would win his heart.

Eyes open, I saw only the bulls-eye of the post. I pulled my arm back. Aramis's life hung on the line. I had to make this throw. The axe flew head over handle and hit the outer edge of the bulls-eye. Good enough to count full points. Whew. Two more throws to free Aramis.

Phillip and Jimmy cheered; Mikey raised his glass to me.

"Lucky throw," Ricky said. He stepped to the line with less swagger and heaved the axe at the post. It hit and stuck in one of the outer rings.

"One throw and already his confidence is blown," Mikey scoffed.

I didn't have to be so accurate this throw but Aramis depended on me. No way would I let him down. Ricky might be trying to lure me into a false sense of security. A perfect throw would prove to Aramis how much I loved him and wanted him to be free.

I focused on the post. I reached back and released the axe a moment sooner than I had the first one. This time the line was better. I hit the heart of the bullseye. Aramis, watching from the tower where he was held captive, smiled down on me, knowing I loved him and that he would soon be free.

"You're being coached, aren't you?" Ricky growled.

I shrugged. "I might be."

"Not fair. You should have said something when I challenged you."

Being coached wasn't cheating, was it? "You never made it a condition of the challenge. In fact I seem to recall you thought you had the upper hand because you'd practiced."

He huffed and puffed for a moment. "I declare this competition forfeit on the grounds of unfair advantage."

"Oh come on, Ricky. Don't be an elf," Patrick called out. "You took the risk when you challenged and didn't set out the terms. The rules state no additions to terms can be made during a contest."

The onlookers chanted, "Throw! Throw! Throw!"

I considered making a bad throw to restore some of Ricky's ego. But dwarves don't lose anything on purpose, particularly a contest of strength and skill. Besides, Aramis needed me to finish this and win it for him.

"Fine." Ricky took his time setting up and focusing on the post.

"Throw the bloody axe already," someone yelled from the back of the crowd.

I agreed. He was playing a mind game, trying to rattle me so I would lose the contest, and Aramis. I shivered and I waited. Aramis blew me a kiss that warmed me from head to toe. I would wait as long as I had to.

Eventually Ricky threw. He kept himself straighter and tighter, a much better line, the way I remembered it being last time. He hit a middle ring, second from the bulls-eye. After he retrieved his axe, he glared at me.

The cold might be good for throwing axes, but I had stiffened up while waiting. I stretched my neck, rotated my shoulders, and flexed my arms the way Mikey had taught me. I wanted to get this competition over with so I could go inside and warm up with some ale before heading home.

I focused. One more throw for Aramis. His life rested in my hands. One more throw and his heart would be mine. His powerful yet thin arms would be around me, I could gaze into his sapphire blue eyes as he kissed me ever so gently.

Right. Don't think about his eyes, focus on the target or I'd lose Aramis forever.

I hurled the axe. I'd released a fraction too soon. I could only hope as it flew from my hand. I managed to hit the first ring away from the bulls-eye. Not perfect, but I had won. I had freed Aramis, and he loved me.

Ricky pushed his way into the tavern. He hadn't even grudgingly congratulated me. I didn't care. Phillip and Jimmy were beside me shoving tankards of ale at me. Everyone else surrounded me, hustling me inside as they shouted their congratulations.

"What about her?" someone behind me said.

"Who, the axe thrower?" his friend asked.

"Yeah. She's interested."

Oh. I guess Mikey was right. Maybe axe throwing was a marketable skill after all. This would make Da happy.

His friend chuckled. "I don't think so."

Or not.

"Too skinny and the most pitiful beard I've ever seen. She can throw, but I doubt she can do anything else. Her friend, though, is perfect. Where is she?"

"She's out with someone."

Seriously? Did he *not* just see me throw? Did he think I came in here by mistake? Didn't he see me with Mikey and Patrick? I am a miner. I am a *Goldenaxe* for crying out loud. That should be more than enough for anyone.

Shouldn't it?

I'd like to stomp *his* ass in the throwing arena.

I downed five tankards of ale in quick succession. What was the point of eating and mining and strength training if I would never look right? I could only hope not every fellow in Gilliam held the same opinion as that bloke. In the meantime, at least I had my Aramis who loved me, flaws and all.

Mikey and Patrick walked me home. More like they had to carry me—each holding an arm—as I swayed and stumbled so much from the drink.

"You held yourself well tonight," Mikey said. "Tomorrow I'm moving the throwing line back a couple of feet."

"Hey. Why don't any other females throw axes?"

"They do, just not in Gilliam."

"Why not? Is it repulsive to the males? Because I'm showing my strength and skill but no fellow is asking to court me. So maybe Da's right. Maybe it's the wrong thing to do to find a mate." I stubbed my toe on a twig, tripping. They held me firm.

"Easy there," Patrick said. "You've won yourself a lot of admirers tonight. Male ones, if you didn't notice."

"So why aren't any of them asking to court me?"

"Most of us males are slow at deciding if we are interested in mating, and even slower at doing something about it if we are," Mikey said. "Don't worry. You've only just reached mateable age. Like I told Da when I started coaching you, you have several years to find a good mate."

"No, I don't. I have to find one now, or I'll be like Mam, too old to have as many dwarflings as I can."

"There is no such thing as being too old. And Mam certainly was not," Patrick said.

"Well she must have been because she's dead. Mams don't leave their families unless they die."

We turned the corner to walk up the path to our home. Patrick lowered his voice. "No, Mabel. Mam isn't dead."

I stopped moving and slid to the ground. She had to be. If she were alive, she'd be with us. "Then where is she?"

"We don't know," Patrick said as he and Mikey picked me up.

"Forget about Mam. She isn't worth thinking about," Mikey said, glaring at Patrick.

"Why?" Had she been banished and we were all forbidden to talk about her?

"She just isn't." Mikey opened the door.

What had she done to get banished? "But—"

Mikey frowned and Patrick shook his head. The subject was closed. At least I knew this much now. I wouldn't give up asking. I'd bide my time. When the right moment came, I'd pounce.

CHAPTER 4

I WISHED last night had never happened. I headed downstairs for breakfast, rubbing my head and leaning on the railing as I went. Those fellows who had insulted me were idiots. I shouldn't have cared what they said. I shouldn't have let them ruin my victory party. I should have been drinking to celebrate, not because I felt sorry for myself. Won't do that again. Ever. For any reason, actually. All the ale explained my thumping headache. But Mam was alive. I'd been up all night thinking about her, why she'd left me. Even the most reasonable explanation I could think of made my stomach turn.

Mikey met me at the bottom of the stairs. "I guess I don't need to ask you how you're doing this morning." I would have told him not to yell, but I hurt too much. He chuckled and put an arm around me. "Some toast and tea will help settle you. Come on."

I hoped so.

I shuffled to the kitchen and Mikey set a small breakfast in front of me. He sat next to me with his own breakfast. My brothers and Da were making too much noise. Did they have to chew so loud?

After I'd had a sip of the strong tea, thick like syrup, which did slow the roiling in my stomach, Mikey placed a parchment on the table. "What's that?" I asked around a mouthful of toast slathered in butter.

"This, my dear little sister, is your training schedule. The Gilliam Games are coming up in a few months from now. We have a lot of work to do before then."

"You've been busy." I squinted through the pain of speaking and sipped more tea. "You've already entered me into the Gilliam Games?"

"I'll be picking up an application today at lunch. Training will be hard, and you'll need to put in a lot of hours between now and then, but I believe in you. Your composure last night after all the shenanigans Ricky threw at you was incredible. That composure alone will qualify you for Regionals. Your focus, too, was amazing. Whatever you did last night, I've never seen you so focused. Keep that up in training. Focus, composure, and technique. I'm telling you, Mabel, you're a natural. You will have no problems getting through to Regionals."

My focus? Did he mean when I imagined winning Aramis's heart? I'd love to do that in training more. Best not tell him that's what I was doing, though. Somehow I didn't think he'd appreciate it if he knew I let myself daydream while I threw. "But Mikey, I'm so new at this. Shouldn't we wait a while, maybe a year or two, before entering me in anything?"

"Hardly. The Dwarf Games are coming up in a year. Now is the perfect time for you. As of today, I am increasing your training. From now on, no more trips to the Prospector after work. I want you to come home for training. As you can see from the schedule, I've mapped out your expected progress. With the extra hours, you'll peak at exactly the right time to succeed at the Gilliam Games. Once you qualify for Regionals in Mitchum, I'll re-visit your training schedule so you can succeed and qualify for the Dwarf Games." Mikey patted me on the back and folded up the parchment. "Have yourself a good day, and I'll see you out back right after work."

"Mikey," Da said, a warning edge in his voice.

"Da, she'll be fine." To me he said, "Tonight we start with moving objects."

"Moving… I'm sorry, did you say moving objects?" I'd forgotten about those.

"Of course. Anyone can master throwing axes at a stationary post."

This was insane. I couldn't do that. "Yeah, but I haven't even mastered that yet. Shouldn't we wait?"

Mikey leaned in and patted me on the shoulder.

"You are a champion. Trust me," he said softly.

By mid-morning, my headache had mostly disappeared and my stomach had settled. The more I thought about competing in the Gilliam Games, in Regionals, and even the Dwarf Games, the more I wanted it. I wanted to see more than just the Gilliam mines. Competing in axe throwing would allow me to do that. I wanted the crowds cheering for me like they had at The Bearded Prospector. I wanted to be an athlete. I wanted to be champion. I wanted to compete. I loved the pressure and excitement of it all, with everyone watching, judging my performance. Sure I was nervous during the contests at the tavern, but the challenge was exhilarating.

I imagined Aramis watching me compete, admiring my throwing skills. "Do you think I can do well enough to qualify for the Dwarf Games?" I asked him. "You'll help me train, won't you?"

And then it occurred to me. Competing in the Dwarf Games would be incredible. But it would be even more amazing if it was decided that a movie should be made of my axe-throwing career. Me, the only female axe-thrower in Gilliam. Radier might be the one to record it. If that happened, I could actually *see* how movies were made, not just read about it.

"I bet the moment we step into the Prospector, you're going to have several blokes lined up to challenge you to a contest," Phillip said, breaking into my thoughts of making axe-throwing and movie history.

I had to refocus on the tedium of scratching at the stone wall of the stope. "Thanks for the vote of confidence, but I won't be going to the Prospector today."

"Did you get a date?" Emma asked, a sparkle in her eyes. "Who is it? A mountain dweller I hope. Don't settle for anyone less. No offense, Phillip."

He grunted. "None taken."

"I wish." And I almost did. It would get everyone off my back. And I wouldn't feel so horrible for not having any male interest. And maybe it might even be nice to have a date. On the other hand, I didn't want dating to interfere with my axe-throwing glory. "No. Mikey has entered me into the Gilliam Games and stepped up my training. I have to practice right after work."

Emma stopped scraping the rock and put her hands on her hips. "Mabel, how do you expect to find a mate if you don't come to the Prospector with us?" All she needed to do was shake her finger at me to make the scolding complete.

Didn't she think I was being asked the same question at home? I didn't need my best friend berating me. I just wanted to enjoy mining and axe throwing for a bit without this constant need for a mate hanging over me. "This is just temporary. I'm sure once I start improving, Mikey will ease up on the training schedule."

Maybe if I was good enough to get to the Dwarf Games, Aramis would hear about me from some of his dwarf friends, and he would come and watch me compete. Then I wouldn't have to imagine him. He would see me and fall in love with me and be in my life for real. I had a lot of work to do to get to the Dwarf Games.

I was packed up and ready to leave the mines before the shift-ending horn had finished sounding. I'd already proven I was a part of mining tradition by going to The Bearded Prospector after work, and sharing the story of finding my first emerald. Now I had the opportunity to be a part of another incredible dwarven tradition, competing in the Dwarf Games.

I hurried home, Aramis at my side the whole way, listening to me prattle on about how only the best dwarves competed, how winning, even in Gilliam, brought fame. Winning the Dwarf Games, simply *competing* in the Dwarf Games, would make me a legend. Everyone knew the names of those competing in every discipline.

My stomach flipped.

If I was famous, Mam might hear about me. If Mam heard about me, maybe I'd get to meet her, or at least hear from her, and find out why she left me.

CHAPTER 5

"KEEP YOURSELF loose, feel the air around you, the ground beneath you," Mikey instructed as we walked.

We—meaning my entire family, including my brothers who worked the night shift—were on our way to a practice competition Mikey had set up. Winning was for reputation only, it wouldn't count toward the standings of the Gilliam Games, or even my chances there, but it was still my first real competition. He said it was impossible to re-create the exact conditions I'd be facing at the Gilliam Games, but the more actual competition experience I had, throwing at both posts and moving objects, the better prepared I'd be.

Throwing axes at moving objects changed everything and I loved it. Once I'd mastered the technique for throwing, the post became nothing. I didn't even know why it was used as the first round of any real competition. In tavern competitions, sure, anyone with a little too much ale in them could mess up a throw. Moving objects, though, required a clear head, sharp reflexes, great instincts, and perfect technique. And it wasn't just moving objects. Targets also popped up at random. The challenge was thrilling. So much better than scratching at a stupid rock wall in the hopes of finding some gems, so called "gifts from the gods", which would be there if there were gods or not.

"Mikey, can I talk to you for a minute?" Da asked.

"Of course."

Mikey and Da walked a few steps behind me. "I've spent the day working on our accounts," Da said in hushed tones so I wouldn't hear, but the wind carried his words toward me. I practiced the fluid motions necessary for throwing in different directions and pretended not to listen. "I thought you might be interested to know that we have, as of today, with the addition of Mabel's income, finally achieved the savings we'd had when it was all taken from us and *she* left."

"Great news, Da."

The "she" Da mentioned had to be Mam. I knew we'd been poor when I was little. I had no idea Mam was the reason my family had to build our wealth from nothing. That was why Da hated her, why he talked about her like she was dead, why he wanted me to believe she was dead. If others in Gilliam knew about Mam, and they probably did, it made sense that Da was eager for me to find a mate.

How much more could be stacked against me? I was already too thin and my beard too scraggly to be attractive. It was bad enough when I thought Mam was dead and had to live down weak female biology. No one wanted a mate who would die during child-birth. Yes, my brothers had done a lot to build our family reputation from having nothing, back to the respectable status we had now. But knowing that we'd had the status taken away from us because of something Mam did... Everything she did or didn't do reflected directly on me, affecting my ability to attract a mate and subsequently how I carried my family in the decades to come.

Being an excellent miner was not going to be enough to negate everything I had against me. I had to build a stellar reputation for my family. I would start by qualifying for Regionals at the very least. Then everyone would know that I upheld dwarven tradition and values, that I was not my mam.

I'd qualify for Regionals in Mitchum, for the Dwarf Games, and prove to everyone, including her, that I didn't need a mam.

We walked to the Gilliam Mountain—not to the mine entrance but to the city entrance. Other than visiting friends, we really had no reason to be in the city side of the mountain.

Mikey hadn't told me anything about where the competition would be because he said I should focus only on my form and throwing technique. My heart beat fast and my thoughts raced faster. There were two small taverns, but Mikey would never hold a competition there. That left the Gilliam arena, where our Battle-Axe team the Dragon Killers competed, and where the Gilliam Games would be held.

"The arena?" I asked as we walked into the city. The streets were a mass of layered labyrinths cut into the mountain, the homes carved into the walls distinguished only by the doorways and small windows. Torches in iron sconces lit our way through the winding roads to the far side of the mountain.

Mikey sighed. "Yes, the arena."

I grinned, suppressing the adrenaline and excitement pumping through me.

"Don't get nervous, I just want you to get some experience in the competition site itself."

I'd dreamed of competing in the arena as one of the Dragon Killers since I could pick up my first toy axe. In my practices, I had often imagined competing in the arena with Aramis watching, cheering me on, or being in a battle with the epic fight for Gilliam happening in the arena and I save Aramis and my city.

Mikey walked us around the side of the arena to the competitor's entrance. He held the door for me and the rest of the family. He told me to wait for him at the door, while he led Da and our brothers through to the spectator seats.

The corridor broke off into two directions, the arena itself to the right, and the warm-up and dressing rooms to the left. I strolled to the left a little ways, not too far though, so Mikey could still see me. I walked the same corridor my heroes walked every time they went to battle. I ogled the more than fifty championship plaques lining the walls. I wanted to be a hero for my family, for my city, just like the Dragon Killers.

I wandered into the dressing room, the same one my heroes used, sat on the bench where they sat, imagining myself in there with all the other competitors, with Aramis, the whole of Gilliam celebrating my win on the throwing range.

Mikey found me staring at nothing. He sat beside me. "I was going to give you a little pep talk, tell you to imagine yourself here during the Games, but I see by your grin I don't have to. You are a Goldenaxe. You have our competitive spirit. You'll be fine. Let's go."

We walked out of the dressing room toward the arena floor. "During the Gilliam Games, this area will be packed with competitors and coaches, and the crowd noise will be deafening, but try and imagine it."

"No problem." I'd been to enough Dragon Killer's matches and Gilliam Games to know the noise level. Though I supposed it would be different hearing it from the floor of the arena and not from the stands being a part of making it.

Mikey chuckled. "Didn't think it would be."

He said it in such a way that I got the distinct impression he was proud of me. Like he didn't hold Mam's flaws against me. I liked that, a lot.

We entered the arena floor and my breath stopped for a few moments. A throwing range had been set up at the center; the red dirt combed into perfect, lengthwise lines. Spectator seats surrounded the arena rising from floor to the naturally domed ceiling. Although only a small section of the spectator seats was filled, I imagined the crowds there would be, the cheers all for me, Gilliam Games Champion.

A dozen competitors and coaches milled around, the throwing post set up at one end of the arena and participant benches along the edge of the range. I saw Da sitting near the wall surrounding the arena, in the section behind the participant benches.

For Da, for the family, for me… I needed to do well for all of us, and for our reputation. Would it matter how great a reputation we had if I never found a life-mate? Today was the chance for me to prove to Da that Mikey was right, that throwing would boost my selection of mates.

Emma was a natural with a great family reputation and even she had to work at it, flirting with all the males. I wasn't sure I'd be able to flirt and be at the top of my competitive game at the same time.

It wasn't like I was *opposed* to courting with someone. In fact, it sounded pretty good from the way Emma talked about it. And if I were completely honest with myself, I wouldn't mind having someone interested in me, or being interested in someone. If I had a choice, though, I would have preferred to focus only on the competition and forget about courtship or finding a mate all together. At least for today.

I looked Da's way again. I didn't have a choice. I had to do both.

A couple of the competitors wore two braids in their beards. I didn't know them but I knew *of* them and both were from decent mining families. I think they even had brothers who were warriors patrolling the dwarven territories keeping the peace between us and the elves, goblins, and trolls; a career as honorable as mining.

Mikey called for everyone's attention. "Welcome to the Gilliam Games Exhibition Axe-Throwing Competition. While this is an exhibition event, your coaches and I decided there should be some reward for winning. To that end, we have combined our resources to come up with some prizes. Third place gets a handful of rubies." Smart, as all of us were likely still emerald miners. "Second place, a handful of sapphires. For first place, a handful of diamonds." All of us gasped. A diamond was an incredible prize. A handful, that was worth fighting for.

After Mikey explained the rules as it would be done in the real Gilliam Games, the order of competitors was drawn from a cap.

I watched the first few throwers, evaluating them

and my chances. From what I'd seen, I had full confidence I could win.

My turn to throw and I took my place at the throwing line, axes in hand. On instinct, I began to imagine a battle scenario with Aramis. I stopped myself. I am a dwarf. Dwarves do not think about saving elves. Even though no one else knew I imagined saving an elf, it didn't feel right. Not here, not now, in the heart of a dwarven mining city, where true dwarven strength and skill was celebrated. No Aramis then.

At the line, I stared down the throwing post, left foot slightly in front of my right, arm up and back, I heaved the axe forward. The blade hit the post too straight on, and bounced off. Dear gods of iron and wood, I hadn't thrown so bad since I started training with Mikey. I didn't need to be the best, but I couldn't be the worst either. No dwarf wants to be with a loser.

My second and third throws were only better because the axes stuck in the post, but they were well off the center of the target. Thankfully everyone else seemed to be as bad as me this first round.

"Good thing we set up this contest," Mikey said when I sat next to him. "You're letting your nerves get the best of you. Relax. You're losing your focus, on the target and your form."

My nerves weren't really the problem. Focusing on the target—well, I saw it, I could aim for it, I threw where I was aiming, but it just wasn't connecting in one smooth chain like it usually did. I needed to think about Aramis.

During a break before the second round, I over-heard some of the other contestants talking with their coaches. I should have been focusing on what I had done wrong and how I was going to fix it. Instead, I took the opportunity to try and find out more about the males who were interested in mating. Maybe I could hear something that would help me flirt with them and get their attention after the competition. I wasn't a natural flirter like Emma was. If I was going to succeed at this, I needed to be as prepared as I was training for competition.

One of the interested males, Spencer, talked about his throws. He'd done all right but wasn't the best. He hadn't hit the center of the target and his form could use a lot of work. But Spencer was a mountain dweller and would be promoted to the ruby mines soon.

"Try putting a little more force in your throw," his coach said. "And don't lock your wrist. You've got to give your wrist a little flick at the end." I turned in time to see Spencer practicing the instruction. No wonder he did so poorly.

Still, when Spencer caught me looking, I smiled and tugged the braids in my beard the same way Emma always did, drawing attention to my avail-ability. It was much more effective when Emma did it, her beard was so much thicker than mine. Maybe she was still gluing bits of hair onto her chin to make her beard thicker than it actually was, like she'd done when my beard had started growing before hers and she wanted one too.

The second round. By the end of it, the top six competitors would move on to the finals. I concentrated on my form and on the post at the end of the range. While my axes stuck in the post, they were too far off the target. My performance had hardly been spectacular, but I made the top six. So had Spencer, which surprised me, considering his disastrous form.

The judges pulled out the gems, setting them on a pedestal off to our right for all to see. I wanted the diamonds, but I didn't know if I should. Would Spencer like me more if he beat me?

Spencer sat next to me. "Mabel, right?"

"Yeah, hey, congratulations on making the cut," I said, pulling on my tunic to make me appear more stout.

"You too. Um, you're friends with Phillip, right?"

How did he know about my friends? "Phillip?"

"That's him sitting with your brothers, isn't it?"

I turned around, and sure enough, there was Phillip sitting with my family. He smiled and waved. "Yes."

"Awesome. Could you introduce me to him after?"

Right. Da was going to be disappointed. *I* was disappointed. At least he hadn't asked about Emma. "Sure, no problem."

I knew Phillip was interested in finding a mate, but I had no idea if he preferred males over females.

I guessed I'd find out.

"Okay, Mabel," Mikey said. "Third round. You need to relax. It's just like throwing at home. Do what you do at home. You can do this, Mabel. I believe in you."

Doing what I do at home meant being too thin, scraggly-bearded, with too high a voice, dreaming of an elf, and throwing axes perfectly in a highly respected dwarven sport.

Why not? There was nothing more dwarven than winning.

I stepped up to the line, feeling the air around me and the ground beneath my feet. I closed my eyes and pictured myself on an adventure with Aramis. The arena was a cave we wandered into, now swarming with goblins attacking us. Three goblins grabbed Aramis. I threw my first axe, piercing the goblin's heart. Screaming, blood gushing, he let go of Aramis and collapsed to the ground, dead. With my second axe, I aimed for another goblin's head. The blade lodged itself dead center, slicing him in half. The third goblin had a hand around Aramis's throat, choking him. I threw my axe, severing his arm, freeing Aramis.

Mikey clapped me on the shoulder when I sat down. "That's my girl. Whatever you did, don't change it, ever. Your focus was incredible."

"Thanks, Mikey." If he only knew.

Maybe none of the fellows were potential mates yet, but they knew who I was and that I was a competitor. Best of all, at the end of the competition, I walked off with second place and a handful of sapphires, and the praise of my family, especially Da, who only spoke about the brilliance of the final round.

And I hadn't given up on finding a mate just yet.

"MORE TRAINING? Mikey's a task master," Phillip said when I waved goodbye to him and Emma at the turn-off to my house.

I didn't really want to leave my friends to throw axes. I loved the training but I could murder a few tankards of ale after the day's hard slogging in the mines. "The Gilliam Games are in two weeks. No time to rest."

"But you haven't joined us for over two months," Emma said. "How do you expect to find a mate if you don't socialize with anyone?"

Da kept saying the same thing. I liked what Mikey said, that I had time. And in the meantime, I could enjoy my standing as the only female axe-thrower and maybe use it to my advantage. I shrugged. "I'm not worried. I'll join you after the Gilliam Games. I promise." As much as I would rather be at the tavern, I was grateful for the practice time. Once I started throwing, I loved the serenity of it, just me and the post and the pop-up targets Mikey had rigged up. And I couldn't deny how much my improvement over the last couple of months pleased me. If I didn't enjoy throwing, if I didn't think I had a chance at winning, I would have quit ages ago.

Mikey met me in the back garden. "I bought you a little something." He brought out his old leather axe-carrying satchel from behind his back. He pulled a trio of throwing axes, diamonds and sapphires embedded into the handle, and passed them to me. "With your own set of axes, you won't have to think about constantly adjusting for the weight."

Such a magnificent gift knocked me speechless. He had a lot of faith in me to give me something so special. "Dear gods of iron and stone. Thank you Mikey. I don't know what to say. Thank you so much." I tested each one's weight. They were perfect for me. Not too heavy and in total balance. "These are amazing."

"I'm glad you like them."

"Mikey, it's too much."

"You have a lot of talent and a good chance to be champion. You deserve the best. Besides, I have a reputation I believe you can equal, even surpass."

I could never match Mikey's reputation as the top axe thrower in Gilliam history and Dwarf Games champion. "I think the best I can do is not embarrass you."

"If you keep up your technique and continue to work hard, you will accomplish much more than I ever did."

"Thanks, but no one can beat being Dwarf Games champion. Especially not in my first year of competition."

"No, not in your first year. But you can if you win and then successfully defend your title." Mikey paused for a moment, head down.

He'd quit throwing after the championship. He had never picked up an axe again until he started training me and then it was like he'd never stopped. This was the first time I'd seen a hint of regret and loss in Mikey. I got the feeling that quitting throwing hadn't been his choice and it hurt him too much to remember. And yet he'd put it all aside for me.

In a flash, whatever had given him cause for grief vanished and he was all business. "I want you to throw these, get used to the weight, make them a part of you, and think about the technique we've been working on."

"That's all?"

"For today."

I had a great time practicing. The axes were so comfortable in my hands, like they were made for me. Mikey watched, only commenting every now and then to correct my form a little. With each throw, I improved.

When the sun set, he lit lanterns. The bitter wind cut through the sweat on my face, though the rest of me was hot enough to warrant stripping off all my clothes. "I'm tired and sore. Can I stop for today?" I asked.

"No. I want you to throw for another half-hour. It's important to build stamina and strength. It's the ones who can throw through fatigue and pain who become champions."

A dull ache in the muscle of my right shoulder made it hard to lift my arm and throw. "Please, Mikey. My arm really hurts."

"Stretch it out then throw for thirty more minutes. I'll have a gorgeous piece of venison waiting for you."

I flexed and rubbed my shoulder and threw again. If I wanted to be a champion, no one knew better what I needed to do than Mikey. It hurt to raise my arm and throw, but I clenched my teeth and kept going. I was wrecked at the end but pleased with myself for pushing through the pain and throwing not too badly. My throws were pitiful, but at least I still hit the targets.

I sank onto the table bench. A huge plate filled with juicy venison right off the spit lay in front of me. My right arm and hand cramped up. I stared at my meat and I stretched and massaged my muscles.

"You've done well today, but there is a lot of room for improvement," Mikey said.

Unbelievable. No axe-throwing competition made the contestants throw for two hours straight. I always threw my best in the middle of each practice session so with the warm-up throws I should be fine. I couldn't do any better, not with only two weeks to go. "How much more?"

"Perfection and nothing less."

I groaned.

"To win you have to push yourself harder than you ever have. Being the best will either break you or you will be crowned champion. You do want to be champion, don't you?"

Of course I did. I also wanted to go to the Prospector with my friends, and sleep.

For Da, for the family, for me—I had to think beyond my aches and pains to the fact every male in Gilliam, whether he was interested in mating or not, would be watching and admiring me, and thinking I would be a suitable mate for himself or a friend. As champion, I could have my pick of mates. "You know I do."

"Then don't be afraid to work hard and keep improving. The Gilliam Games are just the start. The greater your skill, the greater the competition."

That night, I curled up in bed with my movie magazine. I hadn't looked at it in a while. I loved dreaming of Aramis. I loved axe throwing and competing. I did want to be champion. But right now, all I wanted to do was go to the movies with a friend, sit in the dark, and watch the wizard's crystal flash the images on the screen.

All I wanted was to do something else, be someone else.

CHAPTER 6

THE RUMBLE of the crowd shook the ground and reverberated up my body. We were still in the tunnel of the Gilliam Arena. I cowered at the thought of the noise when we would step onto the competition floor. I couldn't hear any of the games official's last-minute instructions. Rock-sludge-like acid from my stomach soon joined the mine-dust-like dryness of my mouth.

"You'll be fine, Mabel," Mikey screeched into my ear. He put his massive warm hands on my shoulders and pushed me forward. The younger contestants, the ones like me competing in our first Gilliam Games, were also pushed by their coaches. The experienced competitors were relaxed, joking, going through the motions of throw and follow-through.

"Ignore them." His breath was hot on my ear. The end of the tunnel loomed. "Tune everyone out. Focus on your own game and no one can beat you."

I nodded ever so slightly to let him know I heard him. If I moved anymore I'd lose everything I'd eaten this last week.

Mikey and I were among the last of the competitors to step into the arena. The noise in the tunnel was nothing but muffled growls compared to being in the cavern. Two to three dwarves crowded into each seat and dwarflings sat on the closest available knee.

Mikey said something to me, but I couldn't hear. I only felt his moist breath. I shook my head and pointed at my ears to signal to him. He smiled and dug his thumbs into my shoulder muscles in a comforting massage.

The games official paraded us around the arena. The confident competitors waved to the crowd, smiling and laughing. I took their lead, hoping it would help my nerves. I smiled and raised my arm, which felt more like an anvil had been tied to it than a well-muscled part of my body that could throw anything. Twisting my wrist I waved as best I could.

My friends waved. Da and my brothers crowded in behind them. Their seats were close to ring-side and right behind the competitors' benches, the same place they'd sat in for the exhibition competition. I'm sure I imagined it, but I thought I could hear my family and friends chant my name amid everything. I relaxed. Smiling became more natural. My arm didn't feel quite so heavy.

We found our place among the benches. Mikey handed me my bag of axes.

The official waved his hands and the crowd quieted down. He then called the first competitor. As the twenty-fifth of thirty contestants, I had plenty of time to prepare. I held my axes, weighing each of the finely sanded and lacquered handles in my hands, deciding which order I would throw them. I closed my eyes and centered my breathing. Lots of dwarves in the stands were eating skewered pork, and the aroma of stout ale made it all feel like being back at The Bearded Prospector, throwing for fun with my friends. Except it was a lot louder in here, and really hot. Sweat pebbled on my brow. I swiped at it with my hand, which only made my palm slick. I dried my hand on my tunic.

Though I didn't watch the competition, I knew exactly how everyone had done from the reaction of the crowd. My stomach clenched and my arms stiffened. I desperately wanted a few ales in me to calm me down.

The official called my name.

"Take a deep breath, shake out your arms, forget the scoreboard and ignore the noise. Focus, relax, and do what you do." Mikey patted my back and nudged me into the throwing range.

I weighed the first axe in my hand. The crowd quieted. Even the vendors selling sweets and roast meats were quiet. I found the silence almost more distracting than the noise. All eyes were on me. This was nothing like throwing at the Prospector.

I focused on the target. At fifteen feet, I knew I could make this distance easily. I stepped up to the throwing line. The target didn't look so different from the practice post at home. I rested my axe on my shoulder. I did this a hundred times a day. Feet spread, one in front of the other for leverage. I pulled the axe back and heaved it forward, my whole body moving with it, the perfect release and follow-through.

It arced, end over end, the diamonds and sapphires in the handle sparkling. It soared toward the target. I thought the intake of breath from the crowd as they gasped might suck the axe off course.

Thunk. The head stuck in the second outermost circle of the target. I stared at it. That would not do.

I had lost all the focus I'd gained from my practice throws. I'd let the noise and the venue get to me and change the way I prepared. I needed to do more than visualize perfection. The more-experienced competitors may have merely visualized their throws, but I could do better. I had Aramis and he depended on me to win his freedom. No, not his freedom. Today we were in a fierce battle and I had to slay his enemy.

The Evil Lord of Darkness cast his shadow on the allied army of dwarves and elves. His masses of minions surrounded us. Aramis battled a dozen of them on his own, freeing me to slay our greatest enemy. The head of my axe, forged in the elven fires, could pierce the toughest armor and the most powerful fields of magic. The Evil Lord of Darkness raised his sword above his head, exposing his heart to my axe.

I had to be careful and accurate. Only one chance now. If I missed, we would all die. I pulled my arm back, narrowed my eyes to see only the Evil Lord's heart. I put all of my body's momentum into the throw, releasing the axe at the right moment. *Thunk.* My axe pierced his armor, an inch off target. The Evil Lord of Darkness roared, mortally wounded. The next throw would finish him off.

Quick, before he recovered! I raised my axe, focused on the Evil Lord's heart. The axe disappeared from my vision as it arced up and over until it descended, the head piercing the armor and slicing the outer vestiges of his heart. I had slain the Evil Lord of Darkness!

I sat next to Mikey. "How am I doing?" I asked, afraid to look at the scoreboard. I hoped my last two throws could make up the points I'd lost with my disastrous first throw.

"You're fifteenth."

With five more competitors to go, it should be enough to get to the second round but I had a lot of ground to make up if I had any hope of making the top ten and moving on to the Regional Competition. I didn't know if I'd be able to move up enough. I should have focused earlier. I shouldn't have let my nerves get to me. "I'm sorry, Mikey. I've let you down."

"You're hardly out of the competition. You did a great job of shaking off the nerves for your second and third throws. I have no doubt you'll make it to the next round. At the very least, that clown Spencer, and a couple of others who have the same coach, have yet to throw. I'd be surprised if they come anywhere near the perfection of your last two throws. With six throws at twenty feet in round two, you've got plenty of time to get into the top ten."

I finished the first round sixteenth overall; hardly a satisfactory result. Perhaps I should have been happy with my score, considering I competed against warriors and dwarves much older and experienced than me, but I could place higher. I had to. With the scores of the first round now negated, competing with a clean scorecard, I would place higher. Aramis and I were at war against the armies of the Evil Lord of Darkness.

I stepped up to the throwing line. We had slain our enemy but the shadow of evil remained in the form of his minions still fighting a losing cause. With the Evil Lord gone, I had every confidence I could slaughter them all. Six minions attacked. With absolute clarity I aimed for their hearts. My axes pierced their armor, three dropped on the spot as my axes sliced through their hearts. The remaining three would die in the night from their wounds.

That was more like it.

On my way back to my seat I looked up at the

scoreboard. I sat eighth with four more competitors left. I'd moved up but I wasn't satisfied. Second-round points accumulated with the third-round points. The possibility of winning hinged perilously on a spectacular performance by me, and an even more spectacular fall by one or two of the top-place competitors. I couldn't win, but I could maybe make the top five.

"You're doing fine, but you're still off by a couple of inches. You're rushing the throw, releasing too soon. In the next round, take your time. Your focus on the target is excellent. Remember the technique of the throw, when to release, and the follow-through."

I remained in eighth place heading into the third round.

I faced nine moving and pop-up targets—and Aramis and I were swarmed by the last of the Evil Lord's minions. Though their numbers had greatly diminished, the battle had worn us both down. I slaughtered the first five minions with blades straight to their black little hearts. My arm burned but they kept coming. I had to slow down, take my time to focus my energy and not get sloppy on my follow-through to make sure the axe flew with full force. I felled three more minions.

One last minion raced at Aramis. I had to stop it. Pain stabbed through my shoulder. One more. I pulled back and put my full body's energy into it. The axe soared in an elegant arc, blade over handle over blade. I grazed the edge of the minion's heart, enough to destroy him.

At last the war was over. Aramis and I and our allied armies were victorious, exhausted, sweaty and sore.

I'd done it. I'd placed fifth. Far from being champion, but high enough to get to the Regional Games.

My family led my cheering section, my friends a close second in volume. I smiled but I couldn't lift my arm enough to wave. "Well done, Mabel," Mikey said. "You've earned yourself a day off from training."

My friends met me at the arena exit. "You were brilliant," Jimmy said, putting a casual arm around my shoulder. "Let's go to the Prospector to celebrate."

"All drinks are on us," Phillip said.

I loved being with my friends. It had been so long since I'd gone to the Prospector and had some fun with them, but I was exhausted and yawned several times on the way out of the mountain. When we reached the turn-off to the Prospector, I stopped. "I'm sorry, but I really want to go home."

"What you need is some proper ale in you to celebrate," Jimmy said.

"And some time with your friends," Emma added. "Besides, there might be some potential mates waiting for you there."

She was right. Now was the time to meet my admirers given how well I'd placed, but I really, truly, just wanted to go home. "I'm sorry, maybe tomorrow."

I didn't feel like celebrating. I'd qualified for Regionals, but I wasn't happy with my overall result. It wasn't a *bad* result, I just couldn't get over my disastrous first throw. Besides, it had been a long day. This level of competing took a lot out of me. Maybe I needed to put my exhaustion aside, for my family and myself, to take advantage of what celebrity I may have. But quite frankly, at the moment, I didn't care about socializing and finding a mate.

CHAPTER 7

"MABEL," EMMA said in a soft sing-songy way as she shook me awake. "Mabel."

"What are you doing here?" I was stukk exhausted frin yesterday's competition. After I'd come home I'd gone straight to bed. Max had tried to wake me earlier, to join them to watch today's events at the Games. I pretended to be asleep then. Emma was too persistent to allow me the same opportunity.

"I'm not going to the Games." I pulled the covers up.

Emma tugged them off me. "Me neither. I want to spend a quiet day with my best friend before your fame makes you too busy and popular to have time for me."

I snorted. "Fifth place doesn't make anyone popular."

Emma smiled as she yanked me out of bed. "You'll see. Come on. It's lunch time and I'm hungry."

"Okay, but then I need to practice. Regionals are coming up." I got to my feet and automatically moved into my stretches.

"No practice. You've earned a day off. Mikey said so. Get dressed. If you're not downstairs in five minutes, I'm going to come up here with a bucket of ice water."

"All right. All right." I reached for my blue tunic.

I dressed, brushed and braided my beard, while at every one-minute interval Emma yelled out how much time I had left. She was on the ten-second countdown when I reached the bottom of the stairs. I'd expected to see all my friends in the living room, but it was just Emma. We used to do everything together, just the two of us, but hadn't since our beards started growing in. This would be nice. "I'm here. What's the plan?"

"There's a new movie playing. I thought we'd go watch it."

"Will the theater be open with the Games going on?"

"It is. I checked on my way over. Let's go or we'll be late."

"What about lunch?"

"I've packed us one." Emma picked up her bag, which had been sitting by the door.

Gilliam's roads were empty. Everyone was in the arena watching the Games. It was kind of nice not having to see or talk to anyone but Emma. "Are you *sure* the theater is open?"

"Yes. I told you, I checked first."

"You walked all the way to the theater then back to my place?" And she packed us a lunch? That was a lot of unnecessary effort on her part. It wasn't like today was a special day.

"Well, first I checked The Bearded Prospector, but it's closed, as are all eateries and taverns in Gilliam. I passed the theater on my way home to pack us a lunch and saw that they were open."

How did she have the energy for all of that? I wasn't sure I had enough energy to walk from home to the theater, never mind anywhere else. "We could have just stayed at my place."

"Do you want to go or not?"

Emma sounded hurt. "Of course I do," I said. "This is really nice. I just can't believe all the work you went to."

"Which means you should be all the more grateful. Come on, Mabel. Lighten up. It's fun. The city is empty. We're not mining. You don't have to practice throwing. When was the last time you had a day, or even just an evening like this?"

I didn't have to think hard. "My second day at the mines. I see your point." I *had* been itching to get back to the theater to see a movie. "Thanks."

"Of course. That's what friends are for."

We arrived at the theater. I was surprised to see a few others in the lobby buying tickets. I really thought everyone else would be watching the Games. There were almost as many dwarves here as there had been the last time I'd come. The theater's reputation must have been building.

"Hey Mabel," Oliver called out. "Emma." He'd just bought his ticket. I waved as I put down my payment and picked up my ticket. I hadn't seen Oliver since my first week at the mines when he'd been moved to the night shift.

"Congratulations on qualifying for Regionals," he said with a big smile.

"Thanks." I blushed and lowered my head. It was kind of him to congratulate me but I wished he'd been able to say "Congratulations on placing in the top three." Or, "Congratulations on winning the Games."

"We're so proud of our Mabel," Emma said, putting an arm around my shoulders and hugging me.

"You should have heard Ricky in the stands," Curtis said, joining us. "He was bragging to everyone who would listen that you wouldn't be throwing if it weren't for him. He practically took credit for your success."

"I wouldn't go that far but it's probably partly true," I said. "If it hadn't been for that challenge, I doubt Mikey would have ever offered to coach me."

"Don't let Ricky hear that," Oliver said. "Do you two want to join us?"

"Sure," I said.

Oliver and Curtis walked in ahead of us, holding hands. Ah, the joys of being a male dwarf, free to love whomever you want.

I picked up a new movie magazine on my way in. "So what brings you two here to the theater instead of watching the games?" I asked.

"With me on the night shift, we hardly have a chance to see each other," Oliver said. "With the mines closed, we thought it would be nice to spend some time together."

They were on a date. If I were on a date with someone I hardly got to see, having people join us would be the last thing I'd want. "It was kind of you to ask, but we don't want to intrude on your time," I said.

"It's hardly an intrusion," Curtis said. "We just didn't want to be surrounded by thousands of dwarves."

"Oh, all right. If you're sure," I said. "You'll hardly know we're here."

We gave our tickets to the usher at the door to the main theater. Emma kept elbowing me for some reason on our way to our seats. Emma and I left a couple of spots empty between us and Oliver and Curtis.

I loved the theater even more this time. Last time, it was all just so new, I didn't know what to expect. Now I knew and I wanted to watch it all, from the way the screen was hung, to the candles lining the walls, to the wizard's crystal at the back of the room.

Even though neither Aramis nor Sevrin were in this movie, and I didn't know what it was about, I didn't care. I knew I was going to enjoy it all. Or I would if Emma stopped poking me with her elbow.

"What?" I asked, turning away from watching the projectionist at the back of the room.

"He likes you."

What was she on about? "Who does?"

"The usher. He smiled at you."

"Specifically at me?"

"Yes. Here he comes."

"Excuse me," he said walking up to us. "Are you Mabel Goldenaxe?"

"She is," Emma said before I had a chance to answer.

"Great job in the Games yesterday. It's nice to see someone who actually still lives here compete and do well."

"Thank you." He wasn't interested in me. He'd only watched me compete. "I just want to make my city proud."

"Well, good luck in the Regionals." He hesitated a moment longer then left.

I turned back to watch the projectionist prepare the wizard's crystal.

"Argh. Mabel. He was totally flirting with you and all you could say was 'I just want to make my city proud.'"

"He wasn't flirting," I said, wishing she'd leave me alone so I could watch the projectionist and the precision required for him to tap the tines of the fork just right to project the pictures. "He was just being nice."

"He went out of his way to talk with you, leaving his job post to do it."

"Whatever."

The projectionist readied the crystal in the tines.

"Even if he wasn't actually flirting with you, which he was—and Oliver and Curtis would confirm it if they weren't so busy—any time a fellow talks to you, it is an opportunity to turn it into flirtation, and, even better, courtship. You do know that, don't you?"

"Yeah, yeah," I said, and missed the moment the projectionist tapped the tines. How did he know how hard or light to tap them? Or where? What if he tapped them too high or too low? How much training did he have for the job?

"That's how I got Zach." Emma's voice was smug with satisfaction.

So that's why we were having this day together, so she could brag about courting Zach. It was a great accomplishment. She'd been trying to get him to court her for ages. "Congratulations. You two will make a cute couple."

I found that no matter how much I tried, I couldn't concentrate on the movie now flashing on the screen in front of me—a drama of the treacherous expansion of an early dwarven settlement. I kept dwelling on my performance at the Gilliam Games and how I needed to do so much better if I was going to qualify for the Dwarf Games and raise the reputation of my family. And yet I knew that for Da, what would help the family most was if I had a mate. How could I find a mate if I didn't know enough to figure out if a male was flirting with me or how to turn plain conversation into flirtation? How did Emma even know about that stuff? Sure she had an older sister, but they were hardly close. They were always in competition with each other. There was no way Rachel would ever give Emma advice on finding a suitable mate, not until she had one herself.

By the time the movie ended, I'd made up my mind. I decided to find a way to understand males. Rather, I needed to find out what everyone else inherently knew about relationships and flirting. I decided to try the Gilliam library, hoping there would be a book that could help me figure this out.

I told Emma I wanted to go home and have time to myself. The house was never quiet and there would only be a few hours before Da and my brothers returned home. I wanted to take advantage of the break. I thanked her for the outing and left her at the turn-off to our cottage.

I had to take a few side streets to avoid Emma seeing me, but eventually ended up on the road to the library.

I huddled into the crevice of the mountainside to protect against the chilly afternoon. Snow and ice covered the path.

If Aramis were in Gilliam, I'd know exactly what

to do. Nothing with Aramis would be mixed signals or guessing if he were flirting. He'd know right away I loved him, and I'd know he loved me too. Why did my mate have to be a dwarf?

The librarian sat behind her counter. "May I help you?" she asked without looking up from her book.

"Just browsing, thanks," I said. Shelves of books filled the cavern from floor to ceiling and wall to wall. As the only patron, I took my time searching the categories: Geology, Mining, Weaponry, Self-help. Self-help? The top shelf, back corner of the library carried the self-help section, the books covered in dust and out of alphabetical order. But Gilliam had a self-help section!

I wiped off the spines of the books: *101 Signs He's Interested: Male Dwarf Body Language of Love; 102 Sign's You're Interested: Female Dwarf Body Language of Love;* and *Meet Him and Mate Him: 1001 Ways to Meet Your Perfect Dwarf Mate.* Who knew there were these kinds of resources? I also found books on the history of Dwarves in movies and the art of movie making. I signed the books out and prepared for a full night of studying. I might start with the books on movies, to ease myself in.

THE DIMNESS of the crosscut made me sleepy. I'd stayed up late the night before reading the books from the library.

Yawning, I scratched at the surface of the rock, still marveling at the origins of movies. The technique had been discovered by Radier when he had led an adventure with Aramis and Sevrin. He'd used his crystal in his staff to light their way. His staff was bumped against the wall, the crystal vibrated, and suddenly they were seeing, and hearing, themselves on the wall of the cave. It took some time for Radier to figure out how he had recorded their travels, but once he had, he knew he had something special. It wasn't until the original recorded material could be accurately duplicated to dozens of crystals that movies became a viable enterprise. By the time I went to bed, I couldn't sleep for thinking about what it would be like to see the original recordings of those first movies. They were still around, archived in Leitham. Maybe someday I'd get to travel there. It wasn't in dwarven territory, but there were enough dwarves there that I could, maybe, one day, find a reason to go.

When Phillip arrived in the crosscut, he joined me. After half an hour of mindless scratching, I put my hand on his arm to stop him then pulled his axe back. I tapped my own axe on the rock.

He tapped his axe on the rock and felt its texture. "Do you want to do it?"

"You do it," I said.

Using his medium pick, he cracked the shell.

Excellent. I couldn't wait to tell Frankie. Every emerald bed we found confirmed his beliefs in this crosscut from the start. If only the earlier miners hadn't given up so quickly on this crosscut. Frankie always said that sometimes you had to cut away a lot of rock before you found the gems, and the gods always rewarded those miners who were patient and persistent.

Phillip and I pried away the outer shell hiding the emeralds.

Emma rushed in. "Sorry I'm late. Zach wouldn't let me get away from him."

"You've been late a lot recently," Phillip said, not looking away from his work. "Your excuses wouldn't pass with most other miners. Your first priority is work, not Zach."

"Sorry," Emma replied. Though I didn't look at her, I heard the pout in the tone of her voice. "What's going on?"

"Mabel and I found more emeralds," Phillip said.

"Fabulous." Emma sorted through her tools to help us.

"Get your larger axe and start working to Mabel's left. There's still a lot of rock to get through before we can find the edges of this bed."

"Can't I help you? I still don't have my first emerald," she whined.

"We need you to keep searching. Besides, you have to find a new bed to get a first emerald."

"Is this a punishment for being late?"

"Nope. It's where you're needed." Phillip brushed away stone and grit from the gems.

After a long day, we had excavated several dozen emeralds and I was ready for a celebration. It had been so long since I'd joined my friends at the Prospector, I'd almost forgotten the wonderful aroma of ale and pipe smoke, the crush of the crowd of fellow miners, and most of all, how comfortable it was to be with friends.

Jimmy and Ben joined Zach, Emma, Phillip and me at our little table. "One of the top axe throwers in all of Gilliam and she still graces us with her presence," Jimmy teased, setting down a round of ales in front of us. "Congratulations, Mabel. Phillip was also bragging about you and the productive stope you have."

If I believed what it said in *101 Signs He's Interested: Male Dwarf Body Language of Love,* then I might think Jimmy had just flirted with me. But I knew Jimmy far too well. Just because he smiled didn't mean that he was interested in me. We'd been friends since we'd learned to walk. Jimmy smiling was no different than what he normally did. "We're doing all right. Phillip and I just found another bed of emeralds this morning," I said.

"The mining gods must *love* you. If you ever get tired of working with Emma and Phillip, we could use someone with your talent working with us," Jimmy said.

According to *He's Interested,* he just flirted with me, except I knew that wasn't true. We'd worked well together in the toy workshop and he probably wanted to work with me again. Still, if he had flirted, I should tease back, but not make it obvious, in case I misunderstood. "I'll keep it in mind."

"There's no way I'm letting her go." Phillip put an arm around me. Definitely flirtation, except after today, I shouldn't be surprised he didn't want to let me go. We were a great team.

To prove me right, as quickly as he put his arm around me, Phillip withdrew it and chatted with Ben about the day's find.

"How many first emeralds do you have now? Three?" Jimmy asked.

"This is my fourth."

Jimmy whistled. We were lucky to have such a productive crosscut. I thanked Frankie every day for getting me in there.

"You'll be moved to rubies soon," Jimmy said.

"I'll need to find dozens more emerald beds before any promotions come my way," I said.

Why did this have to be so hard? Why couldn't a fellow just say "Hey, you have two braids in your beard. I'm interested in finding a mate too. I like you. Want to go out with me some time, see if we're a fit?"

"How many firsts do you have, Emma?" Ben asked.

Emma straightened her cap and stuck out her bottom lip. "None, yet."

"But you'll get one soon," I jumped in. "Besides, getting a first isn't everything. Emma's been great at exposing the fullness of the beds."

Emma looked past me, her mouth gaping open. What had I said? I hoped I hadn't offended her.

"Dearest gods of ale. Mabel, would you look at that?"

Everyone at our table looked in time to see Emma's sister chatting up the fellow standing next to my brother Max. Emma smirked. "Oh thank gods. For a minute there I thought Rachel was after Max."

"You say it like courting Max would be disgraceful," Jimmy said. "He's a great fellow."

"There's nothing wrong with him. I just think Rachel should aim a little higher, that's all."

"Higher than what?" Jimmy demanded. "Mabel's family has a fine reputation. You would be lucky to attract one of her brothers."

"Please. Mabel's brothers are fun, but there's a reason they're uninterested in mating. No one would have them."

If Emma thought so poorly of my brothers, she might as well believe no one wanted me either. My stomach muscles clenched painfully. She probably meant females should want mountain dwellers first. Still. Maybe we weren't the wealthiest of families, but in my lifetime alone my da and brothers had started with almost nothing and earned a fair fortune. Maybe that was the real problem. My mam had absconded with all our income. No one would want to take a chance on our family. Not with that kind of history.

Jimmy sat back and glowered at Emma from behind his tankard. He oozed aggravation. He knew she was right and there was nothing he could say to defend my family.

I liked that he wanted to but it embarrassed me even more because he couldn't.

Then, as though she hadn't insulted my family, Emma said, "Mabel, we found out this morning my mam is pregnant again. She and Da were so excited. They barely got the words out they were giggling and kissing so much. At the rate they're going, they could have a dozen more dwarflings and still not get tired of each other."

I would never be able to say my mam and da had been so in love, or that they'd had dozens of dwarflings. Had my mam left because she tired of my da? She must have, if she weren't dead. Why did she have to leave us? Why couldn't she be dead? At least then it wouldn't look bad on me. Only if she died in battle, of course. If she died giving birth it would be a life sentence to never being loved by anyone.

"Excellent news. Good thing there are others to look after the wee ones now that you're older, looking to start a family of your own, eventually, I mean," I said.

"Thanks." Emma beamed at Zach.

Poor Da. I could forgive his constant questioning me about finding a mate. My brothers had done what they could to elevate the family name. I had to re-focus and do my part. I wished it didn't all rest on my shoulders, but I would deal with it. I needed to take a more proactive approach to finding a mate. I'd read my books again tonight—the relationship ones, not the movie ones—and decide which one had the best method.

CHAPTER 8

I WISHED males didn't want their mates to have stout bellies. However, as it said in *102 Signs She's Interested: Female Dwarf Body Language of Love,* a stout figure is the key to attracting a male. Still, I needed to increase my appetite, or at least eat as much as I possibly could, even if I felt like I was going to burst. I didn't think I could finish all the spit-roasted pork and deep-fried dumplings the cafeteria staff stacked on my lunch tray, no matter how delicious it looked. I pulled on my tunic to appear thicker, not like it made any difference since the belt cinched my waist.

With my figure, I'd fit in so much better with elves I bet. Aramis would love me the way I looked. No. I had to stop thinking that way. No more dreaming of elves or of Aramis. No matter how much I loved him, I had to turn my attention to finding a mate. A real one. A dwarf.

It was up to me to make this happen.

I would much rather focus my energy on training for Regionals but I had to do this for my family. It was my duty as the lone female. I'd known this all along. I had to stop dithering.

I wasn't going to miss a smile from a male and I most certainly was not going to give anyone any reason to insult me or my family the way Emma had.

I'd considered all the available males I knew and decided to aim for the one who had the most to offer. Ben. Perhaps there could have been a more ideal choice considering how he had chased Emma. She had picked Zach so Ben had to choose someone else. Even if he still wanted her, he'd soon realize he could do worse than courting me.

Emma and Zach were always together, which meant whenever Ben and I were with our friends, we were together too. I had my plan all worked out: I was going to make him want me by showing him I possessed the qualities he looked for in a mate. If it didn't work with Ben, I'd have to pick another fellow, find out what he wanted, and basically start over. Ben had to want me or I'd be so exhausted from the search I'd have no energy to love, or mine, or have dwarflings.

According to *Female Dwarf Body Language of Love*, the number one way to let a male know you are interested in him, specifically him, is to be beside him at all possible times, whether it be at the pub, at work, or out with friends. Focus all your attention on him, laugh at his jokes and be interested in what he says. Emma hovered around Zach, laughing at everything and never letting him out of her sight. It worked for her, and it would work for me.

I hoped Ben hadn't found himself someone to court since I saw him yesterday.

Zach and Ben sat alone at a table in the corner. My heart skipped a beat. As Emma and I neared their table, I ran my fingers through my measly beard. I really had to do something to thicken it. There must be some kind of conditioner or product. Maybe I could do what Emma did and trim some of my hair and glue it onto my chin. Or maybe I could get Ben to like me whatever my beard looked like.

Ben smiled at us and Emma grabbed the seat next to him, which meant I could sit across from him. I smiled, willing Ben to look at me so I could hold his gaze for a few seconds, then look away demurely.

"I've had the most frustrating morning," Emma said the moment we sat down. Ben leaned toward her and I gave up trying to catch his eye.

"What's wrong, pet?" Zach reached across the table and held Emma's hands.

"I have been working here almost a year now and I still have not found my own first emerald. This morning I thought I'd found a bed of emeralds. I did exactly what Frankie taught us to do. Turns out I was working nothing more than a rough patch of rock. I am such a failure." Emma covered her face with her hands.

Poor Emma.

"No, you're not." Ben put an arm around her shoulders and Zach stood on the other side of her, rubbing her back, hugging her.

"Why didn't you help her, Mabel?" Zach asked.

Excuse me? "I would have if I'd known. Emma, why didn't you say something? You know Phillip or I would have helped you." She should have told us first, not Zach and Ben.

"Why? So you could get another first emerald?"

What had I done to make her accuse me of stealing from my workmates? How could she think I was full of greed? Goldenaxes have always worked hard for every gem.

Emma sniffed and both Ben and Zach raced to pass her a handkerchief. "Doesn't matter anyway," she said, taking them both. "It's just another useless place to mine."

"Nothing is useless," Ben said.

"A lot of miners go years before they get their first gem," Zach said. "You're doing fine, pet."

"You really are," Ben said. "It took some of my brothers over five years before they found their first emeralds. Now they're among the top in their fields."

"True." She wiped her eyes, though I hadn't actually seen any tears.

"And don't be afraid to ask Mabel for help," Ben

said.

I appreciated his belief in my skills, and that he knew I could help. But Phillip, Emma, and I were a good team. We didn't need him or Zach telling us how to work. I pushed back my tray with half the food untouched. My stomach turned and I trembled under the accusatory stares.

I had to get out of here.

I left them and walked back to our crosscut in a fog of anger. How dare she accuse me like that? We were supposed to be best friends. She was not going to get away with those lies and accusations. She knew better than anyone that I would not steal. No one in my family stole.

I clutched my axe and took my frustration out on the stope wall. I scratched at the rock and ignored Emma when she sauntered in, humming, happy, like she hadn't just tried to ruin my reputation.

When Phillip returned, I stopped working and said, "We have to talk. All of us."

"What's going on?" he asked.

Emma chipped at the wall, ignoring me.

"Emma, stop," I said. "We have a problem."

"We do?" Phillip asked.

I rested my axe on my shoulder. "Emma is unhappy working with us. Instead of telling us, her workmates, who she should be telling, she's running off telling everyone else." Only then did she stop working and face us, blushing deeply, and her lips pressed tight together. I couldn't bear to bring up her accusations of theft. They hurt too much. "If there's a problem, you should talk to us first. How can we fix things if you don't tell us?"

"Why would I tell you? It's the two of you who don't want me to find my first emerald."

"Excuse me?" Phillip asked, taken aback.

"You keep making me work in areas where you know there are no emeralds so you and Mabel will get all the firsts."

So it wasn't just me she was accusing, but Phillip as well.

"No one knows where the emeralds are until we get there," Phillip said. "You're doing as valuable a job as Mabel and I, eliminating places there aren't emeralds, digging us to a place where we will find them."

"Exactly. You want me to do the grunt work, keeping me from finding my first-ever gem."

"You're paid your share of the beds," Phillip said.

"But they aren't firsts," Emma said.

"Keep working. You will get there. And you can always ask for help if we're working somewhere else."

"I don't need help. What I need is a better place to mine."

"Then I suggest you get to work," Phillip said, "because you're not going to find a more productive stope than this one. Stop whining, stop flirting, and maybe you will find something." He picked up his axe and returned to work.

In spite of everything she'd said, the accusations, the hurt, I felt bad. She was wrong. We didn't know where the emeralds were until we found them, but maybe it wasn't fair that we had her working on her own.

"Is there a reason Emma can't work with us?" I asked.

"There are only three of us and a huge cavern to mine," Phillip said. "We need to spread out."

I needed to do something to prove to Emma she was wrong, that I hadn't deliberately kept her from extracting gems or finding her first-ever emerald, that I wasn't at thief.

"Fine. Emma, you work with Phillip and I'll be here where you were. I only wanted to make sure if any of us had a problem with our arrangement, we talked to each other first. Okay?"

"Sure." Phillip shrugged and returned to excavating the emeralds.

"No problem," Emma said just as casually as Phillip. "Mabel, why don't you come help me? I don't think he wants me working with him right now."

I didn't really want to work with her right now either, but if it would stop her from ruining me then I would.

I felt the stone. I couldn't see why she'd been so frustrated by it. By all signs of the texture of the rock, one tap and a bed of emeralds would be exposed.

"Not there. Feel this."

I ignored Phillip's snorts disguised as grunts. Emma pointed me to the pure granite stone she insisted on working. Hadn't she paid attention to Frankie? I continued to feel the stone while I decided my best option for fixing this situation without embarrassing her, and without her thinking I intended to get the first emerald.

I cleared my throat. "Right. This stone is too solid. We need to work around it, get at the emeralds from behind. Maybe if we chip away at the other stone. Why don't you start? I have to step out for a few minutes."

"Are you all right?" Phillip asked.

"Ate a little too much. Maybe you can help?"

"I can do it myself. Besides, I wouldn't want to distract Phillip from his most important work."

I hoped this worked. If it did, they would stop fighting. If it didn't, Emma might become unbearable.

I hovered outside the entrance of the crosscut. Emma chipped at the stone, grumbling. If she didn't hurry up, I'd have to get back in and help her, and she would not want me to. Besides, why shouldn't Emma experience the elation of finding her first-ever gem?

Emma grumbled louder the harder she hit the stone. I cringed. I could just see the emeralds cracking inside. At last the chipping settled into a rhythm, then a pause and a gasp from Emma, followed by a high-pitched squeal and, "Dear gods of diamonds and mortar!"

I ran in. "What? What is it? Are you okay?"

"Look. I found it. I bet this bed is huge, bigger than any either of you have found. And you told me to dig here to get behind rock a few feet over." Emma pocketed her first emerald, half the size of the palm of her hand.

Phillip stood at my side, studying her find. "Well done. You don't seem to need Mabel, so can I have her back?"

"Please, take her."

My insides turned.

"That first belongs to you," Phillip muttered as we headed back to our own emeralds. "If you hadn't told her where to look she'd forever be chipping the wrong stone."

"Maybe, but she needs it more than I do."

First emerald in hand, Emma became much more talkative than she had been in a long time. Every few minutes she said things like, "I am so relieved. I can't believe it took me this long. This is only the first of many. Rachel had her first-ever in her first year as a miner and she's been boasting about it since I started. She says with all of her firsts, profits, and the earnings of her future mate, they are going to buy themselves a mountain dwelling."

I was glad I didn't have a sister to compete with. My brothers were nothing but supportive of me. Phillip and I kept on working. I did my best to ignore her but Emma's constant babble was difficult to shut out.

"It doesn't matter," she continued. "Even if Rachel marries the wealthiest dwarf in Gilliam, they still can't buy a mountain dwelling if he needs Rachel's income to help him. She doesn't have as much as she says she does. Besides, there aren't any mountain dwellings for sale. There never are. Anyway, I am so relieved, like a huge weight has lifted off me. Now I can prove my worth as a miner. Rachel's always telling me I started working here too soon and I hadn't really reached full maturity, even though I looked it. Now my first-ever is bigger than hers."

I wished she hadn't insulted me in front of Ben and Zach because of her rivalry with Rachel.

"Sorry about being such a grump earlier," Emma said. "Da couldn't understand why you two were finding so many emeralds and I hadn't found any. It's all he would talk about. He'll be so proud when I tell him how I found this one, and how big this bed is."

I'd never tell her I tricked her. Hopefully she'd ease up on me and my family after this.

After our shift, we headed to the Prospector. Taverns frequented by co-workers was one of the top places listed in *Meet Him and Mate Him* as ideal for finding a mate, because that's where I'd find someone with similar interests as me. Ben was still my best option for a mate, if I could convince him to forget what Emma had done to me at lunch.

We caught up with Ben and Zach on the road to

the Prospector. Emma squeezed herself between the two and I pushed my way between her and Ben. She launched into her tale of finding the emeralds. Ben leaned forward to see her so I moved to his other side, making it easier for him to hear her, and I didn't have to be so close to her, listening to her tell how she found the emeralds without any help.

"Mabel, a word please." Frankie stood outside the Prospector, Phillip beside him. Great.

"Frankie, please don't be upset." Emma stepped in front as if to protect me from my brother. "It was just a lapse in judgment, that's all."

Phillip opened the door to the pub. "Come on, I'll get the first round," he said to Zach and Ben.

"What did she do?" Ben asked, as the door closed behind them. Fantastic. She was going to tell him I didn't know how to mine and I'd have to try even harder to win his affection.

"Frankie, I—"

He put his arm around me and led me away from the tavern. "You're not in trouble. Mikey asked me to come get you. He wants you to start practicing again. Regionals are coming up."

"Right." Thank the gods. I didn't want to sit in the tavern listening to Emma all evening. It would feel great to throw some axes again.

"Phillip told me what you did to help Emma."

And here it comes.

"He is concerned word will get out and you will be disgraced. I assured him I would stop all negative rumors and make sure your reputation as a miner is upheld."

Then maybe he should be in the Prospector right now instead of walking me home.

"It really can't be disputed since you've got five first emeralds to her one," he continued. "I understand you didn't want to embarrass her, but Mabel, don't do it again."

"You weren't there, Frankie. She accused Phillip and me of purposefully stopping her from finding emeralds. She practically accused me of stealing. I had to do something."

Frankie pressed his lips together and he tensed up. He breathed deep and relaxed. "She had no right to accuse you of anything, especially theft. If she can't pay attention long enough to figure out where the emeralds are and how to mine them, then she doesn't deserve to work in the mines. I know she is your best friend, but if it were up to me, she wouldn't have been hired so early."

"You're not being fair. Phillip and I have been lucky."

"It's more than that. More than being blessed by the dwarf gods. You have a definite talent at spotting the right stone. Who knows how many beds have been missed because of her. I'd like you to go in early tomorrow and go over all the stone she worked and see if she missed anything."

"I'm not going to embarrass her like that," I said.

"If it makes you feel better, tell her I made you

do it, as punishment for telling her the wrong place to excavate. No, don't, it might make her gloat more than she already is. I'd rather you tell her you're checking to see what she's missed, or not say anything at all."

What would Emma say about me if she saw me going over her part of the crosscut? "She'll hate me."

"Mining isn't about being nice or mean or making friends or enemies. There is nothing personal about mining. It is about serving the gods of the mountains and receiving their gifts. If someone isn't good at mining, if they are too impatient and not devout in their worship of the gods, they shouldn't be mining. You have talent and are building a strong reputation. I don't want Emma to take it away from you because you feel bad for her."

"Okay, okay, Frankie. I get it. I won't help her anymore. But I'm not making a fool of her."

I turned the corner to the back of our house. Mikey stood there, throwing axes in hand. I grabbed an axe, imagined the throwing post was Emma's gloating face, raised my arm and hurled the axe. It felt amazing to take out my frustration on the throwing post.

CHAPTER 9

I DREADED going to work. While I'd been practicing for Regionals last night, Emma had probably told our friends, and anyone who would listen, that I couldn't mine. Even though Frankie said he'd silence any rumors, I doubted he'd be able to. Emma could be very convincing when she wanted to be.

Besides, I had no one to blame but myself. I made her think I didn't know how to mine. She had every right to tell all of Gilliam how she found her first emerald. I just hoped Emma was happy now and focused on her own mining. Maybe she'd even learned how to detect the right stone.

I decided to go in to work early to avoid the change-of-shift rush. I arrived at my crosscut before the horn blew for the end of the night shift. I took my time lighting the lanterns, watching the sparkle of the exposed emeralds.

The light on the craggy walls reminded me of my conversation with Frankie last night and how he suggested Emma might have missed a number of emerald beds.

I walked along the walls, smelling the mild sulfur veins in the granite. I ran my fingers over the stone, lightly touching, sometimes tapping at the rock. With a bit of excavation, there might be a few places where emerald beds lay. They were places Emma had worked, but it might be understandable why she stopped. Maybe. More likely she had given up too quickly.

"You think she missed something?" Phillip asked, coming in and lighting the rest of the lanterns.

"Maybe. I don't know. I should be angry with you for talking to Frankie, but you were looking out for my reputation, so, thanks."

"You're welcome," he said with a sheepish smile. "You're right though. I probably shouldn't have. I just had a bad feeling about what Emma was going to tell everyone and if anyone could quiet the rumors, it would be Frankie."

"Was it bad, last night at the Prospector? Am I going to have to do major damage control?"

"It wasn't great, but Jimmy and I rebuffed most of her accusations and assertions. Your reputation will recover. You have the track record to prove your skill, she doesn't."

"Thank you."

"Of course. What do you want to do about the beds she's missed? We'll have to start over."

I shook my head. "I don't want to say anything to her but I don't want to repeat what I did yesterday."

"We'll finish excavating the two beds we've got, then we'll start back," Phillip said.

"I can probably get an order from Frankie or one of the foremen, if they believe me," I said. "On second thought, maybe it would be better if you got the order. It would spare all of us embarrassment," I said. Especially my own.

"In the meantime, we should be working closer as a team." Phillip laid out his tools next to mine.

"I'd appreciate it," I said. "It has been uncomfortable the last while," I said.

"Maybe now Emma will take her work seriously and not worry so much about status and finding a mate."

If only it were that simple for us females. We sorted through our tools, preparing for the day's work. "I doubt it," I said. "She talks a lot and seems pre-occupied, but it's how she is. Whatever is on her mind, she tells you, and she's always positive things will work out in the end," For her, anyway. "If nothing else, she is competitive, so there shouldn't be any problems getting her to focus and work hard. She wants to prove herself."

"Don't we all," Phillip said.

We had excavated several emeralds when Emma

arrived, groaning. "I should have stayed in bed. Drank too much last night. You should have been there, Mabel. We had quite a celebration. Where'd you go anyway? Frankie wasn't too upset, was he?"

I wished she'd forget about yesterday. "I was training for Regionals."

"So Frankie wasn't upset? He didn't say anything about your mining?"

My stomach clenched. Why was she, my supposed best friend, so determined I should be in trouble? I feigned ignorance. "No. Should he have?"

"No, I guess not."

Did she look disappointed? Maybe I should tell her what really happened. Somehow, though, I didn't think she'd believe me.

"Speaking of yesterday," Phillip said. "I decided we should all start working together. Perhaps you were right. Mabel and I have—at least I have—been taking all the good spots."

"Sure, fine. But I'll excavate my own emerald bed. We can negotiate when I've finished," Emma said.

"Emma," Phillip said.

"Just let it go," I said. "We can work it out later." I was kind of glad not to have to work with her just yet.

Her hangover hadn't cleared by lunch. I gave her credit for sticking out the morning. We'd worked hard excavating and we were coated in sweat and dust.

As we had the day before, Emma and I joined Ben and Zach. She didn't complain about her hangover or about her lack of sleep.

I couldn't worry about what she may or may not have told Ben last night. I knew the truth. And I had an asset Emma didn't have, and never would.

I set my tray down. "I heard you all had a little party last night. I wish I had been there, but Regionals take precedence now."

"I'm sure you'll make Gilliam proud," Ben said, though he looked at Emma. "Are you all right? You've hardly eaten anything and you look the wrong shade of green."

Wow. It wouldn't matter what I did, he would never notice me if he thought he had a chance with her. For a moment, I considered fighting back. I could tell him that Emma was still hungover, she couldn't hold her ale, she didn't really know how to mine, and that I'd come in early and found several possible emerald beds that she'd missed.

What was the point? Emma was so desperate to have Zach and Ben that she would slander me. Surely they would see through her lies and fake tears eventually. They had to, or they were pure idiots who weren't worth the effort.

And of course, according to *She's Interested*, I should play it calm, not draw any unnecessary negative attention to myself, even if it was in my own defense. It would only make me look bad.

I ended my lunch break early and retreated to

the refuge of my work. With my medium pick-axe I chipped away at the stone until my muscles ached, which felt great. It kept my mind off Ben, kept me from questioning why he still wanted Emma when she technically wasn't available, kept me from questioning why he wouldn't choose me.

Aramis would never chase after a female who was spoken for. He would have noticed my interest in him. I desperately wished Aramis would come to Gilliam, tell me he loved me, and take me away from here. We could go on all kinds of adventures and make movies together. I would love to learn how to direct one. It would be so exciting and different every day. And I wouldn't have to worry about finding a mate, or mining, or winning Regionals.

Emma returned to work before Phillip. "Hey, Ben mentioned a new movie is opening at the theater. Why don't we go tonight? It's a romantic comedy. I can't remember who is in it, but Ben said it should be good."

"You're not going with Zach?"

"He has to watch his brothers because his parents are going out."

"What about Ben?"

"He offered to take me but Zach roped him into helping. I don't have to do everything with Zach, do I? So are we going?"

"I'll have to see, with practicing for Regionals and all." I wasn't particularly keen on going out with her, but I wouldn't mind the chance to see a movie.

By the end of the day, after much pestering, Emma convinced me to join her for the movie. I still had to get my practice in—Regionals were important to me—so we agreed to go to the late show.

Okay, it wasn't just Emma who persuaded me. I'd seen an advertisement for the movie and Aramis was in it. This was a great excuse to go see him.

After work, I shortened my practice a little.

"You're done early," Da said when I came in from my practice session.

I didn't have time for chatting. I expected Emma at the door in a few minutes and I needed to change out of my sticky, sweaty tunic. "I'm going out to-night."

"With whom?" he asked as I reached the stairs.

He wanted me to say I was going out with a fellow. "Emma."

"Anyone else?" Da followed me.

I stopped half-way up the stairs and turned back to face him, deciding to play dumb. I was doing this a lot today. Would it work in helping me find a mate? It wasn't one of the tips given in any of the books I'd read, but they were written before movies existed. "No. Why?"

"Where are you going?"

"To the movies."

His voice dropped an octave. He was serious about something. "Mabel, we need to talk."

I didn't have time for one of Da's lectures on finding a mate. "Emma's going to be here any minute. We can talk about whatever you want when I get back."

"We'll talk now."

The cold firmness of his tone didn't leave me any choice. I glanced at the door, hoping Emma wouldn't come yet. I didn't want her to hear Da lecturing me. That was all I needed, her telling everyone at the mines that Da lectured me on finding a mate and how I needed to make myself more attractive and available. "What is it?" I returned with Da to the kitchen and sat at the edge of the chair, ready to jump up the second he finished.

Da sat across from me. "I'm concerned, love. Have you had anyone ask to court you yet?"

This really could wait. "No. Da, we can talk about this when I get home." I stood.

"Sit down, Mabel." Da had that look on his face, all scrunched up and hard as rock—the don't-mess-about look. "You haven't been socializing with your friends since you started axe throwing, and now you're going out with Emma and no others. If you hide yourself away you'll never find a mate."

Thanks for your faith in me, Da.

"I want you to quit axe throwing." He signaled for me to keep my mouth shut. "I know Mikey said competing in the Gilliam Games would give you more admirers, but it hasn't, has it?"

I couldn't quit. So what if there weren't floods of admirers coming at me? The Gilliam Games had just ended. I had a better chance at Regionals, anyway.

Besides, this wasn't just about finding a mate; it was about building the reputation of the family and proving to everyone that I wasn't like Mam.

"But Da, Regionals are just around the corner. I'm so much better now than I was at the Gilliam Games. There will be loads more fellows at Regionals. Most of the fellows my age haven't decided if they want to mate or not." Okay, maybe not entirely true, but Patrick had said males tended to be slower at deciding.

"You don't have to stick with fellows your age. Your brothers have plenty of friends who are interested in mating."

No they didn't.

Max entered the kitchen. "Mabel, Emma's here," he said, walking to the cupboards and digging out some bread, meat, and cheese for a snack.

"Thanks," I said.

"I don't like you going to these movies all the time," Da continued as though we were the only ones in the house.

"This is only my second time." I hadn't told him about the last time Emma and I went during the Gilliam Games.

"They're disgraceful. No miner should be seen there. And how are you supposed to meet anyone? I know you think you have a lot of time, but you don't."

I stood. "I'm doing the best I can." I left Da calling for me to come back. "I'll see you when I get back," I yelled. "I'll be quick as an elf," I said to Emma as I ran upstairs to change.

Moments later I returned in a clean red tunic. "Let's go," I said, hurrying out the door, Emma close behind. "Sorry."

"No worries." Emma sniffled.

Only then did I notice her puffy, teary eyes. I could be so self-centered sometimes. "What's wrong?"

"Zach broke up with me." Emma sobbed into her sleeve.

"What? Why? When did this happen?"

"After work," Emma said between sobs and sniffles. "He said I was still in love with Ben. I've never loved Ben. I have only ever been in love with Zach. He kept saying I flirted with Ben. But I never have. Then he kept going on about how I flirt with every fellow I see and if I loved him I wouldn't do it anymore. Who do I flirt with? No one but Zach."

Not exactly true, but he should have known Emma wouldn't be with him if she wanted someone else. Besides, he knew she flirted with every fellow when he started courting her. I put my arm around her shoulders. "I'm so sorry, Emma. I thought Zach was madly in love with you. I never imagined he would ever break up with you."

"He *is* madly in love with me, and I'm madly in love with *him.* I don't want anyone but him."

We joined the line for the movie. The poster for the movie, *On Pointe,* featured a close-up of Aramis. My Aramis. I stifled a smile.

"I'm sorry. I'm not in the mood for a movie after all," Emma said. "Can we go back to your house?"

I didn't want to go home to more of Da's lecturing. She'd heard him telling me I had to find a mate and not to go to the movies. Did she want to hear more of my humiliation? "I'd rather not. I had a bit of a falling-out with Da."

Emma sniffled again. She needed me though, and I supposed Aramis could wait until another time. "How about the Prospector, or your house?"

"Not with all those couples at the Prospector and my parents all kissy at home. I can't bear to be around happy, loving couples right now."

The line crept forward and we stepped into the foyer of the theater. "We could go somewhere else. Maybe just walk for a while."

"I can't believe he broke up with me. I can't think straight. I don't know what I want anymore." Emma sighed. She looked around at the others in line and she no longer sniffled or had tears in her eyes. "See that one?"

"Who?" I looked around but didn't know who she was referring to.

"The fellow there in the yellow cap."

"The one behind us?" I asked.

"Yes. Don't look. He is totally checking me out."

The dwarf in the yellow cap talked to his friends, not even facing our direction. The only reason for him to look our way was to look for some of his friends. Or because Emma talked so loud her voice echoed off the ceiling catching his attention.

"Och," Emma held a hand up to her face. "He's coming this way. What should I do? What should I do?"

The yellow-capped dwarf walked past us without a glance in our direction, and joined some friends not far ahead of us.

"Nothing," I said.

"He's gone? Oh, good. I bet Zach dumped me because all the fellows flirt with me and he's too insecure to take it. Enough about me. What happened between you and your da?"

I opened my mouth to tell her how ridiculous Da was being, but she was distracted, continuously looking around us, standing on her tip-toes to see the fellows in front, and leaning out to look at the fellows behind. Yellow Cap walked past, returning to his place in line. Emma twirled a braid around a finger. I didn't think he saw, but she giggled in his direction anyway. She didn't appear distraught. She didn't need my comfort anymore. I wanted to see Aramis and forget what Da said. "If you want to go, I'll understand. You don't have to see the movie with me. But I'm going to stay."

Emma put a hand on my arm. "Are you sure? I'm just too upset about Zach to be here."

She had a funny way of showing it. "Yeah, fine. We'll do something together some other time." I didn't feel like listening to Emma talk about her boyfriends or which fellows at the theater flirted with her. I was happy for her, of course. It was just hard to take sometimes. Even though I knew that wasn't her intention, it made me feel like something was wrong with me because no fellow ever showed any interest in me.

"Thanks so much. I promise we'll do something soon." Emma hugged me then fluffed her hair and walked away. It must be exhausting living your life thinking everyone wanted you. Exhausting or really conceited. Except fellows really were interested in Emma. Maybe not the one in the yellow cap, but I'd bet a whole emerald bed if he looked at her he would be.

Maybe I was being too harsh. I should have gone with her. Aramis could wait. I stepped out of the line and watched slack-jawed as she strode up to Yellow Cap.

"Yellow is a great color on you," she said.

"Thanks."

"Hi. I'm Emma." She'd lowered the pitch of her voice to a solid bass, lower than her natural baritone.

"Hey. Um, Mark." They shook hands.

"Listen, I'm here by myself. My friend decided she didn't want to stay. She ditched me. Can you believe it? Anyway, I hate watching movies on my own and I really want to see this one. May I join you? Great." She hooked her arm in his. "I haven't seen you around Gilliam. Where are you from?"

I didn't bother to hear the rest. I stepped back into line. Unbelievable. If she didn't want to be here with me, why didn't she just say so? And I'd felt sorry for her, believing her sob-story about Zach. She didn't have to use me. She could have just said she wanted to go talk to Yellow-Cap. Was she *trying* to humiliate me?

I considered leaving, but I really didn't want to go home and face Da. And I'd agreed to go out tonight as much for myself as for Emma. Maybe if Aramis wasn't in the movie I'd feel differently. I wouldn't mind taking my frustration out on the throwing post. But since Emma wasn't beside me, I could spend the next couple of hours dreaming of being in the movie with Aramis and not worry about Emma saying anything mean about him.

"How many?" the ticket clerk asked.

"Um, one, thanks." I glanced back, watching Emma. She clung to Mark, chatting like she hadn't abandoned her best friend for a stranger. Maybe it was a good thing I was going to watch the movie on my own.

The clerk handed me my ticket. Was he smiling at me? The clerk stared at me as I walked into the concession area. What was his problem? I wiped at the corners of my mouth in case there were crumbs. Emma could have at least told me so I didn't make a fool of myself. She probably hadn't told me on purpose.

What would Emma say if I spoke to her when she walked in? I stood to the side. Minutes later Emma and Mark entered as intimate as though they'd been courting for ages.

My stomach turned like cream in a butter churn. I should have been happy for her. After being dumped by Zach, she had a new fellow interested in her. I was happy for her. I could even go home and tell Da Emma found someone at the movies and if she could do it, so could I. I should also contact the author of *Meet Him and Mate Him.* Let her know there was a new location she could add to the list of places to meet potential mates.

Emma smiled and laughed. She deserved to be happy. And it wasn't like she hadn't been hurt when she wanted to leave. She was the one who had told me to take every opportunity to find a mate. She was just quicker at it than I was. I shouldn't be upset with her. Except that I was. I walked past so she saw me but I didn't stop. I didn't know what to say to her. That's not true. I wanted to yell at her and call her a skinny liar who used me.

I kept walking to the magazine stand outside the theater door. I picked one up to hide behind and grabbed a seat close to the front so Emma had to sit behind me. I couldn't bear to look at her. I flipped the pages of the movie magazine without reading. I was angry at Emma, and angry at myself for being angry at her. I hid behind the magazine and wiped my eyes. I'd see Aramis soon enough and I'd be a lot happier then.

Or I'd see him now.

Thanks to the magazine and the five-page interview of Aramis, and another three pages of pictures distracting me, I began to put Emma behind me. I slouched and absorbed everything Aramis.

By the time the oceans of his eyes filled the screen in front of me, I'd forgotten Emma and Mark existed. "Aramis," I mouthed. "I love you. I'm so glad you're here. You understand what I'm going through. I wish you were here with me instead of on the screen with that she-elf."

I lost myself in more than Aramis's stunning eyes. I was on the edge of my seat as Aramis fought to save the life of his lover who had become mortal by an evil wizard's spell.

I walked home alone, happy and full of images of Aramis. I opened the front door as quiet as I could, hoping Da wouldn't notice I'd returned and want to pick up where he left off. I started up the stairs thinking I had succeeded, but I stopped when I heard Mikey and Da arguing in the kitchen.

"You saw how well she did at the Gilliam Games. Regionals are only three months away and she needs to train. She's good, but she'll need to be ten times better to be competitive," Mikey said.

"Her focus needs to be on finding a mate, not training."

"Da—"

"Do you know where she went tonight?"

"The movies. So what?"

"Think about it."

The argument lulled for a moment then Mikey

said, "Ooooh."

"Exactly," Da said. "With elves. We have just recovered from that fiasco. I am not going to allow something like that to happen again. The longer she goes without a mate, the greater the chance someone will raise it and ruin her chances forever."

What? What about movies and elves? How could going to the movies possibly ruin my chances at finding a mate? All my friends went. What were they talking about? I thought we were ruined because of Mam, not because of movies and elves.

"I understand. How about this. She still trains, but I'll reduce the hours, to give her some time after work to socialize with her friends. If she does well at Regionals, I'm sure she'll have some high-profile males interested in her."

"Fine."

Mikey entered the front room, surprised to see me at the bottom of the stairs. "Mabel, you're home."

"Yeah, just got in."

"I've been pushing you quite hard. Why don't you take some time after work to go to the Prospector, have a few drinks, then come home and train?"

"I heard," I whispered. "Were you talking about Mam? Could she ruin my chances of finding a mate?" If I framed the question about her that way, I hoped this time he would talk. I held my breath. Mikey didn't answer though. He walked out the front door. I turned to follow but saw Da scowling from the kitchen door.

CHAPTER 10

I WAS not prepared for Emma's cheeriness when she met me on the road to the mines the next morning.

"Good movie last night," Emma said. "For a movie about elves, it sure drew a crowd. Mark said it was more scary than funny or romantic." Emma laughed. The laugh of the newly in love. I'd heard it from her several times. She'd nearly perfected it.

"Mark? Oh yeah, that's the name of the fellow you were with last night, Yellow-Cap. What happened? I thought you were going home because you weren't up to a movie. I'd turned around to go with you and there you were flirting with him." I tried to sound casual but ended up more accusatory.

Emma looked at me with a blank expression, like she didn't get my question. "That's what happened."

She was as good at playing dumb as I was, but I wasn't in the mood for games. "Why did you lie to me? Why didn't you go home like you said you were?"

Emma furrowed her brows for a moment then smirked. "What's the problem, Mabel? You said I could go. I could do whatever I wanted. I didn't have to stay with you if I changed my mind about seeing the movie."

"Except I think you never intended to go home," I said. "As soon as you saw Mark, you said you wanted to leave. If you didn't want to be there with me, why not tell me? Why not just tell me that you wanted to go chat him up? I wouldn't have minded. Instead you lied to me, and him."

"I didn't lie to him."

How dare she deny it? "You said I'd ditched you, when it was the other way around."

"Don't be so sensitive," she said condescendingly. "I met a fellow. If I hadn't met Mark, I would have left. Thanks for ruining my excitement over finding someone. I thought you would be happy for me, especially after Zach treated me so badly."

She hurt me, but she was my friend, and it had been a difficult day for her. "I'm sorry. I am happy for you." Did I just apologize? Shouldn't she have apologized to me? No matter how right she might be, what she'd done was still rude. "Tell me about Mark, then." I faked a smile.

"He kept me laughing the whole time," Emma

said all happy again. Her ability to change her moods amazed me. "He is so handsome too."

I didn't think he looked very good. Not compared to Aramis, though he couldn't really be compared to Aramis. No one could.

"Too bad he's not a miner, which means he's not a mountain dweller. He'll be good to help me get over Zach, but it can't be a long term relationship. I mean, I'm a miner. I can't mate with someone who isn't. What a shame, because I could easily fall in love with him. Although I suppose as a blacksmith, he has a fair amount of respectability. Still, I have to mate up. It will be fun until I find someone else, someone more perfect for me."

I seethed inside and I felt horrible for it. "Who would be the perfect one?" I asked.

Emma sighed. "I don't know. I thought Zach was. He was just too jealous. He wanted me all to himself. Because Ben was there all the time, Zach thought we were flirting. I love Zach. I want a mate exactly like him, just not so possessive."

"Well, Mark sounds great," I said without any enthusiasm, trying to find something safe to say to keep her in a positive mood. "Do I get to meet him?" At the theater, she had denied I existed. Would she introduce him to her friends or would she keep these two worlds of hers separate?

"If you want. I'm meeting him after work."

"Bring him to the Prospector," I said.

Emma rubbed her forehead. We were close to

the mines now and she whispered. "I can't bring him there. He's not a miner. I'll be laughed at forever." She grabbed my arm. "I can't go anywhere with him in case someone I know recognizes me. I'm with someone I can't be with. I might as well be alone. Forever."

She spoke like her destiny was doomed to the fiery depths of the cursed delved-too-deep mines of legend and childhood horror stories. At least she had found a potential mate, unlike me who truly would be doomed if I didn't find one soon. Da said as much last night. "What are you going to do?"

"The only thing I can. I'll have to dump him. He might be fantastic, but he's no good for me. What a shame. Oh well, at least I had fun last night." Emma shrugged. "Please don't tell anyone."

"Of course I won't."

"It is going to be tricky, keeping Mark secret until I've dumped him."

Emma didn't say a word all day. She must have spent it planning how to keep her relationship with Mark secret. I knew what she was going through and I could sympathize, having my own secret love that occupied every thought and every breath. I thought of the two hours I'd spent with Aramis last night and warmth spread through me.

After our shift, Emma disappeared before I raised my head out of the cleansing pool.

"Coming to the Prospector or do you have to rush home to practice for Regionals?" Jimmy asked as he,

Phillip, and I wrung the water from our beards.

"I'm coming for a drink or two before practice." I looked forward to an evening with Phillip and Jimmy and a few ales. I know Da had pushed for me to have this time to socialize so that I could find a mate, but I just wanted to spend some time with friends, just for tonight. Tomorrow I'd get back to putting into practice what I'd read in the self-help books.

Inside the Prospector, Ben waved us over to his table, which was covered in tankards waiting to be drained. "Help yourselves," he said.

"Thanks." I lifted a mug. "The next round will be on me then."

"Not to worry," Ben said. The way he said it—if I hadn't witnessed his interest in Emma—I might think he liked me. The author of *He's Interested* stressed the generosity of buying drinks and the refusal of allowing the female to buy a round as an important sign. If only. I dismissed his comments as nothing more than a courtesy between colleagues.

I forgot all about Ben and his misdirected love for Emma the moment the cool, sweetly bitter liquid grazed my lips, swirled over my tongue and satisfied my belly. The drink of the gods is what ale is.

"Where's Emma?" Ben asked.

A simple, easy question with a complicated answer. I expected Emma to be breaking up with her new blacksmith lover. "I'm not sure. She hurried off kind of quick today." I should have stopped there but I just couldn't. Apparently I was a terrible liar. "Maybe she had to look after her siblings. She didn't say." I hoped I sounded believable.

As I sipped my ale I thought about all the things I could say to Ben. I could question his loyalty and friendship to Zach, if a day after Zach broke it off with Emma, Ben chased after her as a suitor. Most of all, I wanted to ask him why he didn't want me.

He didn't have to like me now. I just wanted to know what was wrong with me. Why no one showed any interest. If I knew, maybe I could fix it.

I drained my ale to keep myself from talking.

"Do you think she'd want some help?" Ben asked.

I released a solid rumbling belch, my best ever, which no one heard over all the talk and other belches around me. I patted my belly while I glanced around the Tavern and didn't see Zach. Probably home nursing his grief, or he and Ben had a falling out. Unless he was with Emma apologizing.

"What?" I asked, though I'd heard him well enough. I didn't like his boldness, it made protecting Emma's secret difficult.

"Do you think Emma might want help looking after the wee ones?" He leaned closer to me.

He smelled extra nice today, like worn leather and pipe smoke and salt-spice. I leaned back. He smelled nice for Emma, not me. "I don't… I doubt it. She's quite good with them." Oh great, way to make a better case for him to like Emma. "I mean, if she's even with them. She didn't say where she was."

I put my tankard on the table. "This has been too short but I'd best get going before Mikey hunts me down." And before I said something else I'd regret.

"I'll walk with you," Ben said. "It's on the way to Emma's."

Maybe he would walk in on Zach apologizing and Emma taking him back. Then he would stop chasing her. "Suit yourself."

We crunched through the snow, a welcome silence compared to the din of the Prospector. I had nothing to say, and thank the gods Ben was content enough to stay quiet. A perfectly romantic moment, the two of us walking in the early moonlight after a social evening with friends. At least he didn't ruin the illusion by talking about Emma, or any other female he fancied.

"Who was the nice young lad walking with you?" Da asked when I walked inside.

Why did he have to see Ben? Now there would be endless questions and prodding for information and pushing for a relationship that didn't exist.

"Ben Stronghammer." I walked past Da into the kitchen.

He followed. "A Stronghammer. Good family. Mountain dwellers too. Very good. I knew if you spent more time with friends you'd meet someone."

He had such a big, happy smile it almost hurt to destroy his joy. Almost. "He's interested in Emma, not me." No fellows are. I walked outside and slammed the door before he could say anything else.

I stretched my arms and back muscles while I waited for Mikey. I hurled my axes in rapid succession with no attention to form.

I scratched my feeble beard as I retrieved my axes. No wonder no fellows were interested. I couldn't be more hideous: what with my thin, scraggly beard, my alto voice, and I had no stoutness about me. A poor model for the future generation.

All this exercise might prevent me from gaining weight, but it made me strong. If any of the fellows in Gilliam were aware of my strength, they'd look past my thinness. They would fall at my feet begging to court me. They had no appreciation for what I offered as a mate. Aramis did. No fellows here cared. Their loss.

I hurled the axes hard. A sharp twinge pinched in my shoulder. I sucked in my breath and held it. The twinge turned into a searing pain like forged iron running through me. I pushed my breath through my nose, making myself breathe through the pain.

I picked up my next axe. I raised my arm and thought I heard my shoulder muscles tear.

I MASSAGED my shoulder. I'd felt no pain this morning when I first woke up. I thought I was better and then I moved. It was worse than yesterday and had been progressively declining all day in the mines. I'd hoped a few quick ales at the Prospector would help deaden the pain enough to get through tonight's practice but it hadn't done anything for me. Neither had the stretching.

The axe felt like lead in my hand and for the first time I dreaded throwing it.

"How's it going?" Mikey asked coming into the back yard to coach me.

"Fine," I said. I couldn't let him know how hurt I was. He'd think I was weak, not a champion. I cherished his respect too much. I cringed as I raised the axe. My breathing was labored but I focused on it to ignore the pain. A grunt escaped as I hurled the axe, which fell woefully short of the throwing post. I hadn't thrown so poorly since I first began training.

"When did this start?" he asked. His voice was quiet. He stood close to me.

I should have known I couldn't fool him. "Yesterday."

Mikey took the axe from me and checked out my shoulder, pressing on it, raising my arm to the side and front but only until I grunted or winced, which didn't take much. Simply breathing made the pain throb.

"This isn't great, not with Regionals coming up, but we can work with it. You'll need to take some time off."

"No, Mikey, I can't do that," I whispered. "Da can't know. He'll make me quit throwing and I don't want to quit. And I can't stop mining because then he and every other dwarf in Gilliam will know something is wrong, which will hurt my reputation."

"Mabel, it wouldn't be quite that bad. Da, maybe, but not your reputation. Nothing that doing well at Regionals wouldn't fix. And you can't do well at Regionals with this injury."

"I can't afford to take a break from training, Mikey. Fifth at the Gilliam Games is *not* going to get me to the Dwarf Games. I need to practice and work hard. I can't take time off. I shouldn't have taken the day off after the Gilliam Games."

Mikey looked at me without saying anything for several minutes. How much more did I need to say to impress on him how important this was to me? That I'd heard him when he'd said that champions didn't let anything stop them? That I had what it took to be a champion?

"Will you tell Phillip and Emma and ask them to take on some of your workload? Tell them you have to take it easy, my orders," Mikey said at last.

"I will."

"And do you promise you will tell me if the pain gets worse, the moment it happens?"

"I promise," I said maybe a little too quickly.

"You have to tell me or we stop training right now and withdraw you from Regionals."

"I promise, Mikey. I swear to the gods I will tell you. Please don't make me stop throwing."

"We'll have to modify your training schedule, but I can do that and not raise any suspicions in Da. Have you been doing your stretches?"

"Every morning, night, and before and after each practice. Always."

"Good. Do them again, right now. Just the stretches, no weight lifting. While you're doing that tell me what happened."

I told him about the pain as I threw and about hearing the muscle tear. I hadn't done anything different in my training. I'd been paying attention to my form and technique. I'd done my stretches and strength training. I didn't know how this happened, or why it happened now.

Mikey showed me a few more stretches and ways to protect my shoulder as he mulled over what I told him.

"I still don't want you throwing any axes for the next few days," he said. "If Da asks, I'll tell him we're working on your concentration and other aspects of your conditioning. The moving-target portion of the Regional competition is going to be more difficult and we should spend some time working on developing your senses anyway. I'll be right back."

He returned moments later with an ice pack, which he strapped to my shoulder. The chill felt great on my muscles, like it might actually put out the fire that smoldered there.

"Close your eyes, breathe deep, feet firmly on the ground. Feel the wind around you, feel the earth move beneath you. Point in the direction of the pop-ups the second you think they're up."

My concentration was off. Either I missed the

first few pop-ups entirely, or I pointed in the wrong direction.

"Take another deep breath, Mabel. Be aware of everything around you. Take your time. Nod when you're ready."

Birds sang overhead, no, to the right of me. The wind rustled in the trees. Wisps of the breeze chilled on my ice-pack and caressed my right cheek. Mikey breathed behind and to the left of me, close to the back door.

I heard Radier's voice in my mind directing me in a movie. I was a great dwarven warrior and my people relied on me to stop the goblin throngs attacking us.

I nodded and the targets popped up in random order, much quicker than Mikey had made them when I prepared for the Gilliam Games. This time I was ready and pointed out most of them accurately.

"Better," Mikey said. "Let's do it again."

It turned out to be a pretty good training session. We'd worked hard on sharpening my concentration and accuracy. I could see how spending time on that alone, without actually throwing any axes, would help me during Regionals.

We'd removed the ice-pack for the second half of the session. I had it on now as I prepared for bed. I lay under the covers and read the latest movie magazine, reading and re-reading the profile on Aramis. He and Sevrin had survived so many battles. If they could do what they had and still be alive, surely I could persist through a little shoulder pain to get to the Dwarf Games and even win them.

The ice was already making me feel better. I'd still tell Emma and Phillip about it because I would need to take things easy for the next few days.

Maybe.

The way I was feeling right now I was sure that by tomorrow or the day after I'd be fine.

I CRADLED my arm to prevent my shoulder from jarring every time I took a step. Five days had passed since I told Mikey about the pain and it was only getting worse. No amount of ice or special exercises helped. I hadn't told him though. I couldn't risk him pulling me out of competition.

"Going somewhere?" I asked Emma, pointing out the waterskin slung over her shoulder as we walked to work.

"Don't hate me," she said. "I told my mam about your injury. Only I didn't tell her it was you, just a friend, and I asked if I could do anything to help. She said this kind of thing isn't altogether uncommon among dwarves and she mixed up some medicine to stop the pain." Emma handed me the waterskin. "She said to take a small sip whenever you need to. And she also made this herbal poultice she says you are to rub on your shoulders at night." She searched her bag and pulled out a jar, which she handed to me. "It's supposed to relax your muscles so they can heal."

Emma could have Ben and Zach and every first emerald in Gilliam for all her help. In fact, if this medicine worked, I'd never begrudge her anything ever again. And I wished her mam a dozen more dwarflings.

She was lucky to have a mam she could talk to and ask for help without any trouble. I could never talk to Da about this. What would have happened if my mam were still here and I told her about the pain right from the start? If I had told her, I bet she wouldn't bellow and stomp around the cottage like Da would. "Thank you."

"You're welcome. I thought talking to my mam eliminated a lot of your complications. You really do need to tell Mikey it isn't improving. I'm sure he wouldn't pull you out of Regionals. He's fought too hard to keep you competing. He'd probably take you to a doctor or something, to see what could be done."

"I'll think about it." He might. Or he might tell me to quit, with the unstated implication that I didn't have what it took to be champion and that I disappointed him. I'd rather try and fix this on my own first. The pain couldn't last forever.

"Mam says this stuff tastes awful, but," Emma shook her finger at me in a mock imitation of her mam, "you're not to spit it out no matter how much you want to."

I pulled out the stopper on the waterskin. It reeked like rotting goblin carcass. I sipped the thick slimy and gritty liquid, like gnarled and solidifying ogre fat mixed with crushed dragon scales. I pressed my lips together and the back of my hand to my mouth to keep the sludge down. My stomach heaved, desperate to expel the horrid stuff, but I kept my hand at my mouth. With a violent shiver from head to foot, my body accepted the medicine.

"Awful doesn't come close to describing it." I put in the stopper. "I hope it works fast. I don't want to drink much more of it."

"Mam said you should drink it whenever you feel the pain, and to not let the taste stop you. Otherwise neither the drink nor the poultice will work. Somehow they're supposed to work together. I don't know. That's what Mam said."

However disgusting the taste, the medicine warmed my insides. Its warmth spread from my stomach out to every muscle. "If it works, I can survive the taste."

"Good. You are never going to guess what happened yesterday. Ben and I were together at the Prospector. Zach saw us together and it didn't faze him. He joined us and we chatted like he and I had never been together. He didn't blink when Ben put his arm around me, or when he kissed me. Can you believe it? Did I mean nothing to him?"

I was happy for Emma and Ben, I really was, but I didn't need to hear every detail of their relationship, especially about Ben kissing her. If she really loved him, why did she care what Zach thought? Unless she didn't love Ben and only used him to make Zach jealous. Did she care about anything other than fellows? Was there nothing else we could talk about for an entire conversation? Or half of one, before we talked about boys?

"They're best friends," I said. "If they're going to stay friends, Zach can't exactly be showing his jealousy, can he? Not if they want to work together."

"I guess that makes sense."

I was kind of in the same situation as Zach. "And, you're not exactly acting like Zach broke your heart."

"Of course he did," Emma said.

"*I* know it, and *you* know it, but *he* doesn't see it, does he? He sees you with Ben now. I bet he's imitating you."

"If Zach thinks just because he devastated me I'm going to mope around, he better think again. I haven't got the luxury of time like males do. I need to find a mate before it's too late. Males are so lucky, they can take all the time they want.

"Anyway," Emma continued. "I left the Prospector early. I told Ben I had to help Mam with the baby, in case he asks. I really went to see Mark. He showed me around the smithy and we found a cozy dark corner where we cuddled for a while before he walked me home. My family might have seen him, but the kiss he gave me made the risk totally worth it."

I thought she'd broken up with Mark. "You're still seeing him? And Ben? At the same time? What if Ben had come to your house to help you out and saw you with Mark?"

"He does tend to pop in unexpectedly, doesn't he? I hadn't thought of that. Well, next time, I'll make sure Mark doesn't walk me home."

"How long do you think you can keep this up?"

"As long as I can without anyone getting hurt," Emma said. "It's all for fun. Mark is so perfect and sweet except he's not a miner. I'm sure I'll tire of him soon enough. Ben is a miner and a mountain dweller, and he is a fine enough lad so he will win me in the end. I just can't give up Mark yet."

"Be careful," I said, though a part of me almost admired her ability to juggle two relationships, and her nerve for even trying it.

"I will. I'm so glad I can talk to you. I might go crazy otherwise."

I might grumble a lot, but I was glad Emma was free to talk to me about her worries. We were best friends after all. She might not always show it, but today, with the medicine and poultice, she did care about me and what I was going through too.

The medicine worked fast. Only a dull ache remained in my shoulder.

I felt great all day. Still, I took care not to work too hard and I kept the waterskin close by. I endured the vile medicine whenever the pain increased, which was maybe only four or five times.

After work, I parted ways with my friends as I usually did, to go home and practice. Emma stopped me before I went too far. "Come join us, just for a couple of drinks."

"I'd love to but I really need to practice."

"You're swallowing the medicine like it's better than ale. Are Regionals so important?"

I appreciated her concern, I really did. But there stood Emma, Ben two steps behind her, and every male walking past us glanced at her, not me. She'd done a fairly decent job not long ago of trying to ruin my mining reputation. If no males here were interested in me, then Regionals might be my best and only hope of finding a mate and restoring my reputation. I didn't have the options she did. But even more importantly, I loved axe throwing. I loved it over almost everything else. There was no way I was quitting or even reducing my time on the throwing range. "Yes, they are."

I didn't tell Mikey about my pain, or about the medicine I took. I warmed up longer and focused on my form. I pushed through the pain.

"Good work," Mikey said, clapping his hand on my sore shoulder. I bit back a whimper. "You must be feeling better."

I knew then I'd done the right thing not telling him. I'd finished the practice session like a champion. Too bad it hurt so much.

I quickly ate supper and retired to my room. I dug out the poultice and smeared it onto my shoulder. It smelled like ale and honey. Thank the gods I didn't have to stink like rotting goblin corpse all night.

I opened up the movie magazine with the feature

article on Aramis and I read and re-read it. I flipped through the pictures and advertisements until I came across an ad for the same cloak fastener Aramis wore in the movie *On Pointe*. I decided to treat myself.

I filled out the order form and prepared to take it to the traders first thing in the morning. Then I curled up on my bed and took out a rock I'd chipped out of the mine wall that morning. It had been a while since I'd done any stone carving. I'd enjoyed it when I worked on my masterwork, and doing it now didn't hurt my shoulder. With my smallest carving tools, I scratched at the surface, etching in the design. A model of Aramis.

DAWN HADN'T broken when I rushed out of the house to get to the traders and back before I had to meet Emma for work. I had a handful of small emeralds in my pocket along with the order form. The waterskin banged against my bag in rhythm with my hurried steps. I had enough medicine until tomorrow and then I'd need to get more.

I headed to the trading post at the outer edge of Gilliam, a place I hadn't been to since the field trip in my early days at the toy workshop when we were shown how our products were sold.

The pre-dawn light made the shadows longer and the cracks in the road deeper than I remembered. Whatever the reason, I walked with greater caution than I liked. I stumbled over a loose rock in the road. I had to swing my arms to keep my balance, making my shoulder hurt more than usual when I walked.

Farther into the valley, the tree line receded from the road, a relief for my nose. Instead of trees, houses crowded the edge of the road and each other, much like they were inside the mountain side of the city. Lanterns were lit in some. The thick scent of cooking oats surrounded me from the open windows along with voices of dwarves getting ready for an early start.

I didn't recognize any of the voices, or any of their faces. This far down the valley, I doubted many of the dwarves I passed worked in the mines. The buildings were too small—only one floor, and too narrow, probably only one room at the front—to belong to miners. Even the lowest level of miners lived in bigger houses. Plus, miners needed more than oats in the morning. But even if miners lived this far away, they wouldn't have to get ready this early.

I shivered, remembering a time when I was little—barely walking—when Da considered moving to this part of Gilliam. I never knew why, except that he had said something about all our wealth being stolen around the same time. Now I knew it had to do with Mam's disappearance. If we'd ever moved here, would we have gotten back to our home where we belonged? Sure I hated the trees surrounding us, and we weren't mountain dwellers, but even if we had nothing else, where we lived represented good standing in our city.

How could Mam have taken it away from us?

Try as I might, I couldn't think of anything anyone would willingly do to destroy her family, even if she hated them all and wanted to ruin them. Surely Mam hadn't hated us. She'd stayed with us long enough to have twelve dwarflings. If she'd hated Da and my brothers, she would have left earlier, wouldn't she?

I tripped over another rut in the road, snapping out of my thoughts. I'd arrived at the trading post, a half-stone half-log cabin, on my right. Behind it waited horses tied to carts loaded with goods. A group of traders at the edge of the road huddled over a fire in a pit, warming their hands, sharing a cask of ale and a few laughs.

I looked over the carts loaded with gems, elven dolls, thick wool blankets, and material goods.

"Excuse me," I said. A few of the traders looked at me. "Are any of you going to Leitham?" They turned back to their friends and continued their gossip. "Please," I said. "I have an order that needs to go to Leitham."

A trader with a face like worn leather shuffled over to me. "I'm going to Leitham. What is it you have, lass?"

I handed over the order form and enough emeralds to pay for the cloak clasp. "Here." I reached in my pocket and pulled out a small handful of additional emeralds, "This should be enough to cover the cost of your troubles."

"It's no trouble at all, lass. This is more than enough," he said only taking two of the emeralds.

Whatever elves and fairies might say about dwarves, we are not greedy.

"Come back in twenty-one days. Your order will be in the trading post by then. Any other orders can be left there."

"Right." My cheeks felt suddenly hot. I should have known that's how it was done. "I'm sorry."

"No problem." He smiled.

"Thank you."

"Hey," another trader called after me. "You're the axe thrower, Mabel Goldenaxe, right?"

They recognized me? "Yes, that's me."

"You were excellent at the Gilliam Games," he said. "Good luck at Regionals."

I smiled. "Thank you very much." I waved but stopped short as pain ripped through my right arm. I wouldn't do well in any competition unless this pain went away quickly. As soon as I saw Emma I'd ask her if she could increase the strength of her medicine.

EMMA HANDED me a new waterskin filled with my fifth batch of medicine. I took my first swallow of the day. The taste never improved, but I endured it because it minimized my pain. Anything to function normally and not slow down.

"You need to take it easy on this stuff," Emma

said. "This is the fourth time I've increased the strength and it's only been three weeks. Each batch is supposed to last ten days."

"It's helping. It really is."

"Not if I have to keep making it stronger. It's a good thing Mam showed me how to make it. She'd have a fit if she knew you were taking it so frequently."

"Well this should do it. I promise, if the pain is still here after Regionals, I will tell Mikey and Da, and I will get it looked at."

"I really don't like what you're doing to yourself. Neither do Phillip and Jimmy."

"What does Jimmy know about it?"

"Jimmy saw you sipping from the waterskin and not eating at lunch. He asked Phillip about it at the Prospector the other day. He thought it was because you're pushing yourself too hard, that you're on a special diet."

"What did Phillip tell him?"

"That it's for an injury and that you'll have it looked at after Regionals."

Thank the gods. I didn't need this spreading. It would make me look even worse.

"We're just worried about you," Emma said. "I hope Regionals are worth it."

Me too. With the pain and medicine and missing socializing at the Prospector, I had to practice harder to make sure I performed at my absolute best. Unfortunately, the extra practice made the pain worse. "I'll be fine."

We were quiet for a few moments then Emma asked, "Can we talk about my problems now?"

And we're back to the fellows. "Yes, of course. Sorry. What's wrong?"

She released an exaggerated, body-sagging sigh. "I broke it off with Mark last night. I know it was supposed to be for fun but my heart feels like it's been ripped out."

"I'm so sorry." It couldn't have been easy and I'm sure it hurt, but I was proud of her.

"Yes, well, he wanted to make our relationship more serious. He wanted me to wear a single braid for him. I could have left in the single braid I wear for Ben, but I couldn't bring myself to let Mark think we were more than something casual."

"Good for you. I know it hurts, but turn to Ben. I'm sure in time you'll see he's the right choice."

"Ugh, Ben." She groaned. "He's so possessive. I thought Zach had a problem with jealousy. I would cut Ben loose in a heartbeat but it just isn't an option."

Perhaps I was better off without any males interested in me. It was so complicated and so much effort. I didn't understand it. And I wasn't sure I wanted to. "Why not?"

"I want Zach back but I'm hardly worth any effort or thought if I'm on my own."

"I doubt you'd be on your own. There are probably a dozen suitors lined up behind Ben."

"I'm glad you think so. I'm not so sure. I think Zach is jealous because I'm with Ben and he might be willing to make a move for me if he sees an opportunity. He flirted with me the other day. If he gets jealous enough, he'll ask me to come back to him."

Or he might give up if she made him work too hard. "Why not tell Zach you want him back?"

Emma rolled her eyes. "Because I did nothing wrong. He needs to come crawling back to *me,* apologizing to *me.*"

"I'm sure he will."

At the end of the day, I hurried out of the mines the moment the horn blew, relaxed and pain free thanks to the new, stronger medicine. The day had finally arrived for me to pick up my order at the trading post. I appreciated Emma keeping my shoulder pain a secret but I wasn't about to tell her about Aramis or my fascination with movies, and certainly not that I'd ordered an elven cloak clasp and a behind-the-scenes movie magazine subscription.

Still, I kept watch for anyone I might know on my way to the trading post. Luckily I didn't see anyone.

The traders' carts were loaded and lined up in the lot beside the trading post, ready to go first thing in the morning. Tightly fastened, treated animal skins covered each cart, protecting their contents from the climate.

At least a dozen dwarves milled about inside the trading post, chatting to each other or waiting in line at the counter for their turn to send or collect parcels.

I had no idea so many dwarves used the trading post. There were eight customers ahead of me in line. I wished I had time to return in a day or two when it might not be so busy, but the lines might be longer tomorrow or the day after. Then again, this might be the slow day. I'd hurry home as soon as I collected my parcel. I'd practice longer and harder too.

Thinking about practice made my shoulder hurt. I contemplated taking some of the medicine now but thought better of it. I couldn't take any with Mikey around, which meant I had to endure my entire practice session on one dosage. I always took some right before I warmed up so it would carry me through. It was too early to take it now.

I tried to distract myself from the simmering fire in my shoulder but there were no goods for sale to look at, only a lot of chatter. One or two patrons left, the rest stayed to talk. Even though more customers came in, the talk quieted to whispers. All talking stopped when I stepped up to the counter.

"I'm here to collect a parcel," I said. My voice boomed into the silence.

"Name?" the postmaster asked.

"Mabel Goldenaxe."

"It *is* her, Mam," a dwarfling exclaimed.

I turned around to see who they were talking about. Everyone stared at me and they all spoke at once.

"You were amazing," one said.

"We'll all be cheering for you at Regionals," said

another.

"It's nice the females are taking up axe throwing again. You do the sport proud," an elderly female said.

The postmaster interrupted them. "Here you are."

I held my package close. The shack had filled up and was now almost as crowded as The Bearded Prospector.

"I want to be just like you," a female dwarfling said—the same one who had pointed me out. She looked at me with dark-brown eyes.

Poor deluded little one. I crouched down to be at her eye level. "If you work hard and don't give up, you can do whatever you want to do. I wager one day you'll be better than every dwarf in Gilliam."

She grinned from ear to ear. Her eyes sparkled and glowed with adoration. I had to practice extra hard so as not to let her down.

I thanked everyone for their support. Cheers broke out and spread to the far reaches of the room. Everyone shouted their wishes of good luck and those nearest me patted me on the back and arms as I passed by them. I cringed every time one of them squeezed my throwing arm. I needed the medicine, now.

At the door I turned to wave to them all. I used my non-throwing arm. I hoped they thought I was protecting my right arm, saving it for competition, and they didn't see the pain on my face when I used it to clutch my parcel.

Once outside, I breathed deep several times to ease the pain, then switched the parcel back to my left arm. I raced home, bolstered by the good wishes. I could get through this. In two weeks, after Regionals, even if I did well and moved on to the Dwarf Games, I'd have plenty of time to get my shoulder fixed up.

"You're late," Mikey yelled the moment I walked in the door.

I didn't stop but ran up the stairs yelling back at him, "I know. Sorry. I'll be right there," before I slammed my bedroom door.

I took a few minutes to slather the salve on extra thick and massaged it into my skin. I felt well enough to open my parcel. I flipped a couple of pages in the magazine.

"Mabel," Mikey hollered from downstairs.

I clutched my new Aramis cloak clasp and imagined I won Regionals with Aramis in the crowd to watch and cheer me on. Aramis asked around and found out where my hotel room was, showing up to give me his personal congratulations and show me how much he loved me.

"Mabel!"

I grabbed my waterskin and took an extra-large swallow. I squeezed my eyes and mouth shut until the sludge settled in my stomach and my body shook so hard I nearly lifted off my feet. "Coming," I squeaked. I waved my hands and whispered, "Come on, work, work, work," on my way downstairs and out to the back garden.

"Sorry, sorry." I lengthened my stretch time, praying the medicine would act faster. By the time I finished my warm-up the medicine had sufficiently numbed my shoulder.

Relatively pain free, I focused on my form and technique.

"Keep it up, Mabel," Mikey said. "You're doing great. Throw like this at Regionals, and you'll be in contention."

I beamed. As much as the support at the trading post surprised and encouraged me, Mikey's faith made me want to work extra hard.

"Twenty-five more throws then you can join us for dinner," Mikey said going into the house.

I was anxious to please. The medicine had worn off but I could get through twenty-five throws.

I hurled the final axe with all the effort and strength I possessed. The muscle in my shoulder tore from top to bottom. The ripped muscle blazed like demon's fire consuming me.

I bent double trying to breathe through the pain. I had done something terrible. I had to quit throwing. I couldn't throw and have a successful career as a miner, not like this. But I couldn't stop. I'd be letting down too many. Not only my friends and family, but those at the trading post. Competing at Regionals was the best way for me to find a suitable mate and prove to Da that all the training time was worth it.

I couldn't eat. Exhaustion and pain overwhelmed

me. I wanted to go to my room. I managed to chomp down a few potatoes and slices of roast beef. "I'm tired. Going to bed. Thanks for dinner."

"It's a long trip to Mitchum so be ready to leave at dawn tomorrow," Da said.

Two weeks. I'd be finished competing at Regionals and I'd have time to get my shoulder looked at. Two more weeks. I could do this.

CHAPTER 11

REGIONALS, HERE we come!

"It's about time," Kenneth said as I settled onto my seat at the back of the wagon.

I clutched a small leather satchel along with my travel bag and axes. The satchel carried my copies of the books on relationships, the two magazines I owned with pictures of Aramis and movies, and my Aramis cloak fastener.

Da snapped the reins urging the two horses we hired into motion. Our overloaded rental wagon jerked forward. I bit back a whimper.

My brothers and Da managed to get extra time off from the mines so they could travel with me to Mitchum for Regionals. It saved costs because we only had to rent one wagon and pair of horses. It also meant the seven-day journey to Mitchum wouldn't be as tiresome since everyone would take frequent turns driving.

"What took you so long?" Max asked.

I'd stalled as long as I could waiting for Emma to bring me more medicine before we left. She hadn't come. I didn't know what I was going to do. "I needed to make sure I had everything," I said.

"Mabel, wait." Emma yelled behind us.

Thank the gods.

"Da, stop." I shouted. Emma ran up to our cart, a large sack in hand.

The cart rolled to a stop. "Thanks, Mr. Goldenaxe," Emma said, gasping for breath. "So glad I caught you. Here." She handed me the sack. "A few gifts from your friends for your trip."

I bent over the edge and hugged her. "Thank you so much."

"See you in Mitchum," she said.

We waved as Da prodded the horses back into motion.

My friends had pooled their funds and hired a wagon and a team of horses to travel to Mitchum. I wished I was going with them. It would be so much more fun. Traveling with my friends would also have been a great time to socialize and maybe even find a mate. With all the dwarves traveling to Mitchum, there had to be at least one male among them who was interested in mating, and maybe even interested in me.

But participants had to arrive a few days early to register and practice in the arena. My one consolation was the few days in the company of all the competitors, the majority of whom were male, and quite possibly a few declared Interesteds. Not to mention all the males from the entire Black Mountain region, in the stands watching.

Really, when it came down to it, who I traveled with didn't matter. All the excitement happened at the games. And I'd be fine thanks to the extra waterskins of medicine and jars of salve.

It didn't take long before I needed some privacy so I could take the medicine thanks to the jerking and rolling of the wagon jarring my shoulder. I kept banging against Bernie or the edge of the wagon. Every jolt or nudge sent me into agony, but I couldn't take anything until I was alone.

I closed my eyes, clenched my teeth and tried to relax enough to let my body roll with the wagon.

We hadn't gone very far before we stopped. "Excuse us," Frankie and Patrick said, stepping over me.

I opened my eyes as they hopped off the back of the wagon and ran into the Prospector.

"Quick stop," Danny said, "to pick up some extra supplies for the trip."

Twenty minutes later Frankie and Patrick returned, each carrying two casks of ale on their shoulders. Wilbur, Kenneth, Ross, and Billy placed the casks in the center of the wagon. "That's not nearly enough," Kenneth said.

"There will be taverns along the way, won't there?" I asked. Frankie and Patrick were already on their way back into the Prospector for more.

"There's thirteen of us, Mabel," Bobby said. "We'll need at least four more just to get us to the next tavern."

I knew my brothers liked to have a good time, but who knew they brought the party with them? I'd been too young to remember what they were like when Mikey competed in axe throwing, which I believed was the last time my family had ever gone anywhere. Either they'd planned this trip in great detail, or they had the routine from Mikey's days of competing. Either way, traveling with my family might be fun after all.

And the ale might help numb the pain until I could take my medicine. I'd tried to drink away the pain once before, unsuccessfully, but perhaps I simply hadn't had enough to drink then.

Another twenty minutes passed before Frankie and Patrick returned with four more casks and two large canvas sacks. We readjusted ourselves to let them back on and make room for the casks. Patrick opened his sack and pulled out pewter tankards for each of us, including Da, and a couple of taps for the casks. Patrick and Danny set themselves up as the family purveyors of the drink. Pulling a hammer from his pocket, Patrick tapped the first cask. He filled a tankard and passed it to Da, then they filled the rest of the tankards for each of us.

Da raised his tankard and shouted, "To Regionals."

Each of us raised our tankards, shouting, "To Regionals."

We drank and released a unified belch. I loved my family.

Da snapped the reins once more and we were officially on our way to Mitchum.

Danny and Patrick kept the ale flowing, refilling our tankards as necessary, and even when it wasn't. Frankie passed out loaves of bread and dried meats from his sack.

"It was the greatest, most profitable battle of the ages," Frankie said between sips of his sixth ale, his voice changing into storyteller mode. This trip was getting better by the minute.

"By the end, not only was Gillis the greatest dwarven warrior, but also the greatest dwarven explorer in all of history," Frankie continued. "It began when Draco, the Lord of the Dragons, sent his minions into the Black Mountains. This very mountain range through which we now travel, was hidden by the shadows of those great winged creatures. Gillis led his army of dwarves, together with an army of elves—" My brothers and I booed. Frankie persisted. "I know, I know, but together they fought against Draco and his minions. Many were lost in those long days of bloody battle. The roads we travel were lined with the bodies of dwarf and elf and dragon alike."

The story of how Gillis defeated the dragon and

conquered Gilliam Mountain relaxed us. We flowed
and rocked with the motion of the wagon. Frankie's
words slurred the farther we traveled out of Gilliam
valley and into the Black Mountains.

I drank a fair bit myself. It didn't dull the pain
like I'd hoped it would, but I didn't really mind so
much. Too bad it was against the rules to compete
with this much ale in me.

I swung my empty tankard toward Danny for my
seventh refill. Mikey put his hand over it. "She's had
enough for today,"

"I've not. You've had a dozen," I protested.

"We're on the road, Mikey, ease up on her,"
Danny said.

"She can't be not drunk when the rest of us are,"
Bobby waved him off, pushing Mikey's hand and
falling onto the casks in the process.

"You need to be sober to practice when we stop
for the night," Mikey said as he helped Bobby back
to his seat.

"What are we practicing?" Bobby asked.

"Not you," Mikey said. "Mabel."

"Ah, Mabel. She's great," Bobby slurred. "Mabel,
you're great."

"You're great too, Bobby." I wished I was as
drunk as he was.

"You all need to slow down on the drinking," Da
grumbled. "It's time to switch drivers and I want us
to stay on the road." Da stopped the horses and came
around to the back.

"If I have to be sober, I'll take my turn," I said.

"You're not taking any turns, Mabel," Da stopped me. "You need to conserve your energy for competing. Mikey. You're driving."

Da and Mikey traded places and we started rolling. Frankie picked up the story where he'd left off.

I fell asleep thanks to the amount of ale warming my insides. It was the only way I knew how to try and escape the pain.

Mercifully my family allowed me to sleep until we arrived at a roadside inn—mostly used by traders—where Da announced we were stopping for the night.

Groggy and blurry-eyed, I looked over at the side of the mountain while my brothers stumbled out of the wagon, unloaded our gear, and disposed of the empty casks. If there hadn't been a wood door and a sign hanging over it with the name *Cracked Wheel Inn,* I wouldn't have seen an inn here at all; just a flattened section of the mountainside where the road cut through.

"Come on, Mabel. Let's get some practice in before dinner." Mikey held my axes for me.

I didn't see a place to practice unless the owners hid a range in the mountain. "Where?" I asked, staying put.

"Inside. Not a lot of room, but there is a throwing post. Management has offered to move some of the tables for you. Let's go." Mikey patted my shoulder, pushing me off the wagon.

I desperately needed my medicine. I picked up my bags and the sack from Emma. I didn't know if I had my own room, but if I did, I could take my medicine quickly before practice. "Can I have a few minutes to freshen up?"

"No time." Mikey held the door for me. "The owners are giving us the extra space until the traders come, and they're expected soon."

I could survive a short practice, I hoped.

The insides of the Cracked Wheel were bigger than I would have thought, but not as big as The Bearded Prospector. Tables were already pushed aside, and a fire roared in the stone fireplace at the center of the room.

I set my bags down and warmed up while Mikey watched and the rest of my family drank and ordered food. Axe in hand, I prepared to throw. I glanced over at my bags and longed for a sip of medicine. I wouldn't be allowed to take it during competition. I'd better practice without it. Blessedly, I only had time for a few agonizing throws before the traders arrived. My brothers helped move the tables back to their places.

"Before you go to sleep tonight, I want you to stretch a lot. It will help keep you loose and limber while we're traveling."

"No problem." Stretching I could do. It always helped, and I could give myself a nice massage while I rubbed in the poultice.

THE NEXT few days passed without much variation. At times the roads were bumpier than others and the mountains were higher or lower. All the inns were as non-descript as the Cracked Wheel. Each morning, before we got back on the road, I took a few large swallows of the medicine. Thanks to the painkiller and a sufficient amount of ale, I slept most of the time.

On the sixth day of travel Da said, "Mabel, pet. Come sit up here in the driver's seat with me."

We rearranged ourselves for Da to take a turn driving in the afternoon. I didn't like these shift changes. They disturbed my sleep. I liked them even less when, at times such as this, I had found, and now had to vacate, a comfortable sleeping arrangement. "Sure."

I yawned and Patrick helped me out of the wagon and up onto the driver's seat. The horses started moving and the wagon jerked forward slamming me against the back of the seat and the side wall. I let out an involuntary whimper then bit my tongue to keep quiet. Da glanced at me, but I didn't know if it was because he'd heard me.

Kenneth regaled everyone in the back with one of his stories of misadventure. Da was quiet, and I didn't care to say anything so I did my best to make myself comfortable to sleep.

"Is everything all right, love?" If any of my brothers heard or were curious about what Da asked me, they never let on as they kept talking and laughing.

He had noticed my whimper then. I shifted to a less painful position, then sat up straighter. I couldn't tell him. Even if I wanted to, we were arriving in Mitchum tomorrow. I had to compete in Regionals to find a mate. "Everything's fine."

"You've been sleeping a lot."

"Saving my energy for the competition, you know."

"Mmm." Da looked at me long and hard like he could read my mind or, failing that, I would break and tell him the truth if he looked long enough. I put on my best smile for him. "You don't have to compete if you don't want to," he whispered.

Yes I did. I'd spent so much time practicing that I no longer had a social group at home. All the desirable males interested in mating were probably claimed. I wasn't about to let down my friends or family, or those at the trading post, by dropping out now. They were all counting on me to do well. "I want to do this, Da. I'm excited. Can't wait."

If it weren't for the pain, it would have been true.

WE CRESTED the ridge overlooking the valley and mountainside containing the city of Mitchum. Houses filled the entire bowl. Pillars of stone lined the streets mapping out distinctive blocks and neighborhoods. The main road we traveled cut through the city to the doorway in Mitchum Mountain, the tallest, widest, deepest mountain in the entire region; the focal point of the Black Mountain Range.

"Mikey, do you have the directions to where we're staying?" Frankie called from the driver's seat as he eased us down the side of the ridge into the valley.

"We're staying at the Diamond Helm Inn. Keep on this road until we're into the mountain. I'll give you more directions once we're inside."

Wow. I'd be a mountain dweller for the duration of the competition.

The grooves in the road were smoothed to near perfection. I couldn't have been more grateful. The lack of bumps in the ride meant there was one less thing contributing to my pain.

Banners of deep blue with sparkling silver images depicting all the different fields of competition in the games hung between the pillars along the road. Flags of each city and town in the region fluttered in the breeze along the street.

Max and I leaned over the edge of the wagon as we gaped and pointed at the businesses displaying signs that welcomed competitors and guests, and offered discounted prices on their goods. The taverns had the biggest and brightest signs, each one purporting to have the best ale and food and as the only place to be before, during, between, and after all competitions.

I did a quick mental check of the itinerary Mikey had set up for me. Until the end of my competition, my days were filled. I'd have no time to participate in any of the goodness Mitchum had to offer. Thankfully, hand-held axe throwing was one of the first events to finish. I could still squeeze in a few days of shopping and drinking and enjoying myself.

As we rolled down the busy street behind a long, slow line of wagons, I did my best to remember the names of all the places I wanted to go. There were too many, and I might not remember them all, but as long as I remembered some, I could wander around and find the others, and maybe even some new places I didn't see today.

The entrance into the mountain side of Mitchum that had appeared as a mere doorway from across the valley, gaped the height and width of two giants. The road continued into the mountain, which housed half the city, their competitive arena, upper-class inns, taverns, and entertainments. Of course, in Mitchum, all miners were mountain dwellers.

The outside part of Mitchum seemed colorless and quiet compared to Mitchum under the mountain. It reminded me of the dining cavern at the mines. Voices from taverns, the rumblings of wagon wheels, and the clopping of horses' hooves echoed off the stone. The roads were narrow here and looked more like criss-crossing tunnels cut into the rock. Forming the walls and ceiling of the tunnels were houses, taverns, inns, and pedestrian walkways. Every few feet, windows, that weren't much more than holes in the walls, revealed candle and lantern lights as families and friends gathered together.

"Turn right," Mikey shouted to Frankie.

After a few more turns in a zig-zagging pattern, we arrived at the Diamond Helm Inn, marked by a sign over the door in the shape of a helm all encrusted in diamonds that sparkled from the lantern light. Beside the inn, a gold sign with silver, diamonds, rubies, emeralds, sapphires, and amethyst marked the entrance to the Mitchum arena.

"Here at last," Patrick said as he stretched and hopped out of the wagon.

My descent from the wagon was a little slower and a lot more labored, but my relief and excitement were greater than anyone's.

The inside of the Diamond Helm sparkled. Crystal lanterns on golden hooks hung on the marble walls, their rainbow prisms shimmered off the marble floor, ceiling, and welcome counter. Oak chairs with feather-stuffed cushions were clustered around the lobby. I'd never seen any place so smooth and shiny. I couldn't wait to see my room.

Mikey didn't give me any time to enjoy it. As soon as he and Da checked us in at the front desk and we were given our room numbers and keys, he said, "We still have time to get ourselves registered. Let's go. The lads will put our bags in our rooms."

Mikey and I left the inn, walked a few paces to our right, through the door into the arena concourse, down a short corridor, and we were inside the practice arena, a space as large as the Gilliam arena.

A dozen tables were set up in the middle of the floor. Signs of the same dark blue and silver as were on the main road into Mitchum, hung over the tables. Hundreds of competitors from all over the Black Mountain region milled around or lined up at the various tables waiting for their turn to register. I didn't see any other qualifiers from Gilliam.

"This way," Mikey said, leading me to the handheld axe throwing table.

I checked out my competition. I didn't know how well they had done in their home games, but the experienced ones were easy to spot. They all chatted calmly with others around them. The new competitors like me fidgeted while looking around, glancing at everything and everyone. I doubted any of us firsttimers would remember anything about today, or the Games. I had a feeling this would all end up as a blur of excitement and nerves.

Two males lined up behind us. Stout figures, full beards, declared interesteds, and they talked about work supervising the mines here in Mitchum. Neither of them came close to Aramis in attractiveness, but they looked better than any dwarf in Gilliam. They were available, and they were top miners. What more could I ask for?

I'd have to work hard to attract their interest. Good thing I brought my relationship books with me. I'd spend the night studying them so I could get right to work.

Mikey pulled my attention back to the registration line as we crept forward. "I need you focused on your preparations for the competition. You can enjoy the thrill of the Games after your part is over."

"I'm focused, Mikey. Don't worry about me." I had to be, to do well in the competition and to impress potential mates. But I had to remain relaxed, casual, attentive. Too much focus might prevent me from being open and responsive to their reactions and attractions to me.

"Name," the bloke at the registration table said without looking up. He held the quill poised over the parchment.

I totally froze. "Um."

Mikey jumped to my rescue. "Mabel Goldenaxe of Gilliam. Coach is Mikey Goldenaxe."

He wrote our names on small cards attached to a chain like a necklace. "Here is your identification. Wear these until after the closing ceremony. Your itinerary is set out in this scroll along with practice and competition times and locations, where the Gilliam team will meet for opening and closing ceremonies, code of conduct—no cheating, respecting the officials, that kind of thing—player and coaches' oaths—please read those over—information on local eateries and taverns, and who you can contact and where to find them should you have any questions or problems. Enjoy your stay and good luck in the competition." He said it all in a monotone voice like he had said it too many times. "Next."

Mikey took the scroll and we stepped to the side
of the room. We put on our badges and Mikey opened
the scroll a few inches. "Your first practice is in here
tomorrow, mid-morning. The rest we can go over at
breakfast."

Good. I had a lot of preparation to do and at least
a little time to do it.

"Let's get to our rooms, wash up, have a good
sleep tonight. It's a big day tomorrow," Mikey said.

Max and Wilbur met us in the lobby. They handed us our keys. "Thanks to the Gilliam Council, there
are only two of us in a room," Max said to Mikey. He
then turned to me and said,. "You're going to love
yours."

A double room wasn't as big a deal for me as it
was for my brothers and Da who all shared one room
at home. If I were them, I'd probably never want to
leave the hotel as long as we were in Mitchum.

We climbed up three long flights of stairs, all
marble with a gold banister. Crystal lanterns hung on
silver hooks on our floor. The doors were varnished
oak with silver door handles and keyholes. This must
have cost the Gilliam Council a bundle, paying for
thirteen single rooms in such an upscale hotel.

"Your bags are already inside," Max said pointing to my door, the one next to Mikey and Da's.

I hoped they hadn't looked inside my bags.
"Thanks." I unlocked the door and it swung open
without a squeak.

My bags lay on an oak chest at the foot of the bed. Two steps led up to the bed itself, which lay on a platform made of marble, an extension of the floor. The bed had white sheets, pillowcases, and a thick white down-filled quilt. Silver and crystal lanterns sat on oak tables on either side of the bed, making up for the lack of natural sunlight.

I unpacked, lovingly placing everything in the chest. I could get used to being a mountain dweller. Starting tomorrow, I had to make the most of my opportunities so I could actually get to be one and not just a pretend one by staying in a hotel.

I took out my books, curled up on my bed and read for maybe an hour.

Tired from traveling and the excitement of the upcoming competition, plus the exhaustion from enduring the pain in my shoulder, I lay down on the thick, soft, feather bed. Aramis's presence would have made this a perfect day and this room a perfect place. I fell asleep imagining Aramis holding me, kissing me with long, luxuriating kisses, massaging the pain away, every inch of our bodies touching, with every kiss and caress an expression of how much he wanted me.

MIKEY WOKE me the next morning by banging on my door. I rolled over to tune Mikey out, and then I saw *Ways to Let Him Know You're Interested.* Time to put the knowledge to work.

"I'm up," I yelled.

"Be downstairs in twenty minutes," Mikey called back.

I sighed, hugging the blankets to me for one more moment before I got out of bed and sauntered into my very own bathroom.

As I soaked in a hot, steamy bath—the running water coming from the hot spring that ran through Mitchum Mountain, incredible!—I reviewed what I had read last night. Every author said no one else would love me unless I felt good about myself. I reminded myself of all I had to offer. I might have a lot going against me, like being thin or at least not as stout, but emphasizing my lean but solid muscle mass showed off my strength. My absent mam was more difficult to turn into a positive but I had a close, strong, and respected family that I was very much a part of.

I drained a waterskin of its medicinal contents. I had one left, enough to last until the end of the competition.

I yawned and stretched at the breakfast table. The air felt tight and old. I found it difficult to breathe. Though I thought I'd slept well, the weight of the mountain and the ever present cold emanating from the stone left me as exhausted as a grueling shift in the mines.

After breakfast, Mikey and I headed straight to the practice arena where a Games volunteer directed us to my practice post. All posts were evenly spaced around the edge of the cavern. I assumed it was for safety and so we could focus on our own throws and not get distracted by the skills of everyone else.

My shoulder sufficiently numb, I commenced my warm-ups and surveyed the room for any Interested males. Only a quarter of the axe-throwing competitors were in the practice arena. Fortunately for me, the fellows I'd spotted yesterday were among them, their practice posts not far from mine.

I straightened my cap and tugged on the braids in my beard the way Emma always did, but that didn't attract their attention. I widened my stance to make myself look bigger, rolled up the sleeves of my tunic, and flexed my muscles. Still nothing. I was the only female in here. What was wrong with them?

"Focus, Mabel. Ignore the competitors. Give us a few practice throws."

A good solid throw could go far to attract interest. I dared anyone here to tell me this practice time wasn't being used to scope out the competition. And if one or two of the fellows happened to be impressed by my throw and found me attractive—well then, all the better for me.

Instead of tossing the axe in the unfocussed manner that I usually did for a practice throw, I paid careful attention to my technique as I threw and hit the bulls-eye. It worked. One of the fellows walked my way.

I ran my fingers through my beard and tugged

at the braids. I smiled the way Emma always smiled at whichever bloke she happened to be talking to or walking past or standing in the same vicinity of, all sweetness and confidence. A smile that said, "I am the perfect one for you."

He walked past me to Mikey. "Excuse me. But you're not Mikey Goldenaxe, are you?" He had a voice like too much mine dust had caught in his throat and the sound had a tough time ripping through.

"I am," Mikey said.

"I thought so. My name is Kyle." He shook Mikey's hand. "I had to grab this opportunity to talk to you and tell you how much I enjoyed watching you compete. Are you throwing again?"

"No, no. I've finished competing. I'm here coaching now." Mikey's right shoulder twitched like he was picking up an axe to throw it.

I'd never seen him do that. It must be the excitement of the competition. Muscle memory, or did he miss competing?

Kyle glanced in my direction without any spark of recognition I was there beaming my best Emma-smile at him. "Wow. Would you mind giving me a few tips? I'd love to learn from the best. I'll pay you, of course."

"I only have, and want, one student. But thank you. If you'll excuse me, I need to give my full attention to Mabel."

"Yes, of course." Kyle walked back to his throwing post, waving and nodding greetings to others around us.

What was I? Invisible?

"Don't let these fools distract you, Mabel," Mikey said quietly to me. "They'll do these kinds of things to waste your practice time so you don't perform as well as they do. If any more interrupt us, I'll deal with them, but you keep throwing."

Great. The one fellow who talks to us doesn't notice me but if any others try to talk to me, Mikey will scare them off. What good were Regionals for finding a mate if I couldn't talk to anyone?

THE TIME had come for the opening ceremony of the Regional Games.

All the competitors and coaches from Gilliam gathered in a group in the practice arena, dressed in uniform sapphire-blue tunics with fingernail-sized diamonds, sapphires, rubies, and emeralds stitched in to form a stripe down the sleeves and around the cuffs and trim. Competitors from each of the other cities were gathered in their groupings with their city's uniforms as well, waiting to enter the arena for the opening ceremonies.

For the first time since we'd arrived, no one surreptitiously compared themselves to the competition. We were too eager to take advantage of our one chance to relax and have a bit of fun before the games started. The Mitchum Organizing Committee had promised a spectacular show. The excitement in the atmosphere alone proved them right.

The doors to the arena opened to the fanfare of trumpets, horns, flutes and drums loud enough to drown out the cheers of the crowd. The cavern vibrated beneath our feet, which only added to the excitement.

Each city entered the arena in alphabetical order, marching in to its own song. On our way past the Mitchum competitors, I tugged at my braids and patted my stomach to emphasize my stoutness in the same way Emma would to attract the attention of the males. In doing so, I also made sure the gems on my tunic caught the light from the lanterns.

When we reached the entrance gate, all instruments stopped. Gilliam musicians took over the place of honor inside the arena, ready to lead us in. They wore the same uniform as the competitors and from the determination on their faces, they were in as much of a competition as we were.

After a pause, the drums began with a single steady beat. They added beats and inflections but kept it simple. Then the trumpets joined in a rousing battle call. We marched around the circumference of the arena, which had three times as many stands as the Gilliam arena. Everyone cheered; spectators from one full section were on their feet cheering and waving the sapphire-blue flags of Gilliam. We played to our part of the crowd, waving, flexing our muscles, blowing kisses and all kinds of carrying on.

"Do you miss this?" I shouted to Mikey as we were marshaled into the center of the arena with the other cities as the parade of competitors continued.

Mikey's shoulder twitched again. "What's to miss? I'm here with you." We continued to play to the Gilliam fans as the other cities played to their own.

As the host city, the Mitchum competitors entered last. Once all the competitors were in the arena, games marshals ushered us to the outer edges.

Two members of the Mitchum Battle-Axe team, performing a mock contest of skill and strength, entered the arena on a platform lowered from the ceiling. Other members of the team joined them on the platform demonstrating each of the contests in the games. The stage rotated so we could all see what they were doing. The band continued to play by the entrance, then they moved in single file, marching around the stage. Their final note resounded as the players reached a climax in battle.

The Head of the Mitchum Council descended from the stands and walked onto the stage. "Welcome to Mitchum," he said to tumultuous cheers. "I now declare the Black Mountain Regional Dwarf Games *open.*"

CHAPTER 12

HAVING SIZED up the competition during practices, my nerves didn't threaten to get the best of me as they had for the Gilliam Games. I figured my talent fit in the middle of the pack, which meant if I did really well, I could make it to the finals. I only wished I could have taken the medicine, especially since the competition began first thing in the morning. A sip or two, or three, and I wouldn't have had enough in my system to get me through.

Axes in hand, I stepped up to the mark. I flexed and rotated my shoulder to keep it loose and rubbed my elven cloak clasp in my pocket for luck. I lifted up the first axe and hoped I'd be able to fight off the pain long enough. I aimed and threw my axe. It arced head over handle and stuck in the third of the four rings out from the bulls-eye.

Not good. I thought I was relaxed.

Focus.

Once the games were all over, I'd get my shoulder looked at and maybe get rid of this pain properly once and for all.

Focus, throw well, forget about the pain for a little while longer.

Pain or no pain, Aramis needed me. Draco, Lord of the Dragons, captured him. I had two axes to free Aramis. With my first I sliced through the magic lock that sealed Draco's lair. The guard dragons breathed their fire and it burned me but I didn't stop. Several of the guards caught up to me. I fought them though their scales scraped me raw and fangs pierced my shoulder spreading venom into my blood, threatening to destroy me from the inside. I fought them off long enough to throw my final axe. The head touched the ropes holding Aramis, and the dragon sinew disintegrated. I had freed Aramis. I only hoped I had done enough to get us free from Draco.

I loved axe throwing. I loved the feel of a smooth release, the sweet sound of the axe head piercing the wood, the knowing that I was doing something I loved, and doing it well. I loved, more than anything, the wash of cheers for me, and the rush of competition.

"I think it's enough," Mikey said. He started to massage my shoulders and I shrugged him off. He meant well, but it only hurt me more.

I made it into the second round. I fought the pain by focusing on surviving the next few throws. Aramis had to carry me out of the lair. Though he ran as smoothly as he could, it still jarred my shoulder. "Hang on, my darling. Hang on," he said. "We're almost there. You saved me. I will not let you die. Do not give up on me. Hang on, my darling."

I could see the exit and only one dragon stood in our way. Draco himself. Draco spat his fire at us. Aramis shielded me with his magic. The flames glanced off the invisible shield and turned back on Draco, striking at his soft underbelly. We were free.

I made it to the finals. A part of me wanted to give up the fight and the competition, but Aramis coaxed me on. We were free of Draco, but we still had a war to fight. When Aramis laid me on the ground to ease my pain, he told me we were not alone. Others had come to our aid. Our victory was complete.

Mikey hugged me. I and three other competitors from Gilliam made it into the top fifteen, the largest contingent from any city.

I made my family proud. I was building up their reputation. And I loved it. If I were courting some-one, what chance would I have had for axe-throwing glory at the tavern, in Gilliam, here at Regionals, and now possibly, the Dwarf Games? None, that's the chance I'd have. I was so thankful Mikey had convinced Da to let me compete. There would be plenty of time for me to find a mate. And I was in no rush.

PAIN? WHAT pain?

I entered the arena with the other finalists, ready to compete for a place on the Dwarf Games team. I felt no pain in my shoulder for the first time in forever. I hadn't wanted any of the medicine all day. Maybe it was just the adrenaline, or maybe it was finally gone. Whatever it was, I didn't care. I felt great.

The official called my name first. With the earlier scores being combined with today's scores, I didn't have much chance to make the top three, but I could move into the top five, if I had the competition of a lifetime. I should have been terrified, or at least very, very nervous. But I had practiced with a bad shoulder, I had made it to the top fifteen with excruciating pain. Now, with no pain, I could go to the top.

Except for a few shouts of "Go Mabel," from Jimmy and Max, the crowd fell silent when I stepped up to the mark. The axe with its polished wood and gem handle was light and comfortable. I pressed my hand to my breast pocket to feel my Aramis cloak clasp. I closed my eyes, aware of the air around me, and the ground beneath me. I was ready. I nodded and the pop-up targets began. With pin-point accuracy I hit the first target.

Nothing could stop me now.

I let my mind relax a little. Aramis was there, as he always was, helping me focus, in practice or competition. This time we weren't at war or in any kind of fight or in need of rescue. Aramis wanted me to show him how to throw. I told him to watch closely. I'd perfected my form and technique. I nailed the remaining throws. Aramis took my hand and we sat down together. He put his arms around me and whispered how much he liked this personal demonstration. His lips tickled my ears.

The second round went as well as the first. I loved throwing for Aramis. Aramis threw after me, but his throws were off. I promised him in the third round, I'd show him again how to do it.

At the end of the second round, Mikey snapped me out of my daydreaming. "You're in fifth place, Mabel," he said. "Keep doing what you're doing."

Fifth place. I had a chance at third. "Thanks, Mikey." I smiled. My calm and confidence didn't waiver. Third would be amazing, though I might settle for fifth as it carried a fair bit of respectability, especially for a first-time competitor like me. And fourth- and fifth-place finishers were sent to the Dwarf Games as alternates. Of course I'd rather be Regional Champion going into the Dwarf Games, but as long as I got to the Games, I could win them and make my family proud.

My turn came for the third and final round of throws. My first throw hit the outer edge of the bullseye. Excellent, but I could hit dead center. The crowd hushed and I focused. I could have sworn Aramis was truly in the arena watching me. His mere presence, real or imaginary, must have been what was helping me.

I released the second axe. Muscles tore and bones ground against each other as my arm extended beyond its natural reach.

"Graaauugghhh!" I grabbed my right arm as it hung like dead weight at my side. Pain like the flaming teeth of a demon of the abyss consumed me. My stomach churned.

The earth spun. Everything turned black.

The medics were beside me. Someone pushed me down onto a litter and carried me out of the arena.

I shrieked and sobbed as hard as I'd wailed.

Mikey held my left hand, never letting go. "It will be all right," he said over and over again. But his voice waivered.

I leaned over the edge of the litter and released the contents of my stomach. The effort and the movement only made the pain worse, if that were possible.

"Mabel, we're going to sedate you for a while," one of the medics said in between my fits of screams. "I'm going to give you a few sips from this flask, and you'll go into a nice sleep. It won't be long, just enough for us to examine you without causing you more pain. All right?"

In between my screams and my sobs the medic pressed the cool metal of the flask to my lips. A watery, smooth and sweet liquid caressed my teeth and tongue. I had expected the sludge of Emma's potion.

"Good girl. Now swallow it. Good." The medic stroked back my hair. He and the pain faded into darkness as I drifted into oblivion.

I WOKE in a curtained off corner of the practice arena, Da and Mikey at my side. My brothers and friends talked in hushed voices beyond the curtain. Mikey sat in a chair, his head in his hands. Da stared at nothing, his arms crossed, his face closed, solid as stone.

"I'm sorry, Da," I said and the tears resumed their cascade.

"She's awake," Jimmy said from the other side of the curtain.

Da's arms uncrossed, and his face softened when he looked at me. "You'll be all right. Won't she, Mikey?" Da tapped Mikey on the back.

"Yes, of course you will," Mikey said. Though I think he only said it to placate Da. "You dislocated your shoulder. The medics reset it. Your shoulder muscles were shredded. It will take time to heal. You'll be in a sling and won't be able to use it for some time, but you will be fine."

"Come now. Let's get you up. The medics left you some medicine to help the pain." Da leaned over me, putting my left arm around his neck and looping his arm under my knees. When he straightened up, I swiveled and swung up into a sitting position. The room swayed for a moment. I'd been lying down too long. I grasped the table.

Mikey didn't look at me. Da held on to me as I stood. My friends and family applauded when I walked around the curtain.

"There's our champion," Wilbur said.

Frankie scowled. I'd let them all down. I wanted to hide my face in shame. I started to cry. Their pity applause stopped.

Jimmy hurried to my side. "We're all proud of you. You did amazingly well for any competitor, and with a bad shoulder..."

His words were sweet sentiments but meant nothing. No male would look at me now. I had absolutely nothing to offer. I would never find a suitable mate, here or at home or anywhere else. I was a liability, a chipped and cracked and impure gem that no amount of polishing could salvage.

"We need to get some food into you," Max said.

"Into all of us," Jimmy joked.

"And plenty of ale," Billy said.

"Let's go to the Crystal Lantern," Kenneth suggested.

"You'll come, won't you?" Jimmy asked me.

"Mabel, Mikey and I need to talk with you first," Frankie said. He pulled a waterskin from behind his back. My waterskin. The one with Emma's sludge. "We'll catch up with you in a few minutes."

Where did he get that from? How could he go into my room? Into my things? How did he even know to look?

Jimmy simply nodded and walked out with the

others. Emma didn't look at Frankie or me so I doubted she'd seen the waterskin.

Mikey still refused to look at me. It might be best to speak first, cut them off before either worked themselves into a full rant. And ignore the waterskin. "I'm so sorry. Mikey, I'm so sorry I let you down. I should have pushed through it. I only had one throw left. I could have made third. I'm so sorry."

Mikey looked at me then, his face crushed in deep sadness, not anger. "Mabel, don't. I wish you'd told me the pain was worse. I could have found something for it, I could have helped you, I wouldn't have pushed you so hard. I never wanted you to work so hard you'd injure yourself like this. Maybe I should have seen the signs. I don't know how I didn't see the pain you were in. Why didn't you tell me?"

My tears flowed harder. "Tell you what? I'm not a champion? I couldn't push through the pain?"

"I didn't mean this kind of pain."

"What other kind is there?"

"Mabel." Frankie interrupted and held up the waterskin. I'd tucked it into the bottom of my bag with throwing axes and a change of clothes, in case the need arose and an opportunity to take it presented itself. If I had taken it today, would this disaster still have happened? "You haven't let anyone down. We're only concerned for your health. Who did you get this from? How long have you been taking it?"

"You went through my things?" I accused.

"I didn't have to. I was told you were taking this

as a pain killer. Do you even know what is in this?" Frankie pulled out the stopper and sniffed. "Whoo!" He held the skin at arm's length, turning his head away and re-stoppering it. "How long have you been taking this?"

I lowered my head. I couldn't avoid it anymore, but I didn't have to tell them everything, either. "I don't quite know. At that strength, maybe a couple of weeks."

"What do you mean 'at that strength'?" Mikey asked. He took the skin from Frankie and had the same reaction.

"I had the strength increased a few times," I said.

"No wonder you slept all the way here," Mikey said. "With it this strong, you shouldn't have been able to walk. Who did you get this from?"

"It doesn't matter."

"Yes, it does," Frankie said. "You never should have been given something this potent. It was incredibly irresponsible of whoever gave it to you. This home-brew made you so numb you may have done irreparable damage to your shoulder."

"I was injured before I started taking it. I'm the only one to blame for this," I said.

"Oh, we know you are hardly innocent in all of this," Frankie said. "Do you even know what you were taking? You don't, do you? It may not have done any more damage to your shoulder, but who knows what it might have done to the rest of you?"

"I'll be fine," I said with much more bravado

than I felt. "As soon as my shoulder is better, I'll get back to mining. It will be like nothing has happened. This didn't do any added damage to me."

Frankie sighed. "You won't be mining for quite a while. The damage to your shoulder is too extensive. When we get home, we'll get you in to see a doctor to see just how bad things are and how it can be treated."

"But I will be able to mine, won't I?" I had to. What else would I do with myself? Everyone in my family mined. I was expected to.

"While your arm is in a sling you can only use your left arm, so you'll only be able to help with the actual excavation of the gems. You may never get full use of your right arm back." Frankie's voice broke and he shook his head. "You came very close to having no career in the mines. You had so much potential as a miner. You could have achieved so much, maybe even mined for diamonds, and now, well, you'll still be mining, but unless you manage to fully recover you won't get much farther than emeralds."

"If you'd only told me," Mikey said. "We could have treated it properly from the start. This never would have happened.

Frankie turned on Mikey. "You don't know that. If you hadn't pushed her so hard she wouldn't have needed to keep it secret from us."

"I didn't push her any harder than I thought she could take," Mikey argued.

"So you're saying I'm weak," I said.

"No. You didn't tell me. If you'd have told me I would have eased up."

"And then I wouldn't have competed as well as I did and I would have disgraced you completely."

"You wouldn't have. I never expected you to place this high."

"Because you think I'm weak."

"Because nobody does their first time competing!"

Not everyone could win, of course, but to say nobody won was unrealistic, especially when I knew the truth. "You did," I said. "And you wanted me to surpass your record."

"Mabel." Mikey sighed and sat beside me. "I thought you'd remember, but I guess you were too young. I didn't win my first year competing. It took me several years to win. I didn't even place in the top ten at the Gilliam Games my first year. I shouldn't have pushed you so hard but I saw you had so much more potential and talent than I ever had."

So I had been pushing myself all this time to live up to a standard, a memory of Mikey that didn't exist? I'd almost reached that standard too, and because of the way I pushed myself, I may have ruined everything I'd worked so hard for.

"Enough," Frankie said. "Enough. We need to get some food and drink in us. We're all proud of you, Mabel. You've proved your strength. We knew that long ago. Everyone does. When we get home, we'll find the best doctor in Gilliam to fix you up so you can mine again. And you *will* tell me who gave you this brew."

Together we walked out of the practice arena toward the Crystal Lantern.

"I thought you might want to know that once all the scores were tallied, even though you didn't get to make the final throw, you came in sixth," Mikey said.

I felt a twinge of disappointment. "Great. Thanks."

"It is great," Mikey said. "It is fantastic."

"I guess, but it doesn't get me to the Dwarf Games. Not even close. At least if I'd finished fifth I could have gone as an alternate."

"Not with your shoulder the way it is, you wouldn't. Not even if you'd won."

"No, I guess not." In spite of everything, this was the closest I'd ever felt to my brother and now felt like the right time to ask a question I'd been dying to ask for ages. "Mikey, why did you quit competing?"

He paused and Frankie moved ahead of us. "I hadn't decided yet if I wanted to mate but I had my eye on a certain male. I knew he wanted a diamond miner who lived in the mountain. There are not too many of those, so I thought if I worked hard enough, I could win his affection. I earned the promotion to diamonds, but lost him to another. By then, I'd worked so hard on getting into diamonds, I had lost more than a year of throwing. And working in diamonds uses a completely different skill set. I'd have had to retrain my muscles. So, I gave up."

"I'm sorry."

"It was a long time ago and I'm well over it. Actually, I couldn't be happier. I love mining diamonds. There is nothing I'd rather do."

"But you miss throwing. I've seen your shoulder twitch when asked about it."

"Sure. I miss the competition and the camaraderie with the other throwers. But after the heart-break, I'd lost too much time and thinking about throwing just hurt more. But you gave me a second chance at it, Mabel. And I've enjoyed coaching you more than I ever enjoyed competing."

"I'm sorry," I said. I'd taken that away from him now.

"Me, too. But you know, there are Mage-Stones competitions. I could coach you in that now, if you'd like. Or we could just play some Mage-Stones together, because that's been the best part of coaching, spending time with you."

I smiled. I had liked spending time with him, too. "You're on. Since I won't be mining for a while, how about we set up a Mage-Stones tournament when we get home?"

We passed a billboard advertising a movie opening soon, *The Goldminer's Daughter.* The billboard featured a picture of a female dwarf. The soft shape of her mouth reminded me of someone but no names were listed and I didn't know who she might be or if I might have seen her in another movie.

I guessed since I wouldn't be mining I'd be playing a lot of Mage-Stones. Maybe I could look forward to more time for watching movies and learning more about them. Da wouldn't like it, though.

It was dark inside the Crystal Lantern. We couldn't see our family until Jimmy waved us over. "I saved you a seat, Mabel," he said. "I've already ordered ale for you. Hope you don't mind."

Frankie patted Jimmy on the shoulder. Jimmy shifted in his seat. Had Jimmy given Frankie the waterskin? Why would he do that? It *was* kind of him to pre-order for me. Was it just to ease his conscience for ratting me out? If he did, by no means was I going to let him get away with it that easily. "Thanks, Jimmy."

"You're welcome. Anything you need, just ask."

Jimmy was my friend. He wouldn't betray me like that, would he? I drained my ale. "Did you give Frankie the waterskin?" I asked.

He hesitated and I knew. There was no point in him denying it now. "Why?" I asked.

"I'm sorry," he whispered.

I pressed my lips together, as though doing so would hold back my tears as well. "How could you?"

"I was concerned about you," he said. "As soon as Phillip told me about your injury, how you were taking this home-brew so often, I knew it couldn't be right. I should have said something earlier but I didn't because Emma kept telling me you knew what you were doing. I shouldn't have listened to her."

"It wasn't any of your business what I was taking

to kill the pain. And I *did* know what I was doing."

"I just thought it would help the medics to know what you'd been taking up until now. Why are you so upset if it was perfectly fine to take?"

Sweat beaded on my face and every conversation multiplied in volume as they echoed off the walls and ceiling. Did no one else mind the heat and noise? Must be the after-effects of the medicine the medics gave me, or whatever they did to set my shoulder. "You betrayed my trust."

CHAPTER 13

"HERE SHE is," Jimmy said as I descended the stairs of the grandstand to my seat.

Phillip looked up and smiled. "Hey, Mabel. We weren't sure you'd join us. How are you?"

My head swam from too much drink last night but I knew he wasn't referring to my hangover. "As well as I can be. The pain medication certainly helps," I said, walking past him and Jimmy, asking Emma and Ben to move over so I could sit between her and Zach. I didn't want to be near Jimmy yet. Several others from the Gilliam mines filled up the row and I briefly considered sitting at the other end altogether. Or maybe I should have joined Da and my brothers who sat a few rows back.

The medics gave me more effective medicine

than the sludge from Emma. The clear liquid, sweet like wild berries, relaxed my muscles enough to ease the pain so hopefully they could heal, but not enough to numb all senses in my arm or make me pain free.

What had Frankie said yesterday about the medicine from Emma? The medics thought it had been one of the causes of the potentially lifelong damage to my shoulder. It couldn't have. She would never give me something harmful. Not on purpose. She gave it to me because she's my friend. She had no reason to be jealous of me.

Although, when my beard started growing before hers, she made a fake one. Maybe she knew I tricked her into finding the right place to mine so she could discover her first emerald and she didn't want to work with me anymore. Maybe she didn't want me to attract the attention of any fellows in the region. Not like I attracted any, but she never noticed if I had a fellow or not. She could have asked to transfer to a different team, or asked me to move elsewhere if she thought I out-performed her. She didn't have to poison me.

Emma would not poison me.

"Ooh, Phillip, look." Emma leaned across me and Zach. "The boulder toss is about to start. Didn't your da compete in that when he was younger?"

And yet, why wouldn't she? I'd made it so easy for her. I kept asking her for more of the drug. I kept asking her to make it stronger. I never asked for the recipe so she had to keep making it for me.

"Yeah. He didn't get very far though," Phillip said.

"I guess it's a good thing losing doesn't hamper anyone's chances of finding a mate." Emma looked right at me.

What did she mean by that? I should be grateful some fellow might pity me and want to be my mate even though I'm a loser?

"If you look at all the beards of the winners, they're Uninteresteds, which is probably why they win," Phillip said. "They spend all their time practicing."

Thanks. Thanks a lot. I should have declared myself an Uninterested because I spent so much time practicing I lost any chance of finding a mate. Mikey had quit throwing because he'd wanted a mate. Except now I'd lost and I was damaged.

"The exception being, of course, Mabel," Jimmy said.

He meant well, I'm sure. I hadn't found a mate. I didn't have a single admirer. Why couldn't he just be quiet and stay out of my life?

"That came out wrong," Jimmy said. "I meant Mabel can do it all: mine, have a mate, and be a champion... if it weren't for your shoulder."

Right. If it weren't for my weakness, I'd have it all. Now I had nothing.

Why had I come to watch the games? They said they were my friends, but they weren't, not really. I stood up to leave.

"Excuse me, miss?" a young female approached us. "You were in the axe-throwing finals yesterday, right? Mabel Goldenaxe?" Her chin had a burgeoning shadow of stubble, no cap yet.

"Yes, I'm Mabel."

"Um, excellent. Ah, I don't know if you, well, with your shoulder, but could you sign my program?" She reached behind her back and pulled out a program.

Really? How sweet.

"No, she can't," Jimmy said.

I wish he'd stop interfering with my life. "I can try, though I can't promise it will be pretty or legible," I said over Jimmy.

Zach made Jimmy and Phillip trade places with us.

"She really shouldn't do this," Phillip said.

"It's only one," Zach said. "She's suffered enough. Let her enjoy the fame."

The young dwarf passed me a quill and held a small jar of ink. I clenched my teeth to hide the pain as I took off the sling, dipped the quill, and attempted to scribble my name on the page. I ended up with only an M.

"You were amazing yesterday," she said. "I hope they can fix your shoulder, because I'd love to see you compete in the future."

I handed back the program and quill. "Thanks. It doesn't look like I will be throwing, not for a while, anyway." I snuck a peek at Emma and wished that dwarves had the same mind-reading capabilities as elves. She didn't look jealous of the attention I received, upset for my injuries, or that I might be well enough to write. Her attention was focused on the start of the boulder toss competition and snuggling up to Ben.

"I'm so sorry. My friends and I," she pointed at a group of females back by the section entrance. "We are so excited to finally have a female thrower to cheer for, one who is a miner, not a warrior. You've inspired us to take up axe throwing."

Wow. Even with my injury I had inspired someone to pursue their dreams. "I'll watch for you, then," I said. She giggled, cheeks a rosy blush.

Her friends were now at her side, thrusting their programs at me. "Please sign ours too," they said.

I hesitated. Emma sniffed. If I'd looked at her, I bet I'd have seen her roll her eyes and get closer to Ben.

"Mabel, don't," Jimmy said.

I ignored him. He had no right to speak to me. Not now.

"Pleeeease," the girls said.

"Sure. Zach, can you hold the ink and programs for me?"

He took the first program and held it steady for me. I had to keep my arm as still as possible and writing definitely hurt, but not as much as it could have. I scribbled an M as best I could.

"Are you sure you should be doing this?" Emma

asked.

Like she really cared if I did more damage to my shoulder.

"It's only a few." I glanced up. A line had formed up the stairs and back to the section entrance. Surely they weren't all here to get my autograph. Most of them probably thought they were in line for someone else. Word would reach them soon enough and they'd move on. Until then, I'd sign as long as my shoulder allowed. "It's fine."

"Right." Emma stepped past us and into the aisle. It didn't take long and we had an assembly line going. Zach held the programs for me to sign. When I finished, Emma handed the programs back to their owners. Every now and then I snuck a peek at Emma. I couldn't tell if she helped because she was my friend and happy so many wanted to congratulate me on my performance and get my autograph, or if she wanted me to do more damage to my shoulder.

To my surprise, the line didn't shrink, it grew. I wanted the potion from Emma. The new medicine didn't numb all feeling in my arm the way the stuff from Emma did. At the moment, I didn't care how much damage it had done and would do to me. I just wanted to keep signing and not disappoint anyone. Especially since every one of them wished me well and hoped my shoulder healed quickly.

"Mabel, stop," Frankie said behind me.

I wanted to, but I had to keep going. I didn't want to be rude and turn anyone away. My M got sloppier and looked more like a squiggle than anything.

"Excuse me, coming through." Frankie pushed his way through the line and down the stairs to my row. "This is the last one, Mabel," he said as I took a program and signed it. He stopped the next dwarf from handing his program to Zach.

"Thank you everyone." Frankie raised his voice. "Mabel will be unable to sign anymore autographs at this time." Everyone in line groaned. "She appreciates all of your support and well-wishes. As I am sure you can understand, she needs to give her shoulder time to heal." He waved the last of them away.

Frankie turned to me, ready to lecture but he stopped before he uttered a word when he saw my relief. I would have stopped earlier if Jimmy hadn't been the one urging me to.

"Thank you," I said, replacing my sling.

Frankie commandeered Zach's seat. "You have to take care of yourself. No one needed to have your autograph. They could have come to wish you well and congratulate you on your performance yesterday." He dropped his voice to a whisper. "Unless you want your mining career to be over forever, you must stop using your arm for a while. If necessary, one of us will feed you and we can get someone to help you dress." Frankie gave the seat back to Zach and turned to my friends. "Don't ever let her sign programs, or anything else for that matter, again."

"Sorry, Frankie," Zach said.

"It's all right. She's a sly one, our Mabel. She

asks you to do something and she's so sweet and innocent about it you can't refuse her. I want all of you,
but especially Jimmy and Phillip, to be firm with her
and not let her get away with anything."

That ought to be easy for them, especially Jimmy.
He had no problem reporting what I do to Frankie.

"Jimmy and Phillip?" Emma asked. "Why not
me? I'm her best friend."

"Exactly," Frankie said.

"What do you mean?"

"You probably knew before anyone else about
how bad her injuries were." Frankie left Emma
speechless and went back to his seat.

We all turned our attention to the competition
floor. I'd completely missed the first round of the
boulder toss. Full-armor sprints were next.

Frankie shouldn't put all the blame on Emma. I
could have, should have, told Mikey how much pain
I was in and gone to a doctor. She only tried to help
me. If there had been something poisonous in the
medicine Emma had given me, of course I wanted to
know if she'd given it to me on purpose or not. Until
I knew for sure, I'd give her the benefit of the doubt.

"Switch," Emma said to Phillip and they traded
places so she sat next to me. "What is Frankie's problem with me, Mabel?"

I didn't want to get into it with her. Not until I
knew if she had poisoned me. Then I would confront
her and ask her if she'd done it on purpose. I kept my
eyes on the competitors lining up ready to start the

race. "Don't know what you're talking about."

"Really. Why is Frankie angry with me?"

The starter flag dropped and the first group of racers ran the perimeter of the arena. Everyone in the stands stood and cheered.

"He thinks your medicine caused more damage than if I'd taken proper pain killers."

"You told him I gave you the medicine?"

How interesting. She cared more that Frankie knew she gave me the medicine, than she did about the damage done to me. "I may never be able to use my right arm again. I am practically useless as a miner. He has every reason to be upset."

"And he blames me for your stupidity? You're the one who kept working and pushing yourself. You're the one who refused to tell anyone about your pain. You're the one who kept asking for stronger doses."

Wow, she was more than a little defensive. "No. He blames me for my stupidity. But without your medicine, I would have never been able to push myself."

"Do you agree with him? Do you think I tried to ruin you?"

I stared at her. Emma, with the perfect figure and beard, who had all the fellows in Gilliam chasing after her, the first of either of us to work in the mines, the first to get a full beard, the first to wear a single braid, the one to find more than one mountain dweller to court her. I could throw axes better, and I found the first-ever emerald. I'd found several emerald beds before her and I had to help her find her first, had to trick her into it. I'd made a fool of her. She wanted to be better than me at everything, to be first to everything. If she couldn't, then why wouldn't she try to stop me? I could have wagered the entire Gilliam treasury on it. "I don't know. Did you?"

"How could you possibly think I would give you something to cause you irreparable damage? I am absolutely sick about what's happened to you. I was the first to the warm-up room to see what had happened."

"Why? Feeling guilty?"

Tears filled her eyes. Real tears, not the fake ones she cried when she couldn't find her first gem. "You're my best friend. I only wanted to help you. Mam said to use an old family recipe. One we've used for generations, since before there were doctors." Emma wiped at her tears but they didn't stop flowing.

Dear gods of pain and sorrow. She would never have done anything to me. Even if there had been something bad in the medicine she gave me, she would not have given it to me on purpose. "I'm sorry, Emma. I know this isn't your fault. I'm sorry." Emma turned to walk away. I stopped her. "For what it's worth, I didn't tell Frankie who gave me the medicine. I think he's just upset at everyone."

"Sure. Whatever."

I slumped onto my seat and wished Aramis were with me. I closed my eyes and wished myself back in my room in Gilliam alone with Aramis. After I've cried and told him how badly I've made a mess of my friendship with Emma, he holds me, his elven calm envelops me like a thick woolen blanket and he kisses me ever so softly and so fully that he becomes my entire being and fills my whole world. In my mind he whispers it will be all right in the end.

"I'll take six," Jimmy shouted.

What? Oh, right, still at the games. I sighed. And no Aramis.

One of the food vendors handed Jimmy six skewers of pork, one for each of us. He paid, then waved over the ale vendor and bought six ales.

"If you need any help," Zach said to me, "just ask. I'll put your ale between us on the floor."

"Thanks." I bit into the tangy and salty pork.

However Zach intended his offer of help, it irritated me. He and Phillip continually bumped me as they ate and drank. I wanted to push them aside. I needed to get out of here. I wanted to leave the oppressive weight of the mountain and go explore the city of Mitchum on my own. I wanted to get away from everyone: Frankie, Emma, all of them.

I walked out of the stands. I couldn't move fast enough. I wanted to run and run until I'd left the mountain far behind.

Jimmy caught up to me. "Are you all right, Mabel?"

"I'm fine." I kept walking.

"Where are you going?"

"Out."

"Do you want some company?"

Not his company. "I want some time to myself."

The moment the door to the Mitchum Arena closed behind me, I began to cry. I marched past our hotel, wiping away tears that wouldn't stop falling. It felt as though the walls of the mountain were pressing in on me. I walked faster, the soles of my shoes smacking the stone.

I had lost everything because of my own stupidity, my desperation to please and impress. If only I had gone to the doctor about the pain. I should have told Mikey when the pain started to get worse. I never should have entered the contest at the Prospector. I should have stuck to mining, nothing else. Mining was the only thing worth doing and now I didn't even have that for who knew how long.

Why was it so hot in here? And where did this crowd come from?

I looked around and realized I'd reached the main road in and out of the mountain. I pushed my way through the crowds, leading with my left shoulder, protecting my right. Ugh. Really. Why weren't these dwarves at work or the Games? So crowded and hot and even though the main street was wider than every other road, the walls were crushing, burying me. I had to get out, away from the stale dead air of the mountain.

A light breeze caressed my face, gently played with the ends of my beard, sweet like Aramis's whis-

pers. It was too far away. The breeze disappeared.
I bobbed and weaved through the hordes, desperate
to get to the breeze before the mountain choked me.
There was a lull in the pedestrian traffic and the exit
was close. I burst out of the mountain and allowed
the cold winter breeze to surround me and carry me
into the openness of Mitchum outside of the mountain.

Finally I slowed to a walk, breathing naturally.
The aroma of the trees lining the street was ever-
present and comfortable. Fresh air, trees, comfortable? Since when? I shuffled over to the nearest
building. I leaned against it, pressing my hot face to
the cold stone, and closed my eyes. Since the open
space didn't make me feel like I was being crushed
or closed in, it took several moments before I felt
safe again.

Exhausted from the panic, I stayed as I was until
the cold penetrated my skin and sank into my bones.
Shivering, I pushed off the wall and wandered past
the shops. The brightness of the sun on the snow-
covered valley blinded me and I welcomed it. Anything was better than the darkness of the mountain.

When we first arrived in Mitchum I had been
so excited to shop and visit all the taverns. Now I
scoffed at the idea. I had no interest in entering any
building, being in *any* enclosed place. And now my
mining career was at best on hold. I didn't know if I
would ever have a decent income again. Sure, there
was a possibility my shoulder would heal, but how

long would it take? What if I'd done too much damage to it?

"Hot apple cider," a street vendor called. "Get your hot apple cider, here."

A hot drink would be great. I had left my coat in the hotel room, and I was freezing.

"All right, love?" the vendor asked when I stopped beside him.

"I'll take a large one, please." I handed the vendor a small emerald.

He gave me a handful of gold coins in change. "Been a rough day, has it?"

"Few days, really." Tears welled up and I blinked them back.

"Very sorry to hear that." He handed me a large steaming cup of apple cider with a stick of cinnamon. "And a little something extra, on me."

"Oh, no, you don't have to."

He waved off my protests and placed an apple pastry into a little bag that he put in my pocket. "A treat for later. Hope things get better for you soon, love."

The tears fell this time and I couldn't stop them. "Thank you."

"Shh, shh, now." He wiped my cheeks for me. "None of that or you'll freeze to death."

I smiled.

"That's it. Have a sip of that cider, get some warmth in you."

I sipped it. The sweetness of the fruit, blended

with malt spice and cinnamon, tickled my taste buds and warmed me. "Sorry about that."

"No worries. You have a better day now."

It didn't take me long to finish the cider as I sauntered on. I pulled out the apple pastry and nibbled on its sticky-sweet goodness. I hadn't realized how hungry I was. Warm and satisfied, I licked my fingers.

A dragon-bone bow in the window of a hunting shop caught my attention. Aramis would love it; long and sleek, the grip decorated with ancient dwarven runes.

Aramis. Would he love me now? Somehow I doubted it. Even elves have their limits as to how much weakness they will accept.

I began to shiver once more, causing my shoulder to ache. I moved on until I discovered a bookstore. Though I had no desire to enter any enclosed place, I needed to warm up and rest for a while.

Inside, a large fire warmed the store, the fireplace filling one entire wall. The rows upon rows of bookcases crowded the room, but it didn't smell old and musty like the Gilliam Library. Here, the scent of freshly cut and bleached parchment permeated everything, leaving me with a feeling of newness and spaciousness. I spotted some chairs in a back corner near the fire. I headed there and found myself in the middle of the magazine section.

I settled on the chair, resting my arm on the armrest as I gazed at the shelf of magazines. There were four kinds: mining, hunting, blacksmithing, and dwarven battle tactics. I sighed.

There was one magazine that was different from the others. It covered dwarven fashions. Fashions? Curious, I picked it up. I had to do something to make myself appear to be a patron before a clerk threw me out for loitering.

I flipped the pages, not really looking, though some of the newer tunics and trousers with patterns of plaids and polka-dots made me chuckle. No self-respecting dwarf would wear those. Maybe on the farthest edges of Mitchum or in Leitham, but definitely not in Gilliam. Mind you, the dark blue one with the lighter blue weave pattern was kind of nice. But some of them, most of them, were just hideous. This was definitely not a typical dwarven magazine.

I looked at the address of publication and sure enough, it came from Leitham. No wonder it was so different. It was published away from the influence of the pure dwarven culture. I was curious and read more. I couldn't mine for a while, and I couldn't throw axes. Maybe I could learn something from this magazine about being a dwarf in a world where I didn't exactly fit in anymore, if I ever had.

Living Your Authentic Life. The title piqued my interest. *The newest book by Psychologist Dr. Thaddeus has reached number one on all the bestseller lists for self-help books. "All of us, at one time or another, feel overwhelmed—whether it be from work, family, demands put on us by society, or any combination thereof. For many, this feeling of being over-*

whelmed leads to a need to run away, leave every-thing behind. This is the mind and body telling them they have ignored their Authentic Selves. They have not found what makes them happy, what gives mean-ing to their life," says Dr. Thaddeus. "With my book, readers will search their inner desires, and learn to feed the needs of their Authentic Selves so they can live their Authentic Life."

I held onto the magazine, open to the article on Dr. Thaddeus, and walked around the store, looking for the book though I didn't expect to find it. A store in Mitchum would not carry a book written by an elf. As with the magazines, they only carried books on mining, hunting, blacksmithing, and war. Thankfully an order form had been inserted at the end of the ar-ticle. I took the magazine to the counter and paid for it with three of my gold coins.

"Excuse me," I said to the clerk. "Is there a trad-ing post nearby?"

"Sure. Out the door, to your left. When you reach the first street, take another left. It's about two blocks."

"Thanks." I grabbed my purchase and hurried to the trading post. It was larger than the Gilliam one, but size was the only difference. The layout inside was exactly the same. At the counter, I asked the clerk for a quill and ink. I gasped when I picked up the quill and I dropped it.

"Here, let me help you fill that out," the clerk said. He tore out the order form and filled it out for me.

By the time I left the trading post, the sun had begun to set and the temperature had dropped. It was time to head back to the hotel. It took two hours to arrive back at the entrance to Mitchum Mountain. I stopped at the entrance. I had no desire to return to my family and friends, to the constant reminder I had ruined everything.

CHAPTER 14

"STOP MOVING," Max said, his brush tangling in my hair as I shifted yet again in my seat. I had my first appointment with Dr. Flint in an hour.

I sat at my dresser while Max brushed my hair. This had become our new routine since returning home from Regionals two weeks ago.

"Sorry," I said.

Max set down the brush and pulled my hair back, tying a black ribbon around it. "You're not looking forward to it?"

I turned in my seat so he could braid my beard. "He's only going to tell me I'll never mine and there's nothing he can do for me."

"I'd be shocked if Dr. Flint can't do anything for you. Frankie says he's the best doctor in Gilliam.

He'll have you mining before anyone else could."

"I'm shocked he even agreed to see me."

"Why? He specializes in mining injuries."

"Exactly. I didn't hurt myself mining, did I?"

"No, but you're a miner, and your shoulder affects your work. Stop talking." Max sectioned off my beard. "I can't braid if you're talking." Two minutes later, he had finished and held up a mirror for me to inspect his handiwork. "Not bad, if I do say so myself."

His braiding skills had improved drastically since he had to braid my beard. They'd improved so much I thought he did a better job of it than I ever had. "It will do."

Max tugged on one of the braids. "Thank you, Your Graciousness."

I followed him down the stairs.

"See you later," he said. "Keep your chin up. You will be able to mine, even if it is only one-handed for a while."

His ever-present optimism made me smile. After he left, I entered the kitchen to have whatever my brothers had decided to leave me for breakfast. Mikey sat at the table. I assumed everyone else had either gone to bed or to the mines. "Not going to work today?"

"Maybe later." He set a plate of eggs and toast and a mug of tea in front of me. "How are you?"

"You're not staying home because of me, are you? I'm fine. I'm not so pathetic I need you to hold my hand or to walk me to the doctor's."

"Of course you're not. Mabel, I am so sorry for all of this, and I thought maybe I could begin to make it up to you, by going with you for support. You know, to celebrate the good news, and if, on the off chance, the news is bad, to commiserate. I failed as your coach because I didn't pay attention, but maybe I can do better as a brother and help you now."

Tears welled up. Gods I had become such a weepy mess. "I appreciate the offer, but I think I want to go on my own."

"Are you sure?"

"I am," I said, digging into my cooled breakfast.

"All right. When you go, take this with you." Mikey handed me a waterskin. "It's what you were taking before Regionals. See if Dr. Flint can identify it. If he can, maybe he can tell you if it made your injuries worse than they would have been otherwise."

Emma wouldn't hurt me. If my family needed Dr. Flint's confirmation to believe it, then I was happy to oblige. "Sure."

"Mabel," Mikey said and sighed. "Who did you get this from?"

"It doesn't matter."

"Why do you continue to protect them, when they could have ruined your mining career?"

"You don't know that," I said. "If Dr. Flint says this painkiller was a bad thing, I'll take care of it."

"I understand why you took it. You didn't want to worry us."

"Then why do you insist on knowing who gave it to me? It doesn't matter. I chose to take it. No one forced me. It's my fault, no one else's."

"If they're peddling this to others, who knows what damage is being done," Mikey said.

"They're not."

"How do you know?"

Because Emma had no time to be selling it to anyone else. She was too busy with Ben and flirting with Zach. "I just do. Can we drop it? Please?"

"All right. For now. Promise me you will tell Dr. Flint everything—when the pain started, how it became worse, how you obtained this stuff," he pointed to the waterskin. "Everything. He won't tell us, doctor-patient confidentiality. It will help him to find the best treatment for you."

I nodded. "Okay."

Mikey squeezed my knee and left.

Less than an hour later I walked toward the mines. Before I reached the turn-off to the mines' entrance, I took a small path to the left into the grove of trees surrounding the base of Gilliam Mountain. The snow was well-packed on the path at the entrance to the stone single-story building.

"Name please?" the receptionist asked.

"Mabel Goldenaxe."

"Welcome, Mabel. Dr. Flint will be with you in a few minutes."

"Thanks." I sat on the stone bench in the empty waiting room. I pulled at the buttons of my coat, wondering what the doctor would say. I had a good idea, and was certain I had been right this morning, but a part of me, all of me, hoped I was wrong, that Max was right, and Dr. Flint would tell me I'd be ready to mine in no time.

The door to the doctor's office opened. An elderly dwarf emerged, followed by the doctor. "I can't thank you enough," the older one said to Dr. Flint.

"You're very welcome, Eli. Say hi to the missus for me, and try to remember your grandlings are getting too big to be picked up."

"I will, and I'll try." The old one shook the doctor's hand.

Dr. Flint shuffled the parchments in his hand, "Mabel."

Dr. Flint's office had a wood desk covered with parchments, and two large leather chairs. An examining table stood in the far corner and on some shelves beside the table lay all kinds of medical tools—metal knives, long silver needles, and round glass on sticks—that I was careful to stay far away from.

"Hello, Mabel. How are you?"

"Very well, thanks." I unbuttoned my coat and eased it off. How was I going to get it back on after?

He pointed at my sling. "I guess I don't have to ask why you're here."

"No, I guess not." I chuckled nervously.

He referred to his papers for a moment. "Ah yes. Frankie spoke to me about what happened. Let's see, dislocated shoulder, and shredded muscles. Quite the injury. All from throwing axes?"

My stomach churned. "Apparently. Though this might have contributed to it." I handed him the waterskin and the salve. "I was wondering if you could test it; maybe see if it compounded the problem. I don't believe it did, but my family seems to think so."

He pulled out the stopper and sniffed it. He wrinkled his nose and quickly re-stoppered it. "I can definitely have a look at it." He set the waterskin aside. "Since Regionals, have you used your arm for anything?"

"Only the basics of getting dressed. Otherwise I keep it in the sling."

"Good to hear. Shall we check how things are healing?" He took off my sling. "Relax and let me move your arm for you." He put one hand on my shoulder.

The heat from his hand warmed through my tunic into my muscles. With his other hand, he held my wrist and slowly raised my arm and rotated it in tiny circles, spiraling out until I whimpered. He let my arm rest for a moment. He then moved it from front to back and up and down, again starting with small movements and making them bigger until I cried out.

He bent my arm at the elbow and pressed his hand against my palm. "Push my hand. Good. Now the other side," he said as he put his hand against the back of mine, even though I couldn't push at all.

He gave my arm a gentle massage. "Very good,

Mabel." He put the sling back on me.

Good? I would be able to mine? I was healing?

"I have some good news and some not-so-good news for you."

Or not.

"The medics did a great job of re-setting your shoulder in the socket. It seems to be healing well, though it did feel like there was some erosion in the socket, or on the joint, or both. We'll know more in time. Your muscles are slowly stitching themselves back together. You are doing a wise thing, keeping your shoulder immobile. I am a bit worried that scar tissue is forming. Again, it is too soon to tell. You will heal from this, though I have my doubts you will ever fully recover."

"So what is the good news?"

"I'm afraid that was the good news. I have seen similar injuries, though never so severe, and in this combination. While I suppose it is possible to do this kind of damage throwing axes, my experience tells me something else was a contributing factor. As soon as I have the results on this medicine and salve you were taking, I will inform you of what I discovered."

"What about mining?"

"I see no reason for you to stay away from the mines as long as you understand that you are only, and I cannot stress this enough, *only* to assist with easy extraction of gems once they have been found. And only with your left arm. If you do anything else, any use of your right arm at this point will reverse any healing that has already taken place. It could possibly cause greater damage."

I hung my head. "So I have ruined my mining career," I muttered.

"On the contrary, Mabel. It will be stalled for several months, but in due time you will regain full range of motion in your right arm, and while there will always be some limitations as to what you will be able to do, you will adjust to it, and you will once again mine as you did before this happened. But it will take time."

I closed my eyes as tears welled yet again. I shouldn't be crying. This was a good thing. Obviously miners were injured all the time or there wouldn't be doctors for us. The delay wasn't great, but it could be so much worse.

"Once we get this shoulder working better you will be able to do most things as before. Don't think the worst. You do have a future in mining."

I wiped away my tears. Why was I so upset? I could still extract gems. Ugh. The only thing worse than the tedium of scratching at rock endlessly, was sitting around waiting for something to do while others scratched at the rock. "Tears of relief," I lied.

"Well, good," he said. "I don't see any reason why you shouldn't return to work any time you like, today even, if you should so choose, again, as long as you only assist in extraction, and nothing else."

Dr. Flint smiled and helped me put on my coat, careful to keep it loose over my right shoulder. I adjusted my sling as he fastened the buttons. "As soon as I have the results on your medicine, I'll ask you to come and see me. Remember to keep your shoulder immobilized. Are you in a lot of pain? Do you need something to ease it?"

"No, thanks. When it's in the sling, it's just uncomfortable, not unbearable."

"I understand, but you need to keep the sling on for some time. I'd like a lot more healing to have occurred before we even think of taking it off. All right? I shall see you soon, likely in a few weeks."

"Thanks, Dr. Flint."

As I left the doctor's cottage, I considered returning to work. I'd have to talk to Phillip about the timing for me to start. It would depend on whether there were any exposed emerald beds or not.

I hesitated at the main road. On seeing the mines' entrance I took a deep breath. I couldn't go in. I didn't *want* to go in. I decided to wait for my friends at the Prospector. I could talk to Phillip there.

It had been so long since I had been in the tavern. I'd missed the aroma of permanent smoke and ale. I ordered enough drinks for my friends and asked that they be carried to our table.

I found a table not far from the door. Zach, Ben and Jimmy were the first to arrive and settled in just as the barkeeper brought the tray of ales.

"Aw, cheers, Mabel.," Zach said.

"It's about time you joined us, even if you're not working," Jimmy said. "You had your appointment today, right? What did the doctor say?"

I hadn't forgiven Jimmy for his betrayal, but if I wanted an evening out with friends, I had to accept he was a part of that group. I still had trouble looking at him. "I can extract gems, but that's about it, for now, anyway." I drank deeply, downing half my tankard.

"That's the best part of mining anyway." Ben said.

I'd thought the same thing dozens of times. Perhaps if I thought about my predicament as an excuse not to spend endless boring hours and days scraping at stone then maybe this wasn't a bad thing.

"Does this mean you can come back to work tomorrow?" Phillip asked, joining us.

I faked a smile, hoping it would help me feel enthusiastic about mining. "If you want me to."

"Absolutely. Don't we, Emma?"

Emma sat beside Zach, who put his arm around her. What happened there?

"Of course we do. We have so much to catch up on."

"I'll get another round," Ben said.

I hadn't realized how close to the door we were until it opened and a great gust of air blew in, carrying the scent of early spring growth of leaves. And I hadn't known how tense I was until I inhaled the spring air reminding me of open spaces, and relaxed. Odd, though, that it should smell like new leaves. They hadn't begun to bud yet. In fact, the snow hadn't melted yet. And no matter what the season outside, it never penetrated the tavern.

"What's an elf doing here?" Jimmy muttered.

An elf? In Gilliam? This I had to see.

His long blond hair, piercing sky-blue eyes and delicate cheek bones took my breath away. Aramis! He was here, for real, in Gilliam. Maybe he could love me, even with my injury.

"Isn't he the actor?" Emma asked.

I had to let him know I was here, that I loved him. Aramis squinted, scanning the crowd for something, or someone. I ran my fingers through my beard. I should go talk to him. He would want to meet a fan, wouldn't he? Maybe he'd like me. I mean for real, not just in my dreams. If his best friend was a dwarf, he might be attracted to me. It could happen. It could really happen!

Our wee ones would be beautiful, like their da.

"Weird folk they are, elves and actors," Ben said, returning with more ales. "No wonder he wandered into a dwarven tavern without thinking twice. How exactly did you hurt your shoulder anyway, Mabel?"

Oh gods. My friends were here, and they could never know I fancied an elf. But this could be my only chance to talk to him.

"Aramis. What do your elf eyes see?" Sevrin, Aramis's best friend, former adventurer, and fellow actor, pushed his way through the crowd surrounding the bar and slapped his friend on the back.

Aramis's cheeks dimpled and his eyes sparkled

when he smiled. "Little more than a blustery wind with the most unruly beard I have ever seen. But if it is willing to buy me some ale, the vision might clear." They laughed and embraced like two friends who had not seen each other in a long time.

It might be the last thing I'd like to re-live, but a tale of battle wounds might catch Aramis's attention without making my friends suspicious. I'd never been much of a storyteller, but my brothers were great at it. I could imitate them easily. I cleared my throat in my best Frankie-as-storyteller voice, I said, "There I was, this young upstart from Gilliam, my first time competing in the Regional Dwarf Games, my first year of axe throwing, and I had made it to the finals." My friends cheered me on.

"I had defeated warriors and past champions, to reach the final ten," I continued. A crowd was gathering. I hoped this would impress Aramis. At the same time, all these dwarves watching, listening, made me nervous. I cleared my throat. "Sure I'd been in some pain, but what athletic competitor doesn't experience pain in their career? On that day, though, I was pain free. If I could compete with enduring pain and make it to the finals, how much better could I be without any?"

"Champion! Champion!" someone in the crowd chanted but was shushed quickly.

I carried on, gaining confidence as I spoke. "With every throw, I had improved and I found myself sitting in fifth place, good enough for a place as an alternate to the Dwarf Games. But I wanted to be more than an alternate. I was in fifth place, but positioned to move up into third with my last three throws." There were more cheers.

I dropped my voice, becoming more dramatic with each sentence. "The first throw was perfect. The gems in the handle of my axe sparkled as it arced end over end. I had thrown it with such force, the entire post rattled as the axe head embedded itself in the bulls-eye. Third place was so close, I could feel it. I could smell it. I could taste it, as tantalizing as this ale." I raised my glass and took a sip. The effect was dramatic, but I'd done it mostly to wet my throat.

"I prepared to throw the second axe, raised my arm, and as I threw it, my shoulder popped out of the socket." Gasps came from the attentive audience. "Pain like demon's fire burned through me. The muscles ripped, shredding like boulders crushing a city in a rock slide." I stopped. There was no more to tell, only disaster. "The rest, you know," I said softly.

"I'm so sorry," Ben said.

Ricky, Patrick's friend, walked up to me. He cleared his throat and that's when I noticed the throwing axe in his hand. He didn't seriously expect me to throw, did he? Ricky set his axe on the floor in front of me, removed his cap and bowed. Without a word, he walked away.

Others approached me with their axes, setting them in front of me, on the table and floor, removing their caps and bowing. What was going on?

This was only the greatest sign of respect a dwarf could show another, putting their axe at the other's feet and bowing. Why were doing this for me? I had done nothing. I had failed.

I looked to my friends for some clue as to what was going on. They only grinned back at me, as pleased and as surprised by the spectacle as I was.

Mikey too set one of his axes in front of me.

"Why are they doing this?" I whispered.

"Your bravery. You've made Gilliam proud," he whispered back and patted my cheek.

Everyone lifted their mugs of ale then and shouted "To Mabel!"

Thirty or more axes lay on the table in front of me and at my feet. I was humbled by the immensity of the tribute. I stood, removed my cap, and bowed to the room.

As things returned to normal, well, relative normal, as my friends gushed about what had just happened, I remembered that Aramis had been here. He'd probably witnessed the whole ceremony. That would have caught his attention.

I searched the tavern but Aramis had gone.

CHAPTER 15

WHEN I woke up the next day, going in to the mines was the last thing I wanted to do. I thought I'd be ready. Being able to mine was supposed to have been my biggest concern with my injury. Ben had been right, extracting gems was the best, most interesting part of mining, and it was what I would be doing all the time now. Somehow, even *that* had lost its luster.

It wasn't like I was getting lazy. I had no intention of staying in bed or not going out at all. I just couldn't face the tedium of mining. And I didn't *have* to work. My friends would understand.

I asked Max to pass on a message to my friends. I was going to go see *The Goldminer's Daughter*, which was opening at the movie theater, if any of them wanted to join me.

Jimmy was the first to the theater door. "The others will be here in a few minutes," he said. "Please, Mabel, I can't have you mad at me. I am so sorry I betrayed you. I should have trusted you. Please, can you ever forgive me?"

He was so desperate. It wasn't like what he'd done had changed the outcome of anything. It hadn't landed me in any extra trouble. "I know you thought you were doing the right thing."

"I was, Mabel, I swear. And I know it wasn't my place to have said anything. I should have kept my mouth shut. Please, Mabel."

It would make it easier to spend time with friends if I did. I shrugged with my left shoulder. "I guess. But I don't know that our friendship will ever go back to the way it was before."

"I understand. I won't stop trying, though."

"Mabel, listen," Emma said walking up to me. "This misunderstanding between us has gone on long enough." It was the first time she had really spoken to me since the boulder toss event at Regionals.

Was today the day for confessions and forgiveness?

"I've missed you too much," she continued. "And there's so much I have to tell you. So I forgive you for thinking I tried to poison you. You were upset and had to blame someone."

What?

Emma linked her arm in mine and let the others go ahead of us. "You will never guess what happened on the way back from Regionals. Zach asked if we could have another try. I told him I was with Ben but Zach convinced me he truly loved me. I told Zach he had hurt me really badly and he apologized. So I said I would give him another chance if he stopped thinking the worst of me for being friendly to everyone and he agreed. Isn't it fabulous? I really think this time it's going to work and he's going to give me a golden ring."

Oh, never mind. I didn't think she had poisoned me. She was too self-absorbed to think up any such scheme. I hadn't seen her this happy in a long time. Not since she first started courting Zach. I stifled a shudder at the thought of living under the mountain like Emma would have to if he gave her a golden ring. "I really hope it works. And I better be your witness at the ceremony."

"Of course you will. I wouldn't have it any other way."

We weren't the first or the last in the line of movie goers, which extended out the lobby and well onto the path. Murmured excitement that seemed to originate from the dwarves next to the movie poster buzzed through the line. I only caught snatches of what they said, only words like "from here" and "family".

When we reached the movie poster, Emma elbowed Zach in the ribs. "Why didn't you tell me she was in the movie?"

Zach glanced at me then and with a half shrug

said, "I don't know. Sorry."

"Do you know her?" I asked. The female on the poster was the same as on the billboard in Mitchum. She looked familiar, but if I couldn't place her, how could Emma?

"We have to talk," Emma said. "Zach, you all go on ahead. We'll meet you inside." She pulled me to the side of the road, too far from the line for me to hear what they were saying, and I assumed far enough away so no one else could hear us.

"What's going on? Did you see Mark?"

"Mark? No. That would be a disaster. No. Mabel. There's something I have to tell you."

"Can't it wait? We won't get a seat if we wait much longer."

"No, it can't. I'm not supposed to tell you this. Really, your da or your brothers should have told you, but they haven't, and now this is happening, and you're going to hear all the talk so it's better it comes from me than you overhearing it in the cafeteria or something."

"Spit it out, already."

"Oh gods." Emma rubbed her face. "Okay. Here goes." She breathed deep. "The lead female in this movie, she's your mam."

"My what?" She couldn't be.

"Your mam. She's not dead."

"I know she isn't. How do you know who this actor is?" How did she know anything about my mam when I knew nothing?

"On the poster, when we walk by it, take a closer look. You look just like her. And also, her name. Everyone knows. Except you, and Max. Your da's done a great job of—"

"You've known about my mam all my life and you never told me? Every time, over the years, when I wondered aloud about Mam, you knew and said nothing." My stomach clenched and my leg muscles ached. I needed to leave, to run, to see the movie. Mam.

"I'm sorry. I really, really, truly am. Our families are friends. My parents agreed with your da not to tell you and they made me promise. They said he would tell you when the time came. He should have. I really thought he would. But he never did and I was forbidden. And now, well, she's been gone so long, no one talks about her much anymore, I thought everyone had forgotten about her. Your brothers I guess have grown up without her so maybe they never thought it necessary to tell you, or to talk about her."

I sank to the ground. "You mean all of Gilliam, all of my friends know about her, and you never thought to mention to me my mam is still alive, acting, to not even tell me her name?"

"Of course I did. But your da thought it best you didn't know, and my parents agreed. I never imagined you'd have to find out this way."

My mam, the actress. No wonder Da never wanted me going to the movies. He didn't want me to know anything about her.

"Is everything all right?" Jimmy asked.

I couldn't look at him. "Did you know, about her?"

"Zach just told me." Jimmy extended his hand. "Do you still want to see the movie? If not, we can go to the Prospector or something instead."

I ignored his offer of help and struggled up on my own. They all knew. They'd *all* betrayed me. "I want to see the movie. I want to see my mam. And then I need some time away from all of you because I don't know who you are or if any of you are really my friends."

"Mabel—" Jimmy pleaded, handing me my ticket.

I snatched it from him and walked past everyone in line. Jimmy and Emma followed, making excuses for themselves which I ignored. I glanced at the poster. No wonder she looked familiar. She looked just like me.

We met Zach in the lobby and he led us into the packed theater. I sat at the end of the row. Jimmy insisted on sitting beside me. I wished he hadn't. I wished he'd left a seat empty between us. I wished I hadn't heard this way, from these traitors. They were going to ruin my first moments with my mam.

Ushers blew out the candles and the screen lit up as the movie started projecting from the wizard's crystal. I focused in on the image the way I had focused on my axe throwing, putting myself into the scene, shutting out everything and everyone around me.

Frerin Gillda, my mam, appeared on screen and I watched, mesmerized by every word she spoke and every movement she made.

The tilt of her head, the crinkle of her eyes, the way she smoothed her tunic over her slightly thin body, all her natural traits were the same as mine. Were those extensions in her beard? Her blue eyes and dark hair were mine. The pitch in her voice echoed a familiarity, as did her vocal inflection.

She cradled her dwarfling and sang a lullaby. Her eyes filled with tears and her voice cracked. I recognized the song and I knew her voice in the deepest core of my being.

Mam.

I wanted to deny it. I wanted her to be dead. I didn't want her on the screen in front of me. Da knew Mam acted. He *knew.* Mikey *knew.* They all knew and no one told me.

I fidgeted and sweat soaked my cap. I needed to get out, go home, make Da tell me everything. I didn't care how angry he might get because his anger could never come close to my fury.

As soon as the film credits rolled I bolted out of my seat stepping on feet to get to the aisle.

Jimmy grabbed my tunic to slow me down. "Where are you going in such a hurry?"

"I have to go home." I pulled away from him, swaying a little off balance thanks to having use of only one arm.

I raced home ignoring everything around me. Frerin's—Mam's—voice filled my thoughts, her mannerisms swarmed around me, the lullaby she sang, the one she used to sing to me. My anger filled me with a burning rage.

"Da!" I yelled slamming the front door. He came into the front room from the kitchen. Tears stung my eyes. "I—" the words stuck in my throat.

"What is it, pet?"

"I saw her." I couldn't say anymore. The walls closed in on me like they were trapping me. I couldn't move, speak, or even think.

"Who did you see?"

I stared at him, the liar. "Mam."

"Ah, pet."

The barrier broke. "Don't 'ah pet' me. How could you keep it from me?" I bellowed. "Why didn't you tell me what she did, why she'd left me? How could you keep her from me?"

Da's face closed into solid granite. "I did it for you."

Not good enough. "Why? Was she mean? An unfit mate? You had twelve of us with her. Was she unfaithful? What, Da?"

"No," he said barely above a whisper.

I stared at him. "Do you feed me extra so I'll be fat and not look so much like her?"

"No."

"Do you wish I had a fuller beard so I won't remind you of her?"

"Mabel."

"Do you hate me every time you look at me because I look like her?"

"Enough. Mabel, I love you, and I loved your mam. But I would not have my family ruined because of her." Da returned to the kitchen.

I followed as it dawned on me. She hadn't left because she'd wanted to. Da had banished her. Had she fought for us? He was not going to shut me up so easily. Not this time. "How is she going to ruin us? Because she's an actor? Is that why you banished her? For acting? She could have done so much worse to us. Why did you let me believe she was dead when everyone else knew she was alive? Didn't you think for one second that everyone was laughing at me because I didn't know the truth?"

He shook, his voice rumbled. "Enough."

I had pushed too far and I knew it. I couldn't look at him anymore. I ran upstairs to my room and slammed the door.

Max sat on my bed, a package in his hand.

"What do you want?" I asked, my anger still burning.

"Did you really see her?" he asked.

"Yes." I leaned against the door. I closed my eyes for a moment and I saw her holding the dwarfling, crying, like it was me she was letting go.

"What was she like?"

I sat next to him. "She looks like me. She sounds like me. She's a brilliant actor. Everything she does is the same way I do it—when she squints her eyes, the way she smiles, the way she walks—exactly the same."

Max bit his bottom lip. "I'd like to see the movie. What do you say to skipping work tomorrow afternoon and going with me?"

"Sure." I had seen my mam and I ached to see her again. Watching this movie might be the only way I'd ever have her in my life. "Do you remember her at all?" I asked.

"Not really. I remember she smelled like these little white flowers we used to have in our back garden. You were tiny. I remember hearing a lot of yelling and you crying the night she left. I sat on the stairs. You clung to Mam's leg and she pleaded to Da about something. Mikey pulled you away from her. Da yelled at her to get out. That's all I remember. But I thought she'd probably died since then, since no one ever talked about her."

Max cleared his throat and continued. "I happened to be at the trading post this afternoon and this package was there for you so I took it with me. Hope you don't mind."

"Thanks." I knew it must be the book *Living Your Authentic Life*. Perfect timing. My life was crumbling like a shell covering emeralds.

Max stood. "I should go. Have a good night. Tomorrow, after lunch, beg off sick and I'll meet you at the cleansing pool."

I thought about the mines, and had no enthusiasm

for returning there, not when I had the opportunity to see Mam. "I'm not going in to work tomorrow. I'll meet you outside the mine entrance."

Phillip and Emma didn't need me anyway.

I ripped the packing paper the moment Max shut my door.

Congratulations, Dr. Thaddeus said, the first words of the first chapter. *You have made an important decision, to find your true happiness and to* Live your Authentic Life. *With your decision will come some big, and sometimes difficult, steps on your way to Authenticity. What you have in your hands now, this book, is your tool, your resource, to help you reach your goal. For this book to be an effective tool, we need to work together. I will give you advice and show you the way, but you will need to do the work. I will help you do that work, right here, in this book. So let's get started. First, I need you to write down what you want most in life. Wait, wait, take a minute or two and think about it. Really think about what you want. Great, now write it down.*

Eager for Dr. Thaddeus to help me sort out my life, I picked up my quill with my left hand, thought for a moment or two then wrote: *a life mate, to work the diamond mines, and a brood of dwarflings.* A moment later, I added *knowing about Mam, Aramis, and everything about movies* to my list.

———

MAX SAID nothing the entire walk to the theater. Only a handful of dwarves were inside. When we claimed our seats he leaned over to me. "I'm nervous," he whispered.

Now that the initial shock of seeing her had gone, I found myself more excited than anything. At least Max didn't have to find out about Mam by surprise. "You'll have to tell me if she's anything like you remember," I said.

The candles went out and Mam appeared on the screen. Max gasped and said, "It's her. She looks exactly the same. You're right, she is a lot like you."

I found myself watching Max almost as much as I watched Mam. It warmed my insides knowing at least one other dwarf in this world knew what I was going through, and understood and shared my need to know Mam.

Afterwards, we purchased tickets for the next showing.

"What about her name?" I asked. "It isn't a normal name."

"It isn't her real name, though I don't remember what it was. She must have changed her name when she left. Frerin is the name of one of her ancestors, a warrior I believe. And Gillda means daughter of Gillis. Maybe it's her way of telling us who she is, that she's from here, that she's our mam in case we happened to see the movie and wanted to find her."

"Maybe. Did it help you remember anything about her?" I asked.

"I remember how she'd sing me to sleep every night. I loved her voice, such a nice alto. She'd hold me and I would fall asleep against her. I never woke up when she put me down but it always surprised me to wake up alone because it felt like she'd held me all night. Do you remember anything about her?"

"No," I said. "Except the singing. But I only remembered last night when I heard her in the movie. Do you think she would have taken me with her if Mikey hadn't pulled me away?"

"I don't know if Da would have let her. I don't think she wanted to leave at all."

"Da had her banished?" I asked. I had accused him of it, but he never admitted or denied it.

"Maybe, but what could she possibly have done to deserve that? Da might think acting is disgraceful, but I doubt the council would banish her for it."

"You don't think acting is disgraceful, do you?" I asked.

"It's hardly as reputable as mining, but shameful? No. And certainly not worthy of banishment."

"What about the money? I've heard Da talking with Mikey a few times about earning back what our family had lost when Mam left us. Did she take it all? Did she steal it?"

Max shrugged. "I don't know. I really don't. I wish I remembered more."

CHAPTER 16

"YOU LOOK exhausted," Emma said, meeting me on the road to the mines, my first day back to work.

Going to see *The Goldminer's Daughter* had become an insatiable need for Max and me. For fourteen days we went to every showing—seeing the first show then getting back in line for the next and the next, until closing. It was all we had of our mam.

And I had to admit, it was a great excuse to avoid mining.

I had memorized Mam's every move, every lilt and inflection of her voice. I burned her image into my memory and craved more. Neither Max nor I told any of our brothers or Da we were at the cinema though they probably suspected. At home, I couldn't bear to look at my family so I spent my time in my room studying *Living Your Authentic Life* and thought about Mam.

"Are you sure you're well enough to work?" Emma asked.

I was fine, though I didn't want to work. I wanted to see Mam but her movie had finished its run at the theater. Mam had left, gone from my life forever, again. "Yeah, yeah. How's Zach?"

"Perfect. No sign of a golden ring yet, but I'm sure it won't be long."

"What's this?" I pointed to a large parchment staked to a post at the side of the mines' entrance.

"Don't know."

Notice to all employees of the Gilliam Mines: Mage Artist Productions has been granted permission to record a movie in the Gilliam Mines. They have promised there will be as little disruption to the working environment as possible.

Additionally, we have been informed there will be a handful of small parts available for Gilliam employees should they wish to participate. Auditions will be held soon.

Please watch this notice board for all updates on auditions and location information.

Thank you all for your cooperation.

And a hearty Gilliam Welcome to our guests.

Gilliam City Council

Aramis!

I'd bet that's why he'd been here, checking out the location, making arrangements. If he was involved in the recording, then maybe I *would* get a chance with him. And maybe, just maybe, if I auditioned for a part, Mam might see the movie, and me, and maybe come looking for me.

I could audition. I needed *something* to do while I waited for my shoulder to heal. What a perfect opportunity.

I stopped myself before I became completely carried away with the possibilities. I reminded myself what Dr. Thaddeus said in *Living Your Authentic Life:* "The first step to taking ownership of your life is to concern yourself with only those situations that are within your ability to control."

I couldn't control much in this situation, only if I went to the audition or not. But it would be so incredibly amazing to see Aramis.

"That looks like fun," I said.

"I wonder if we could take some time off to watch the recording," Emma said.

"Watch? I want to be in it. Don't you?"

"What, the auditions? I would never… Why, are you going to audition? Mabel, don't disgrace yourself like your mam did."

"Oh, come on, Emma. It's for a small part. It isn't like I'd quit mining to act. Wouldn't it be fun to go to the theater with our friends and see our faces up on the screen?"

"More like embarrassing."

Dr. Thaddeus would say I should be unashamed of what I like and my opinions, no matter how different they are from my friends, and I chose to partially agree with him. I could do what I wanted. To keep my reputation, however, no one could know I wanted to audition. Even if I got a part it likely wouldn't change my schedule enough to draw anyone's attention.

The more I thought about it, and the situation with my shoulder, the more excited I became. No one would care if I was mining or not. In fact, Phillip and Emma would probably be happy I was out of their way.

I thought of Aramis and the possibility of being in a movie with him. Please gods, let it be Aramis and let him be here soon.

"THE MOVIE crew is here," Phillip said two days after the notice first appeared outside the mines. He set down his bag of tools.

I jumped up from where I sat on the rock in the center of our crosscut. "Did you see them?" Is Aramis with them?

I wiped at the mine dust on my tunic. The dust only smeared. It irritated me, all this second-hand dust. If I actually chipped at the stone I could appreciate being covered like this, but sitting here waiting for another emerald bed to be exposed so I could help excavate, this dust was unnecessary.

"They're talking to the chief foreman in the entrance cavern. A crowd has already gathered around them. Want to go?"

"Yes," Emma and I said at the same time.

"Did you recognize any of the crew?" I asked. "Were there any actors from any of the movies we've seen?"

"The wizard is Radier," Phillip said. "The one they say went to the lowest dungeon and highest peak in battle against a demon of the depths while on some adventure with the elf, I can't remember his name, the one at the Prospector a few weeks ago. He's here too."

Aramis!

I rubbed frantically at the dust on my trousers. I needed a full-body dunk in the cleansing pool. I couldn't let Aramis see me like this.

We reached the entrance cavern and faced a wall of miners; likely their only opportunity to see a real elf and wizard and whatever other species might be involved in the movie. They'd all deny it, of course. But the truth was, no matter how much we dwarves professed to loathe elves, the only elves most of us had ever known were the ones we'd seen in the movies or heard of in stories. We'd take any opportunity to see one in person.

I weaved my way to the front of the crowd and found myself closer to Aramis than I ever thought I would be. If I were as tall as a troll I could have reached out and touched him. Even from his profile his eyes sparkled clearer, his hair was longer and blonder, and his face more perfect in its fineness, than I'd ever seen in one of his movies. His beauty made his beardlessness irrelevant. I breathed him in, the scent of the deep forest.

I wanted to stay like this forever, standing next to, looking at, and smelling the beauty that was Aramis.

Aramis turned to face us. "Hello and thank you for the warm welcome we have received here in Gilliam." His voice was a touch higher, softer, more melodic, more poetic, and more mesmerizing, than in the movies. "It is wonderful to see how many of you are interested in our little project. My name is Aramis, and I will be directing this movie. I assure you we will do our best to stay out of your way so it will be business as usual for everyone. There are a few very small speaking parts as well as several background parts with no lines, for which I will be holding auditions beginning first thing tomorrow. If you are interested in auditioning, please let my assistant, Althea, know by the end of the day." He pointed to the elf beside him, as tall and blonde and beautiful as Aramis and yet she looked perfectly average standing next to him. If Aramis hadn't pointed her out, I never would have noticed her. "She will tell you where to go and at what time we want you there. Thank you."

We waited for him to say more. I wanted to hear his voice.

The chief foreman cleared his throat. "Back to work everyone." The crowd slowly dispersed.

I took a deep breath and walked forward. Before I reached Aramis, the chief foreman led him and the others away. Only Althea stayed behind, a board and quill in hand.

"Um, excuse me," I said. I barely came up to her waist.

Althea looked down and smiled. "Yes, love?" She flipped her hair over her shoulder. Her fingernails had no dirt or dust under them, and they shone like she'd spent ages polishing them.

"Um, I would, ah, like to a-audition." I barely squeaked it out.

"Most wonderful. What is your name?"

"M-Mabel. Mabel Goldenaxe."

She wrote my name on the board. "Auditions shall be held in the interview cavern. You know of which cavern I speak?"

"I do." It was the cavern where the chief foreman tested our skills before hiring us to mine.

"Perfect. Please arrive first thing tomorrow morning and have this memorized." She reached into a bag at her feet and pulled out some parchment.

A speech, three pages, filled.

I took my time returning to work so I could read over the speech. I laughed. I knew this speech. I'd only heard Mam say it dozens of times in *The Goldminer's Daughter.* I had already memorized it.

I STRODE into the mines and down to the interview cavern thinking of Aramis and my audition. Emma followed, nattering the whole time.

"Is there anything I can say to persuade you not to do this?" she asked.

I stopped outside the interview cavern and tugged at my tunic and straightened my cap. "Nope." I wished she'd stop talking. I wanted to run through the monologue in my head one more time but she kept distracting me. I shook out my legs and my left arm like I did to loosen up before throwing axes. I closed my eyes and breathed deep. This waiting made me more nervous than competing at Regionals. I needed to relax. I knew the monologue and exactly how to perform it. I wanted to get in there and start.

"Honestly, Mabel," Emma said. "Why are you humiliating yourself, your family, and your friends, with this silly audition?"

"Is this really the worst thing I could do? It's for fun; a small part. I have the time. But if you think this is going to ruin my reputation, you might not want to stay here in case yours gets ruined by association."

"No need to get upset. I'm trying to protect you."

The way she protected me by not telling me about Mam?

Thankfully Althea came out just then. "Mabel? Are you ready?"

I took off my sling and stuck it in my pocket. "Yes." I rotated my shoulder in what had become a habitual motion. Though the sling provided a lot of relief from the pain it also kept my arm too immobile. Unfortunately, even the smallest rotation brought back all the pain and I wished I hadn't moved at all. I did not want to be in pain in front of Aramis.

Walking into the interview cavern couldn't have been more strange. It brought back all the anxiety of wanting to impress the chief foreman, wanting so desperately to become a part of dwarven tradition. Here I was, this time trying to impress an elf and be an actor, the very opposite of dwarven tradition. I'd done well then, and I knew I could do it again.

Lanterns lit the entire circumference of the cavern and surrounded a large table set up to one side. Despite the fact we were deep in the mountain, it smelled like we were in the heart of the forest. Three elves sat at the table: Althea sat on one end, another elf who hadn't been introduced yesterday was at the other end, and Aramis sat between them.

He was so beautiful—even more beautiful today than yesterday or in any of the movies or pictures.

"Come," Althea said. "Stand before the table please."

I left my place hovering by the door and shuffled to the table, never taking my eyes off Aramis. My heart beat faster. My skin tingled from excitement. I picked at the dust under my fingernails. I'd scrubbed most of the dirt out last night, but some of it was too far underneath to reach.

When I stood at the table, Aramis stopped talking and looked at me. Really looked at me. I tried to smile, but my face froze solid like a crystallized stalactite. My dry lips pasted my mouth shut. My knees weren't immovable though, they trembled to the verge of near collapse.

Aramis stood, extending his willowy arm. "Hello, Mabel. It is a pleasure to meet you." He bent his slender, graceful frame, took my hand and shook it, his hand ever so soft on my horribly calloused one. He didn't flinch at the grime permanently packed into the creases in my skin.

He looked at my face and a flash of recognition glimmered in his eyes. Oh, no. He remembered me telling that horrid story at the Prospector.

"Althea, Anintae, take a closer look. Does she not look like a younger version of Frerin?"

Dear gods, he knew my mam!

Antinae, female or male elf, I couldn't tell, walked around the table and turned me so I looked at him. How did my shoulder not hurt? He—I assumed Antinae was a he by his firm grip—looked me up and down, then turned my head from side to side and examined my face. He had a more delicate face than Aramis, though, more like Althea's. Maybe Antinae was a she?

"She does." Antinae retook his seat. "All right, Mabel, we shall begin. What is your name?"

I looked to Aramis and Althea. Didn't they already know it? Aramis sat back and flicked the feathered end of his quill on the table. Althea nodded her encouragement.

I cleared my throat. "Mabel Goldenaxe."

"Age?" Antinae asked.

"Seventy-five."

Antinae turned to Aramis. "Is she not a touch young?"

Aramis considered me for a moment. "Not necessarily."

Antinae sighed. "Fine. Why do you wish to participate in this movie?"

Because I love Aramis. Aramis is my world. I want to jump over the table and kiss him. "I'd like to try something new."

"Louder, please," Aramis said.

"Sorry. I'd like to try something new." And I love you Aramis, with all my heart and all of my being.

"Have you prepared the monologue?" Antinae asked.

"I have."

He stared at me for a few moments so I stared back. "Well? Let us hear it."

"Oh, right. Sorry." I felt the blood rushing to my face.

I cleared my throat and breathed in Aramis. I looked at him as he sat back, eyes closed. "I love him, Da. I know he isn't what you wanted for me, but I don't care. It doesn't matter to me if he's a miner or a trader. I love him."

"Stop." Aramis sat up and opened his eyes.

I'd only started. I hadn't been that terrible, had I?

"Are you the one I heard at the pub?"

"Pub?"

"Tavern. You were the one the other dwarves paid tribute to and you told a tale of grave injury to your shoulder, were you not?"

Oh gods. He had witnessed all of it. I didn't know if I should be flattered he had seen me, or die of shame because he saw me completely embarrass myself. "Yes."

"Brilliant. Excellent storytelling. How is your shoulder?"

"N-not good. I have to keep it in a sling, but it is healing. I see my doctor every few weeks. I promise it would never interfere with my schedule if I were to get a part. I can take off the sling for recording, as long as I can keep it on during rehearsals. And—"

Aramis held up his hand. "Tell us the story."

"Of my injury?"

"Yes."

"Okay, well, I was throwing axes in the regional competition—"

"No, no. Tell it the way you did at the tavern."

So sweet, so beautiful, so real. He could ask me anything, I would never refuse him. I know I promised I'd never re-tell the worst, most embarrassing story of my life, but for Aramis, one more time wouldn't hurt. I cleared my throat, doing my best to re-capture Frankie's storytelling voice and style like I had at the Prospector. "There I was, this young upstart from Gilliam, my first time competing in the Regional Dwarf Games, my first year of axe throwing, and I had made it to the finals. I had defeated warriors and past champions, to reach the final ten…"

When I finished, I wiped the sweat off my brow and desperately wanted to crawl into a hole and never show my face to anyone.

Neither Aramis nor his companions laughed at my weakness.

"What do you think?" Aramis asked Althea.

"I think she would be perfect for Ebony."

"My thoughts exactly."

Did I get a part? I think I did. Dear gods of everything good in this world, I'd won a role in a movie with my Aramis! If only I could hurdle over the table and hug him.

He made a note on a parchment in front of him then put down his quill and looked at me. "Right, Mabel. This movie is about an elf who was stolen as a baby then abandoned. He is found and raised by dwarves and becomes a miner before learning about his family identity. This is my first time directing, so we are all taking a risk with this project. I would like you to play my younger sister. As I said yesterday, it is a small part, but I believe it is an important one. How would you like to jump in and take this risk with me?"

I could die of happiness. My lips and throat and tongue finally loosened enough to squeak out, "Yes."

He smiled and the most adorable dimples appeared in his cheeks. "It is truly uncanny. Even her voice is the same," he said to Antinae.

Althea walked me to the door. "Well done, Mabel." She handed me a scroll. "Here is the information you will need for your first day of work. We begin rehearsals in five days. And here is your script." She handed me a stack of parchment bound with leather ties. "We shall see you then."

I tucked the script and scroll under my tunic. I didn't want anyone passing by to know. Then I left the room. Emma had waited for me.

"Emma?" Althea called. "You are next."

I stared at Emma. "I thought you were against all this disgraceful acting business?"

She shrugged then leaned in to tell me a secret, "I am, but I looked into his eyes. It makes you love them every time. I have to now, I'm in love. Can you believe it? I'm in love with an elf. No one can know, Mabel. You have to promise not to tell anyone or I'll be laughed out of town." She giggled and strutted in to the audition.

Hang on. Emma couldn't be in love with Aramis. *I* loved him. She didn't. But she said she did, and she was probably telling him she loved him while I stood out here. He'd fall in love with her and not me because she told him first and he'd be caught in her web of attraction every fellow gets caught in. How could she do this to me? Why would she do this to me? She wanted me to trust her but then she tells me I'm misguided and about to disgrace every dwarf ever to exist then she does exactly what she didn't want me to do. And now she was pursuing the one I love.

My stomach flip-flopped.

Emma came out of the room, a scroll and script in her hands. "I got a small part. With a line to say. Sorry you didn't get a part, Mabel. You're much better off without it. I'm Miner number three and my scene is with Aramis. Isn't he dreamy? A bit distant, though. Didn't really look at me. Probably didn't want me to fall any deeper for him. It must be so hard to be famous and to never be able to look at a female. Or maybe he didn't want to look at me because he knows I'm with Zach and it would break his heart because he can't have me. I should have told him Zach didn't matter to me."

She was so full of herself. At least I didn't have to worry about Aramis falling for Emma. "You might want to hide your script and scroll. I put mine under my tunic so no one could see it." I undid the button above my belt long enough for her to see the parchment.

Blood rushed into her face until it was almost purple. "You got a part?" she asked through clenched teeth.

"I did, actually. A few lines, too. More than a few lines. I get to play Aramis's sister." I relished her shock. She had Zach, she'd had Ben, she had tried to poison me. She was *not* taking acting or Aramis from me.

CHAPTER 17

I SAT on the stone bench in the empty waiting room wishing I could take out my script and read it over one more time. I had it memorized and ready for today's first rehearsal, but I wanted to know every word perfectly.

Dr. Flint emerged from his office. "Good morning, Mabel. Come right in. Thank you for seeing me on such short notice. How are you?"

"Very well, thanks." I took off my coat.

"And your shoulder?"

"A bit better." I wished he'd get to the point and tell me there was nothing wrong with the medicine I'd taken.

"Excellent. I trust you are not using your arm?"

"Not at all."

"Good to hear. About the medicine you took, I have tested it and... well... I am getting ahead of myself. First of all, this is a very old recipe. As such, there is, essentially, nothing wrong with it. But there is a reason it is no longer in use. The study of herbs and medicine has improved a lot over the generations. What you took, in its mildest form, is harmless. But at the strength you were taking, it was indeed quite harmful to your body. Not only to your shoulder. Your stomach suffered some scarring and your heart suffered a lot of pressure. If you had taken anymore you could have suffered severe internal bleeding or your heart might have stopped."

What was he saying? That if I'd kept it at the original strength I'd be fine? Had I done this to myself?

"Under normal circumstances, I'd want to question whoever gave it to you. No one could conceivably increase the strength to such a degree without intentionally wanting to cause you harm. At the same time, I am mindful of the age of this recipe and perhaps its maker did not know the potential for significant harm."

Did Emma know what it would do to me? Or was she really trying to help me? "It's my fault. I kept asking for stronger doses."

"Claiming responsibility is admirable. But it is not entirely your fault. With this particular concoction, there are safer options for a stronger pain-killing ingredient; options that are well known. Again, it is an old recipe and they may have believed changing ingredients would make it ineffective, but I have my doubts."

My stomach cramped, twisted and turned. I had trusted Emma. She told me she would never hurt me, and I believed her. But if I thought of everything—how she changed since we came of age and the mean things she'd said to me and about my family—I don't know if I did, or should, or should have ever, trusted her. She could have killed me.

"While damage was done—intentional or not—we are lucky you stopped taking it when you did. Things could have been much worse. In time most of the damage will be reversed."

"Thank you, Dr. Flint. I'm sorry I didn't come when it first started."

"You will be fine. I'd like you to come see me in about four weeks, and I'll do a thorough check on the healing, all right?"

I made an appointment with the receptionist and shuffled to the mines.

I needed to relax and refocus my thoughts on better things—not on Emma poisoning me. Dr. Thaddeus said to think positive thoughts. He said to think about what makes me think all is well with the world, and always will be.

What made me feel like nothing could ever go wrong? I loved finding beautiful gems in the mines. I'd loved throwing axes. Even though Emma thought acting was shameful for a dwarf, I loved it, more

than mining and axe throwing. Since Regionals, I'd
loved being outside and hearing the birds. I needed
to breathe. Aramis made me happy. Watching him
in the movies, watching any movie really, but especially Aramis's. The idea of being in a movie, trying
something different, made me happy. The possibility
of Aramis being in the movie made me happier. Not
just because I loved him. I couldn't explain it, but I
had a feeling doing something different, something
dwarves like Da and Emma would disapprove of,
gave me some satisfaction, like I was doing what I
wanted, not what they expected of me. I loved walking to the mines alone, washing off the dust in the
cleansing pool at the end of the day, and seeing Mam
in the movie.

I arrived at the mines and strode inside ready for
my first rehearsal. Among my mining tools were my
script and scroll. Althea welcomed me into the interview cavern that she called the green room, now
altered beyond recognition. Gone were the open
vastness and dark craggy shadows. Tables laden with
food and elf-sized sofa chairs set up for lounging
filled the right half. To our left, curtained dividers
took up most of the space with a little room made
for a rack of clothes in every color imaginable, and a
table with mirrors set up against one wall.

"We are still hoping for a different place for the
break room, but this will have to do for now," Althea said. "In the meantime, our change area is on the
crowded side. Let us start you in wardrobe."

I thought we were the only ones there but in moments, from behind curtains, several elven voices filled the cavern, each calling out things like, "Eleanor, I want something more, more, ethereal," followed by various items of clothing from tunics and trousers and even undergarments flying over the barriers and onto the head of an elf.

She gathered the clothes into her arms. "Right away, right away," she said, unfazed by the commotion and the number of demands flying at her.

"Good morning, Eleanor," Althea said.

"Morning, love," Eleanor said, sorting the clothes onto the racks and selecting new outfits.

How did she remember what went where?

"The madness begins," Althea said.

"It does indeed. Always my favorite part." She sounded like she meant it.

"When you have a moment, Mabel is here for her wardrobe fitting."

Eleanor paused and smiled at me. "I shall be with you in a moment. Please, have a seat while I get this lot settled."

We moved to the seating area. I hopped up on to a soft, well-padded chair. I sank into the cushions but not low enough to keep my feet from dangling.

"I do apologize. We shall be receiving some dwarf-sized chairs soon," Althea said.

"There are other dwarves in this movie? I mean besides the ones from Gilliam?"

"Of course. Most of the cast is dwarven. In fact,

most of these chairs will be replaced in the next few weeks, when the rest of the cast arrives."

What a stupid question. Who else would play Aramis's family? What would Da say if he knew how many dwarves acted? What would my brothers say? They'd realize acting held no disgrace, at least not for many dwarven clans.

"May I ask another question, Miss Althea? Who else—"

"Eleanor, you are fantastic!" Aramis said.

I froze. Aramis. In the same room. And me sitting here, my feet dangling like a pixie sitting on a giant's chair.

One of the curtains rustled and he stepped out, fastening the last few buttons of his elf-sized dwarven tunic, his skin elegantly pale with a light pink undertone. The tunic fit snugly, showing off his lean muscles.

"Althea, there you are." He adjusted the dwarven cap on his head. "Mabel, excellent. What do you think? How do I look?" The other actors who had been changing now tossed their clothes at Eleanor as they left.

Perfect. He looked perfect.

"Do I look like a dwarf?"

He could never look like a dwarf.

We walked over to Aramis and Eleanor. "Y-you look like an elf raised by dwarves," I said.

"Really?" he asked.

"Except, well, a respectable dwarven family

would fatten you up." Did I really just call Aramis too skinny? Stupid. Stupid. I am such an idiot.

He laughed. "Sevrin said the same thing. Actually, he says it to me all the time."

His laugh was as beautiful as a bird's song.

He tugged his cap. "I cannot get this right."

"Here," I volunteered. Aramis bent down and I straightened it. My calloused fingers grazed the tip of his ear. I was so close I could kiss him. "You also need a beard." Gods, what an idiotic and rude thing to say.

"Ah, she asks for the two things I cannot do," he said to Eleanor and Althea, smiling.

"Sorry." I pulled back, heat rising in my cheeks. I should just shut up now.

"Elves cannot grow facial hair or gain weight," he said.

I thought of my thin frame and scraggly beard. Was it possible? It would explain so much about me and why Mam was banished. "Neither can I. Maybe I'm part elf."

Aramis smiled. "Frerin says the same thing."

Oh, right. My real da can't be an elf, I look just like Mam. Unless her da was an elf. Was it even biologically possible for the two species to mate? I hoped so.

Aramis examined his reflection in the mirror. "You have something, though, Mabel. Perhaps Radier could create some kind of illusion charm during recording, to give me facial hair. Eleanor, what have we for Mabel?"

"Let us have a look at you then." Out of nowhere, Eleanor unraveled a measuring tape and measured me: my arms, legs, height, waist, and even my feet. Then she stood back and studied me. "You have lovely coloring. Blue, definitely, for your eyes, or the right kind of green. Red too, and light, muted colors. And your size is just right."

"Aren't I a bit thin?"

"The magic is not perfect. When the image is projected from the crystal, you look larger than you are," Eleanor said.

Ooh, I could use that kind of magic all the time. "How much does it add?"

"Only an inch or two so have no fear, you will not look too stout." Eleanor picked a number of clothes off a rack.

"A dwarf can never be too stout," I said.

"They can in this business," Eleanor said.

I smiled. This was the first time I didn't have to worry about my size.

"Right. We shall begin with these. I will put you in this room here." She indicated the nearest change area and hung the clothes inside for me. "When you have the first outfit on, come out and give us a look."

I closed the curtain and removed my cap and sling. Aramis, my Aramis, so close and so real.

The outfits were made from a shimmery silk-like material no dwarven miner would ever wear. The first tunic, a silvery blue, hung past my knees. I opened the curtain and Aramis looked at me and smiled. My heart stopped for a moment as I returned the smile.

"Excellent. Try the green one next," Eleanor said.

"It is amazing. She looks exactly like Frerin," Aramis said.

"She does. Especially in that tunic," Althea said.

"Do you know her well?" I asked before I stopped to think. They were quiet for a moment. I shouldn't have intruded on their conversation.

"I do," Aramis said. "We are fairly good friends."

How good? Had she told him she had a family in Gilliam she'd allowed herself to be separated from without much fight?

"Do you know her?" Aramis asked.

She's only my mam. "I saw her in *The Goldminer's Daughter.* She's brilliant."

"She will want to meet you. I understand she does not usually receive positive feedback from the dwarven community. You can tell her when she arrives a few days from now."

My knees gave out. Fortunately I landed on the stool.

How dare Mam come back after all these years?

"Everything all right?" Eleanor asked.

I steadied my breath, stood and opened the curtain.

"No. Not that one," Eleanor said. "Try the red one."

I closed the curtain quickly. "So she's coming to visit you then?" My hands shook as I took off the tunic. I fumbled with the buttons on the red one.

"Althea, did you not tell her?" Aramis asked.

"We were getting to it when you interrupted."

"Not exactly a visit, Mabel. She is to play our mother."

"My mam?" I wanted to laugh at the idea of the one who abandoned her real-life role as Mam playing her now.

"Right, yes, our 'mam.' Althea, remind me to change the script to say mam, not mother."

"Oh, yes. Red is definitely a good color," Eleanor said when I showed them the third outfit. She held a number of other items in her hands. "Now for the purple."

My mam was coming. Here. In a few days I was going to meet my mam.

ARAMIS AND Sevrin spoke with Radier and some of the other crew to set up the scene for our rehearsal. As I watched, I wiped the sweat off my face with my sleeve. Emma, Jimmy and I waited in the crowded, abandoned crosscut.

Aramis, in his dwarven outfit, rested a large pick-axe on his shoulder as he talked to Radier about what he wanted. Every now and then he pointed at me or one of the others. I heard him saying he wanted to make sure the angles and the lighting were right before they recorded anything. Finally Radier agreed to something and adjusted his crystal.

Aramis joined us by the wall. "Should not be much longer. How do you mine?" He swung the sturdy stone-grinding pick-axe around and back onto his shoulder. His thin arms didn't break like I thought they might. He raised the axe over his head, ready to smash it into the wall.

"Stop, stop, stop." I waved my hand. "Here." I took my own axe in my left hand and showed him how to hold it just below the head. At first his thin wrist bent under the weight, but he straightened it quickly enough. "Now chip away at the rock with small strokes, like this." I tapped the axe against the stone. "Then you wipe away the residue with your spare hand." I wiggled out of the sling and wiped away the dust with my right hand. The scratches I made didn't look good at all. "I usually do it with my right arm, looks a lot better. Anyway, give it a try." I put my sling back on. Though it had been refreshing to move, the bit of work made my arm ache. I welcomed the immobility of the sling.

Aramis followed my instructions perfectly. "How is this?" His lean muscles rippled and bulged under his tight tunic. He pulled away, as clean as before. My breath caught. So the rumors about elves were true.

"Perfect."

"Are there any gems still here do you think?"

"No," I said. "We fully excavated it a generation or two ago," I said.

"Pity." Aramis rested his axe on his shoulder. "How is your arm?"

"It's fine, getting better," I said.

"Are you certain it will not bother you if you have to be without your sling for any length of time?"

Emma stepped in front of me. "She's not supposed to remove the sling. You see, any time she uses her arm, she re-injures her shoulder and further jeopardizes her mining career. She thought with acting she could keep it on. Since that is not the case, obviously you'll want to reconsider your casting decision. I'd be happy to take over. I've been going over the lines with Mabel so I've got them memorized. It wouldn't be a problem, really."

Liar. Traitor. "The shoulder won't be a problem." I said calmly, though I wanted to push her away from my Aramis. "As long as I can keep the sling on while we're not recording, I'll be fine."

"But you can take the sling off for recording?" he asked.

"I can."

"Excellent."

"Well, should you change your mind, I am available," Emma said.

"I shall keep you in mind." Aramis winked at me. I knew it. He didn't like Emma, at least not romantically, and possibly not professionally, either.

"All set," Radier said.

"Places everyone. Remember, this is only a run-through," Aramis said.

On Aramis's signal, we raised our axes and pretended to mine. I kept my arm in the sling and did my best with my left arm. I thought it might be possible for me to work like this all the time if I didn't have to wipe away the dust. After a few minutes, Radier called a halt to our action.

"I need less light and less shadow," Radier said.

"How long will it take?" Aramis asked.

"Not long."

Radier muttered a few words and all the lanterns dimmed at the same time. Then he blew on his crystal and put it back on his staff. "Ready."

"Places," Aramis said.

We raised our axes once more and scratched at the surface of the rock for another few minutes. "Got it," Radier said.

"All right, everyone. That is a wrap for today. Check your call sheets for time and location for recording. Thank you for your hard work," Aramis said.

Emma sidled up to Aramis. "A bunch of us are going to The Bearded Prospector for drinks. Would you care to join us?"

"I thank you for the invitation but perhaps some other time."

"Sure, maybe tomorrow." Emma squeezed his arm as she left.

"See you tomorrow," I said.

"Oh, Mabel, can you come a bit earlier than scheduled? I would like you in costume. If all goes well, as I think it shall, we will do some initial re-cording."

"Great. No problem." Tomorrow we were re-hearsing the scene I had alone with Aramis. Time alone with Aramis!

"Would you like me to come in early as well?" Emma asked. "You know, in case you need me to fill in for Mabel?"

Aramis looked surprised, like he thought she had left already and didn't know why she was still there. "No," he said then walked over to Radier.

I picked up my bag of tools.

"Would you like me to carry that for you?" Jimmy asked.

"I got it," I said. I didn't need his help. And I certainly didn't need Emma trying to take my place in the movie.

"How rude," Emma said as she, Jimmy and I walked to the Prospector. I considered simply going home, but I wanted to see Da and my brothers even less than I wanted to be with Emma and Jimmy.

"He is busy, I suppose," Emma continued, "with all of the responsibility of directing the movie, so I can forgive the rudeness. What if he doesn't love me? He has to. I'll die if he doesn't. Mabel, you can help. He seems to be all right with you, though I can't imagine why he would be with you and not me, un-less… of course, I should have known. He's nervous because he likes me. Like Ben was when we went on those first dates after you started at the mines. Remember how he talked about you the whole time? It was because he was nervous. You said so yourself. This must be the same situation with Aramis. I need you to find out for sure. Casually mention how I've improved at mining, what a fabulous actor I am, that kind of thing, and tell me how he feels about me."

Dear gods of madness. I would rather die a painful death at the hands of the fiery demon of the deepest pit of the mountains than help Emma convince Aramis to fall in love with her. And really, she had wanted to keep her love for Aramis secret because she was right, she would be laughed out of town if anyone knew. And yet here she was talking about it in front of Jimmy.

"What about Zach?" I asked. "Didn't you tell me the other day you thought he'd be presenting you with a golden ring soon?"

"Zach is not Aramis. There is no comparison. But Jimmy, please don't tell him what I said."

Why did she have to pick Aramis? She wouldn't be happy until every dwarf in Gilliam loved her. And now it looked like every elf as well. Should I fight for him? Emma would win. She always did. She'd claimed him by saying she loved him first. By every unwritten rule of friendship, I had no right to fight for him. But if he didn't like her, if he liked me, why should I let her have him? Maybe he would fall for her simply because I didn't tell him I loved him.

I could allow her to talk to Aramis and hope she'd make such a mess of it he'd never be attracted to her, but I knew better. Emma never messed things up with any fellow. I had to keep them apart.

Aramis was everything. Aramis was mine.

"I don't think you need my help," I said. "You had no trouble attracting Zach, or Ben, or Mark." Or gods only knew how many others she had drooling after her.

"Who's Mark?" Jimmy asked.

"No one." Emma glared at me. "I know. But you know how it is. I love him so much I get all nervous and can't find the right words."

I had never, in my lifetime, witnessed Emma too nervous to speak around any fellow.

"Of course you'll be our witness at our golden ring ceremony," she continued. "We'll name our first daughter after you. We'll have dozens and dozens of—"

"He's an elf," Jimmy shouted. "Elves and dwarves don't mix. Friendship is one thing. On rare occasions our armies will fight alongside each other, but there are no inter-species relations. Ever. It is not done. It is repulsive. It is physically impossible."

I didn't think it was impossible, but I had no problem going along with it to make Emma believe him.

"And how would you know?" Emma demanded. Then her demeanor shifted. "You like an elf too. Which one? Althea?"

"I do not." Red rose up his cheeks from his beard line.

"Yes you do. Why else would you have re-searched it?" Emma asked.

"I don't have to research it. Look at history. How many mixed dwarf-elf families have there been?"

"History isn't the best example," I said. "Traditionally the dwarves and elves have been at odds if not in an all-out war."

"Exactly," Jimmy said.

"Exactly," Emma said. "Aramis and I together will be the model of peace between our two peoples."

Dear gods. I'd just supported Emma's claim on Aramis.

"You're hopeless." Jimmy opened the door to the Prospector for us. "Stout ale for you, Mabel?"

"Please." I had a feeling I'd need more than a few ales in me before the evening was out.

"I'll have one too," Emma said.

"You can get your own," he muttered.

"I've made him jealous, haven't I?" Emma asked, as we walked toward Zach, Ben, and Phillip.

"How do you figure?"

"He wouldn't be so upset about my wanting to be with Aramis if he didn't love me, would he?"

I supposed not, unless he was upset because she considered cheating on Zach again, which made the most sense, because he and Zach were such good friends. But this was Emma, and in all likelihood Jimmy did love her. I couldn't tell, though. Whatever signs Emma read I didn't recognize any of them from *Male Dwarf Body Language of Love.*

Emma sat next to Zach, snuggling up to him like she hadn't spent the entire walk here swooning over Aramis and planning her life with him.

"How did it go?" Phillip asked.

"Good," I said. "Mostly standing around waiting for directions, but it was fun."

"Yes," Emma said. "But Phillip, tell Mabel she needs to stop using her right arm. She kept pulling it out of her sling."

She'd do anything to get my part and my Aramis. "Only once, and only for a few minutes."

Phillip shrugged. "Just be careful."

Jimmy came back with ale for the two of us.

"Where's mine?" Emma asked.

"I said you could get your own." He sat beside me.

"I'll go," Zach said. He scowled but Jimmy didn't seem to care.

"How did you like working with Zach?" Jimmy asked Phillip.

"Just like old times at the workshop. I swear his shrieking is getting louder." They both laughed.

"So what you're saying is you like it, right? And you want to switch mining teams?" he asked.

Jimmy did like Emma. He must if he wanted to trade teams with Phillip. The switch meant he would work with Emma and me. Couldn't he see she'd break his heart? On the other hand, if he distracted her long enough, I could get her away from Aramis.

"Not a chance," Phillip said. "I can't wait until

this movie business is over and I get my team back. Unless you want to switch with Emma."

Jimmy didn't want to switch teams with Emma, he wanted to work with her. I decided to help him out. "Dear gods, no. I couldn't take the noise. I nearly lost all my hearing working with you two in the toy workshop. I'd lose it for sure working with you in the mines."

"I guess we missed out on something, not doing a masterwork," Ben said to Emma.

"By the sounds of it, I'm glad no one held me back from mining," she said.

She still believed that having the opportunity to do a masterwork before getting hired in the mines had held me back. I'd believed her at first. It had meant I started in the mines later than she did. But only the most talented dwarves were selected to create a masterwork, a final piece of artistry and perfected skill. My family had been so proud of me. They were the ones who had convinced me that the masterwork was an incredible opportunity. That it would only be to my benefit when I got to the mines, and it had been. I was tired of Emma insulting me for doing a masterwork. But before I could say anything, Ben spoke up.

"If you feel so strongly about masterworks, why are you with Zach?"

Ben still loved her. Ben, Zach, and Jimmy, all in love with her, and she wanted Aramis. Did she really? Or was this her way of making the fellows jealous of her?

CHAPTER 18

I TIP-TOED downstairs as the snores emanating from my brothers' room crescendoed.

"You're up early." Da sat at the kitchen table, reading by candlelight.

Troll droppings.

"Getting an early start. If all I can do is extract gems, I figure I should do more than my share. You know, make up for my general uselessness."

Da smiled. "I am pleased to see you happy to be back at the mines. But as much as we need your income, I don't want you pushing yourself too hard."

"Phillip makes sure I don't."

"Can I fix you anything for breakfast?" he asked.

"No, thanks. Some bread and cheese is all I want. I have to go."

"Mabel, love, sit down."

Mountains of troll droppings.

"I'm worried your shoulder injury is affecting your chances at finding a mate."

A mate. He wanted to talk to me about finding a mate? I hadn't thought about a mate in weeks. Didn't he have more important things to worry about?

"I know, Da. So am I. That is why I'm going in early, working harder." Lying made my stomach turn. I might think it was fine, but if I told Da the truth about acting, he'd say I'd ended any chance at finding a mate.

"Hard work is admirable, pet, but spending all your spare time working doesn't help you meet anyone."

"I'm doing the best I can. And you'd be amazed at all the fellows I meet in the mines working extra hours. Not just day-shift miners, but night-shift too." Aramis wanted me in wardrobe in fifteen minutes. "Why don't you get after my brothers about finding a mate?"

"Don't change the subject. Maybe you think you have lots of time because you're young, but by now you should have several fellows interested in you. Tell me what you think the problem might be and we can try and fix it together."

Problem? I don't have a problem. I've read all the books and put the teachings into practice. I competed in axe throwing to prove my strength and skill. I am a miner.

"They're just not interested." And I didn't mind; at least not while I was involved with the movie. "What more can I say? I'm doing my best. Give me time."

"Whatever you're doing, it isn't enough. And it isn't entirely your fault. You have a few knocks against you that are beyond your control. I'll talk to your brothers, ask them if they can recommend any potential, respectable, mates for you."

"I can find one on my own. Have a little more patience, please."

"It doesn't hurt to have a wee chat with your brothers for some suggestions. It takes time to find the right mate, but to find one, you have to look in earnest. You haven't put in the amount of effort required so I will help you."

Unbelievable. "I have to go."

I slammed the front door. How could Da have so little faith in me? I marched to the mines. It was *my* life, not his. I had enough to worry about without his pushing me to find a mate. I believed what Dr. Thaddeus said, "Relax, do what makes you happy, and when you're ready for love, it will find you."

And what about my stupid brothers? Why didn't Da try to convince one of them to mate? Then he wouldn't be in such a hurry for me to mate and give him grandlings. Well, okay, he would, because it is only through the female offspring that the family line is continued. But still, they'd be helping someone else's line continue. Wouldn't that be worth something to him? And if they were smart about it, they could find a mate in a family that was better off than ours and they could help us out that way too. Did it all have to depend on me?

And really. Did he honestly think my brothers would tell him they had the perfect mate for me? If they did, wouldn't they have already told me?

Stupid, stupid brothers.

Fine. Let Da try and find me a mate. He'd soon find out it wasn't so easy.

A mate. Of course I wanted one, but I didn't understand the rush. I wanted to find the right fellow, eventually. In the meantime, I wanted to do what Dr. Thaddeus said: try new things, enjoy my life and friends, and be with Aramis. As long as I had Aramis, I didn't need a mate.

And I *had* Aramis, at least for today.

I burst into the green room ready, anxious, desperate to see my Aramis. Aramis and some breakfast. Casks of ale and jugs of mead stood on a table surrounded by warm, fresh-out-of-the-oven pastries. I grabbed a custard tart.

"Morning Eleanor," I said, my mouth full of sweet custard.

"Good morning, Mabel. Aramis wants you in the purple outfit today." She came out of hiding, arms laden with clothes. "I shall put you in this change room here." She led me to the second row of curtained areas.

I took the purple tunic, trousers, and cap from the

top of the pile in her arms. She dumped the rest on a stool in the room next to mine and started hanging them up and arranging them in matching outfits.

I shut myself into the tiny space and decided to forget my row with Da and think only of the day ahead. Aramis wanted to see me in the purple which, if I remembered right, I looked best in. I definitely wanted to look my best for Aramis. I slipped off my sling, stretched my shoulder, and pulled off my tunic.

"And this is the green room," Aramis said.

My knees wobbled at the sound of his voice. I buttoned up the purple tunic.

"Wow," a female dwarf said.

I knew that voice. Frerin? Mam.

"This brings back memories," she said. "It's been ages and I'm more nervous now than I was interviewing to mine here."

I sank to the stool. She'd been a miner in Gilliam. On my first day in the mines, Da had let it slip that she was a miner. I'd thought that because the chief foreman had no record of her working here that she'd mined elsewhere. But, of course, Da had made sure there was no record of her existence in Gilliam.

"I think you will have a better experience this time around. I have already met a few fans of yours. Meeting them will put you at ease."

Da may have banished her, but it still felt like she'd abandoned me. She had no right to be at ease.

"I doubt I have any fans here," Frerin said.

At least she got one thing right.

"There are. You shall see. You will not regret re-turning," Aramis's voice came from the direction of the pastry table.

She'd told him about Gilliam? Maybe she had told him about the family she left behind. She volunteered to come here. Maybe she wanted to see her family again. If I weren't in the movie, would she have looked for me? How long has she been back? She hadn't tried to contact us in the last few days.

"I'm not sure coming back was a good idea," Frerin said.

"Please tell me you are not having second thoughts about the movie."

"No, no. Coming back here, to Gilliam, to these mines, it's much harder than I thought."

"Why? You were not banished were you? You do have permission to be here, right?"

"Of course I do." She sounded hesitant. The way I do when I'm not telling the whole truth.

So she wouldn't look for me. She could have come home any time, but she never did. I'd never meet her if I didn't have a part in this movie.

"I never knew how much I missed these mines until now," she said.

She missed the mines but not her dwarflings? What kind of mam doesn't miss her family?

"Do you wish you'd stayed?" Aramis asked.

"Sometimes. But I had to leave."

No she didn't. She could have stayed. She wanted to leave and forget all about us, me.

"What happened? It was not only the acting, was it?"

I leaned closer to the curtain.

"No, not only the acting. It was nothing so bad as to have me banished, exactly. But it was bad enough I had to stay away. For now, I'd prefer it if I didn't meet any of the locals."

I opened the curtain facing the pastry table.

Aramis smiled at me. "Mabel, I want you to meet Frerin Gillda."

Frerin's goblet of mead crashed to the floor and all color drained from her face.

"Is that why you snuck back into town, at night, to avoid your family?" I asked.

She stepped forward as if to embrace me, then changed her mind and stepped back. I was that much of an abomination to her? Is that why she didn't fight to stay here? Fine. I didn't need a mam. I didn't want a mam.

"Mabel. My precious Mabel," she said. "You know who I am?"

"Frerin?" Aramis asked.

"Mabel's my, my—"

"Can't you say it?" I asked. "Are you too ashamed to admit who I am?" She had no golden ring in her beard, nor any braids. Had she intended to keep her family connections a secret?

"Mabel's my daughter." She wept. Not a shoulder shaking sob, but a deep, silent, cry of a heart broken long ago and never healed.

If she was so broken-hearted, why hadn't she tried to contact us? Why wouldn't she hug me?

I kept my emotions close, stayed strong so as not to be weak in front of Aramis. Dwarves don't show weakness to anyone, especially the ones they love. Though I wanted nothing more than to feel Aramis's comfort, he could not make this situation better.

"Eleanor," Aramis said, walking away from us. "Come with me to scout out the dining hall. I shall lock the door."

I trembled the moment the lock clicked.

"I'm so sorry," Frerin said.

"For what? For leaving, or for coming back?"

"For leaving you without any explanation. For slipping into town. For the way everything had to be."

"You had a choice."

"No, I didn't."

I couldn't stand any longer. I sat on the nearest dwarf-sized chair. Frerin sat across from me. She wiped her eyes with shaking hands. "I assume neither your da nor your brothers told you anything about me."

"Until recently, they let me believe you were dead."

"I see."

"When I saw you in *The Goldminer's Daughter*, I asked Da about you. He said you shamed the family." I would never admit Max and I missed two weeks of mining to watch the movie every day and every night just to see her.

"Well, that neatly sums it up, though he left out a few important details; like that my great shame was to act in a mixed species play, and only a small walk-on part, for fun. Your da said I disgraced the family for eternity even though the play ran for one night only. I begged him not to kick me out."

"For acting?" I knew Da hated movies and thought acting in general was disgraceful, but I didn't think it was enough cause for banishment. "Surely you weren't the only one in the play. The only dwarf, I mean."

"No, I wasn't. I spent weeks pleading with him. He refused to listen. He ordered me to leave and never to return to Gilliam or to have contact with any of my family. If I did, he threatened he would have me brought up before the council to have me banished and my existence erased from any records. Unofficial banishment. Either way, I had no choice but to leave. If I'd had any other option, I would have stayed." She said it as though I had not heard what she'd said to Aramis.

The room and everything in it spun in different directions. All but a handful of the lanterns went out, the heat reached unbearable levels, the air so tight I could only breathe in short, shallow gasps. I gripped the arm of the chair.

"Mabel." Frerin touched my cheek, her voice muffled. I pushed her cool hand away from my hot skin.

As quickly as it started, the room straightened, brightened, and cooled. She wasn't telling me every-thing and yet thinking back, everything she said fit too well to be complete lies. She couldn't possibly know how far Da had gone to banish her. "He al-ready erased you. When I interviewed to work in the mines, the chief foreman had no record of you."

"I knew he would hold true on his promises to banish me if I came back," Frerin said. "I knew he wouldn't tell you about me and I couldn't contact you. I hoped you might look for me, but he would do everything he could to prevent you from know-ing about me and being corrupted by me. But I never imagined he would have me erased anyway."

She had no right to say anything against Da. "Don't. Don't make Da the bad guy. He stayed. He loves us." But my resolve was cracking. Da *had* lied to me my entire life, and he was trying to control me now. Was it the same way he had tried to control Mam?

"I'm sorry, but you asked me what happened. I *never* chose to leave. I did what I did because of my love for you, just as much as he did."

She reached for me again and I pushed her away. My resolve and my entire world was crumbling around me like the shell of rock around an emerald bed. "You could have fought harder."

"I fought for weeks, day and night, until I no lon-ger saw a way to change your da's mind."

As much as I hated to, I believed her. Da could

be as immovable as a mountain. "What did you do? Why did Da throw you out? Why does he really want you forgotten?"

Frerin sighed. "The acting was the start of it. Your da saw only shame in it. Then I made everything so much worse when I made a very bad decision. The rest is between me and your da. He was right to throw me out."

She was holding back. I needed answers like they were the only thing I could hold onto and survive. "Why? Why does Da hate you so much?"

"I made a mistake."

"Don't hide it from me."

"You don't need to know."

"Let me decide for myself."

Frerin looked at the floor for a minute or two. I thought she wasn't going to say anything. "It started with the play. Acting, according to Kevin, your da, and most everyone else in Gilliam then, was disgraceful. Anything other than mining was shameful."

Da was nothing if not traditional. So were my brothers. Most miners were. I had been, until I saw my first movie.

"I acted and mined much like Mikey threw axes and mined, or musicians play and mine," Mam continued. "Your da almost accepted it. The play involved elves. There was still a lot of distrust between our two races, then. The troupe traveled between the two communities, including local residents in the production to build a peace. I participated because

I wanted a peaceful future for my family. Kevin disagreed but he indulged me. I had no grand expectations. I wanted to see for myself that elves are not monsters, and pass it down to you and your brothers. Nothing more."

Mam and I were more alike than I ever imagined. Not just physically and in our mannerisms, but we both wanted to be more than a traditional dwarf.

"Elves are charming, friendly, often fun, tricksy, though usually harmless," Mam said. "But sometimes they are manipulative and dangerous. One in particular. I didn't realize how far under his spell I had fallen until too late. He promised a safe future for everyone. If I gave him a little of our wealth, it would support the play and their efforts at building peace. I invited him into our home. He saw where we kept our gems. He graciously received the handful of diamonds I offered as my donation. That night, while we slept, he and several of the others came and took everything."

Oh good gods. That was why we'd had nothing.

"The next morning, they were gone. We sent word to all the neighboring towns but we never heard where they went. Kevin, your da, never forgave me for my stupidity. He said if I had stayed in the mines where I belonged, then none of it would have happened. He said by taking up acting, I had brought this upon myself."

No wonder Frankie was so incensed when Emma had accused me of theft. I'd thought it was simply out of dwarven honor. But Emma had deliberately accused me of the same crime as Da accused Mam because she knew about Mam and so did Zach and probably Ben, or Ben would have soon after. And now every dwarf who knew Da's version of what Mam did would believe I was the same and not someone to trust. But I had eleven brothers who defended me because I was wrongfully accused. Wouldn't they have done the same for Mam if she'd really had nothing to do with the theft?

"For a long time I agreed with him," Mam said. "Since then, I've learned most actors, and elves, are nice and honest, but it is best not to get too close."

"If you were innocent, why let him call you a thief?" I asked.

"Guilt by association," she said. "You see, unfortunately, your da equates acting with thievery. As I knew the thief, allowed him into our home, putting my family in danger, and as I chose to act, he believes I helped plan the theft. Stealing is a punishable offense, and rightly so. Stealing from your family, well, banishment is kind compared to the punishment I believed I deserved."

Did she deserve it? She hadn't stolen anything. If anything, she was guilty of being naive. And who wasn't sometimes? Like her, I wanted to believe everyone was good. Hadn't I been letting Emma get away with all kinds of cruelty toward me because I believed she didn't really mean to hurt me?

"I think deep down, your da knew I hadn't been a

conspirator, but he didn't want me here. When I left, he had not banished me, though he threatened to go to the council if I ever did return. I assume he went to the council and had me banished a few years after I left. You and Max were growing up and would start asking questions. He did what he felt needed to be done to protect you."

"Maybe," I said. "But I'd rather have known all along."

Mam almost smiled. "I need you to know that I had nothing to do with the theft. I would never steal from my family. And most certainly would never knowingly put my family in danger. Should I have been more careful about who I let into our house? Yes. Should I have paid more attention to what our guests were doing? Absolutely. I made a terrible mistake, one I have been paying for every day. It is a mistake I will never make again."

No wonder Da hated movies and elves. It wasn't just the old inter-species conflict. It was personal.

I knew he was desperate for me to have a mate because he hoped that would establish the right reputation for my family, that everyone would forget what Mam had done, they would know I wasn't like her. But everyone knew she'd stolen from her own family. It wouldn't ever matter what I did, or what Da, or my brothers did. No one would have ever wanted to be my mate. It had been a hopeless venture from the beginning.

Da had done his best to erase her existence from

Gilliam but he couldn't erase memories, and dwarves were notorious for their long memories. Especially when it came to something like Mam and stealing from her own family.

"Mabel, please, say something," she said.

As far as Gilliam knew, she'd stolen from us. She'd all but ruined our family. As much as Max and I were desperate to know her, we were also quite fine without her. She must have known I'd be at the age of maturity and looking for a mate. She must have known that her return would destroy what little chance I'd had at finding a mate. "Why come back?"

"I hoped enough time had passed and that perhaps I had been forgotten and no one would recognize me. I dared hope I would get to see my dwarflings, even if only from afar. Maybe I even hoped attitudes had changed here about acting. By the looks of things, they have. And if you're in the movie, maybe even your da has changed."

So she had wanted to see me, but she wouldn't have done anything to make it happen. I wish Da had told me what she'd done. I wished they'd both given me the opportunity to decide for myself if I wanted to see her. Instead, Da told me she was dead and Mam appeared in a movie, then showed up here in the green room. If Da had been honest with me from the start, I might not have ever gone to the movie theater my first week at the mines, or ever. I might not have chosen to audition for this movie with Aramis. I might not have been so desperate to meet my mam. Even if she hadn't removed the gems from our home herself—and I believed her when she said she hadn't—and even if I doubted her error in judgment, at least I would have known and I would have made that decision for myself.

But I'd been desperate to meet my mam and that wish had come true. Did I turn my back on her for something she'd done ages ago? Yes, it affected my future. But she was also the only one who might understand me. Certainly Da didn't. Nor did my brothers, except maybe Max. I didn't have to love her. I didn't even have to be a friend to her. But I could learn from her error in judgment so that I didn't make the same mistakes. Though, if she thought that I was acting because Da had changed, then maybe I was making a huge mistake like she had. "No, Da hasn't changed."

"But you're acting, aren't you?"

"He doesn't know." And he wouldn't know if I had any control over my situation. That was one way I could at least improve on what she'd done.

After a moment, Frerin said, "Then you shouldn't be here. If you quit now, no one will find out."

How dare she give me advice? "Excuse me?"

"Don't go any farther with this, for your own sake," she said.

"Da isn't going to find out."

"He will, Mabel."

"How? Unless you tell him."

"What do you think will happen when the movie

shows in the theater? Do you think no one will see you?"

"Sure they will, but Da never goes to the theater and neither does any of his generation. And of all my brothers, Max is the only one who goes."

"You know how quickly gossip spreads. Someone is going to have too much to drink one night at the Prospector and blurt out they saw Mabel Goldenaxe in some movie and word will get back to your da. Don't make the same mistake I did. Don't throw away everything you've worked so hard for: your friends, your family, your incredible future as a miner. You're not in a one-night play. Your da will think much worse of you than he had of me: you're in a mixed-species movie, with elves, with those he blames for stealing everything from him, and everyone will see you."

"By the time this movie comes out and word gets back to Da, I'll have moved on and found a mate. It won't matter. There will be nothing he can do to me." Besides, how much worse could my life get right now? He already didn't think I had much chance at finding a mate and I had no real interest in returning to mining, just yet. "How do you know what kind of future I have in mining?"

"You're a Goldenaxe," Frerin said with a smile. "What else would you do?"

I snorted and told her about my delayed glorious future as a miner thanks to my shoulder injury.

"Oh, Mabel, my darling girl. I am so sorry. But

you can still mine."

"Sort of. I'll be able to do more, eventually. But
right now I'm pretty much useless. So this acting
thing is to give me something to do. Besides, I'm not
the only one. Some of my friends have small parts
as well. Attitudes have changed. Da is the only old
one."

Frerin poured two goblets of mead. She handed
one to me. "All right, Mabel. If this is what you really want, then I promise I will do whatever I can to
make things easier between you and your da."

She said the things I'd imagined my mam would
say if she had been around. "Thanks," I said, though
really, how much help could she be, especially if she
never saw him?

Frerin smiled. "It will be nice to spend time with
my girl. We have so much to catch up on. I want you
to tell me everything that has ever happened to you
and everything you have ever done. Right from the
start, beginning with when you took your first steps
and what your first words were."

I didn't know what she expected from me. Did
she think we'd be instant friends? That I would call
her Mam? She'd been gone almost my entire life. I'd
wanted to meet my mam, and now I had. I didn't
know who she was, or even if I really wanted to get
to know her. I needed some time to adjust. I was still
getting used to the idea that Mam was alive, never
mind that she was sitting beside me. And now she
thought that with a quick apology I would tell her

everything? I didn't know her. What if she was working with those elves still, and had come back to steal from us again?

Max would want to know she was here. I'd give him the choice I didn't have. "I don't know what my first words were. Max could probably tell you. He will want to meet you, anyway. I could maybe arrange a meeting for you."

"I'd like that, very much." Frerin put down her goblet and gave me a hug. "I've missed you so much." Her voice cracked. "I've thought of you every day, wondering what you were doing, figuring out how old you were, what you might look like, when you would have started at the toy workshop and at the mines. I am truly sorry I missed out on so much. I have no right to ask to be your mam, but I do hope we can be friends."

Frerin's embrace felt nice; warm and safe and loving. I refused to return it. Why could she hug me now and not when she first saw me? I had no idea what to think of her as a mam or as a friend. I didn't know her, though her hug gave me a vague sense of familiarity I didn't want to dismiss. "Maybe we could get to know each other first, and see how it goes."

Aramis knocked as he opened the door. "Everything all right in here?"

Frerin let go of me. "Yes, fine. Sorry for the delay."

A crew of a dozen dwarves and elves came in behind Aramis. "We're behind schedule so we shall have to speed things up. Frerin, Eleanor will show you your wardrobe. Mabel, I want you in full costume in five minutes and I want everyone on set in thirty."

Frerin and I walked to our change areas together. I closed myself into my area and hurried into the rest of my costume and sling. Maybe things would be different. Da might change his mind and she could stay.

"Mabel," Antinae called. "You have thirty seconds."

I slid open the curtain, ready. The crew had already left.

"Let's go." He snapped his fingers at nobody, at least I thought he better not be snapping them at me. I stood beside him before he'd finished the second snap of his fingers. "Finally." He pushed me out the door.

We marched to the entrance cavern of the mines. I ran to keep up with his long elven strides. Antinae turned a sharp right on the other side of the cleansing pool. "But this is to the private houses," I said.

"Of course it is." His voice dripped sarcasm. "Where did you think we should record the home scene, the mines?"

Actually, I had. "No, I guess not." I almost tacked on an apology for my stupidity but thought better of it. Instead, I clamped my mouth shut and promised myself I wouldn't say anything else until we'd reached the set, wherever it might be.

We climbed the worn staircase. Much of it reminded me of Mitchum. I'd only been up this way a few times but I'd been too busy talking with my friends to see the opulence and age of this part of Gilliam. No doubt Emma had noticed and needed no other encouragement to stay with either Zach or Ben or find another mountain dweller.

The natural crystallization that had created the stalactites and stalagmites in the entrance cavern also existed in the stairway, this time producing a marbling effect along the walls and enhancing the light and sparkle of the lanterns to make it look like embedded diamonds guided our steps.

Antinae walked nearly doubled up so he wouldn't hit his head on the dwarf-height ceiling of the pedestrian entrance. This slowed him down, for which I thanked the gods. I knew I'd never keep up if he started taking the steps three or four at a time. It also made him grumble a lot. I didn't catch everything he said but I did hear him muttering something about needing open spaces to breathe and there were minimum standards in architecture and surely this gods-forsaken hole-in-the-ground did not meet those standards.

I thought I might tell him to watch what he said as he entered the hallowed palatial passages of this most glorious cathedral built strictly to satisfy the standards set by the dwarven gods, and that Aramis and his crew were the first elves to enter this part of Gilliam since Gillis and the allied armies drove out the dragon, so he should consider himself lucky, but

I kept my mouth shut. I didn't need to irritate him anymore.

And a small part of me wanted to agree with Antinae, at least about needing open spaces to breathe. Since leaving Mitchum I had been enjoying the outdoors a lot more, including the trees and the birds and especially the fresh air blowing against my face at the end of the day. After particularly long days, or when I'd been frustrated with the state of my shoulder, I'd taken to opening my window at night—but only occasionally. It reminded me of the freedom I'd felt after my panic in Mitchum.

The Gilliam streets were much better for Antinae, at least he could straighten up, and I could run beside him. Most of the dwellings were empty but there were a few that housed dwarves on the night shift and I could smell their fires burning and their meats and breads baking. It made my mouth water. Too much time had passed since my argument with Da, and meeting Mam had made me lose my appetite, until now.

Antinae pinched shut his nose and walked faster. "Thagk the stars we are albost there."

Aside from the crystallization and the smooth marble, I didn't think any of these mountain dwellings were spectacular compared to my family's cottage. They were much smaller and when I considered how many dwarves lived in each one, definitely more crowded than our little house. Still, mountain dwellings were valuable real estate and it meant everything to dwarves to live in the mountain. It didn't mean that much to me, anymore. Dr. Thaddeus would say I was being true to myself for identifying what I wanted, and didn't want, and believing in myself to know I didn't have to want what everyone thought I should. Perhaps, but I supposed I wouldn't balk if I found a mate, or rather if Da found me a mate, who happened to be a mountain dweller. Yes, I would.

"Finally." Antinae released his nose. He entered the dwelling at the end of the road, the biggest dwelling in the mountain. It belonged to the chief foreman.

No one entered the chief foreman's house without express invitation and then you had to be one of the lesser foremen or on the Gilliam Council.

The chief foreman's son greeted us. "Go on through to the back. The crew is ready for you," he said.

I looked around him into the front room. If the other mountain dwellings had half the wealth of the chief foreman, then size might not matter so much to me. I would find a way to live with the crushing weight of the mountain. I would love to own the antique furniture that filled the room, all covered in gold and silver threads in ruby-red suede, and the bookshelves filled with leather bound books that lined the walls.

A glowing fire warmed the kitchen. A half-dozen dwarves sliced potatoes, carrots and rutabaga, salted mutton and pheasant, kneaded dough for bread, and stirred something in a pot that smelled a lot like pheasant stew. One of the cooks cut fruit into a big bowl full of green leafy things chopped up into bite sized pieces. Mountain dwellers ate well, but they also ate peculiar things.

Behind the kitchen we entered a large room, bigger than the front room, nearly the size of our back garden. There were as many cushions as in the front room but no fancy silver and gold threads. A large rug covered the middle of the floor and a fire at one end helped keep everything warm. I used to think mountain homes were always warm but in Mitchum I had quickly learned the stone of mountains held a constant chill.

Despite the size of the room, it felt small and crowded; Radier and the rest of the crew, plus all the equipment like Radier's wizard's staff and crystal, shades, mirrors, and elf-sized furniture, took up a good half of it. How had they managed to maneuver such big chairs up here?

Aramis talked with Radier so I sat by the fire to ward off the cold penetrating my bones through the costume's thin fabric.

Antinae interrupted Aramis to point at me then left. Aramis glanced my way and kept talking to Radier. I wondered what the rush had been to get me here. On the other hand, waiting gave me a perfect opportunity to study Aramis up close without worrying he'd think I was strange for staring at him. I wished I had my Aramis carving to compare with the real Aramis and see how accurate I'd made it, not that I'd ever want him to see it.

The way he moved amazed me. Every movement of his hands, every step, even the way he held himself: graceful and light, like he really did belong in the trees, not in a cavern. Maybe in the forest, his natural setting, he would look normal but I could not imagine him looking any other way.

Warmed from the fire, I wandered over to a chair to get closer to Aramis. His hair had a natural ripple to it. Not a kink or wave, but an actual ripple, like he had a personal fan gently blowing a breeze on him. The other elves in the room had the same kind of ripple, but nothing as beautiful as Aramis's. His voice mesmerized me and I hated it when anyone interrupted him. I closed my eyes, leaned back in my chair and listened to him and the melodious bird-song of his voice and the lilt of his accent.

"Mabel," Aramis said.

I snapped open my eyes. He smiled at me. Oh dear, I think I'd fallen asleep.

"Sorry to make you wait so long."

"No, no problem," I said.

"Hurry up and wait tends to be the movie business. I want you to sit over here." He led me to a chair beside a small games table with Mage-Stones laid out in mid-play. "As we go through our dialogue, we will play." He turned the board so I played the black stones. "Because of the delay this morning, we will not bother to rehearse."

"Of course." I flung the sling onto a chair behind

Radier and went over to the fire place. I flexed my arm and rotated my shoulder a little. He didn't sound angry or upset, but it wasn't comfortable either. My Aramis had seen me at the worst possible moment of my life. No wonder everything felt so awkward and strained.

Aramis moved me into the spot he wanted me so I sat half facing the table and half facing Radier. My right arm tingled under his touch and my knees almost gave way. His eyelashes were so long and curvy and dark and framed his eyes so beautifully. His small and perfect nose had a few freckles on it that I wanted to kiss.

"Excellent. Right there," he said, then let go of me. He sat across the table from me. "Radier, let me know when you have the lighting right."

"Won't be long," Radier said.

"Sorry about this morning." I didn't know what else to say except maybe "I love you." I had to regain his trust and I needed him to know I was a devoted and reliable employee. "It won't happen again."

"No, I suppose it will not. You only meet your mother for the first time once." He smiled.

He wasn't upset with me. Any tension must be because we're working. I could handle that. "Did she tell you about her family here?" I blurted before thinking.

"Not in so many words, but I had a feeling she had not told me everything. Frerin and I have been friends for many years. She frequently speaks of Gilliam, but always with a sense of loss."

He didn't mind if I asked him questions. He didn't mind talking to me and he was so easy to talk to, so I stopped feeling nervous around him. "Did she know you wanted to record here before you asked her to star in your movie?"

"I spoke to her of the kind of movie I wanted to make. We discussed locations and then I broached Gilliam. I had not yet scouted a location, but she knew of the possibility. When you auditioned, I understood Frerin's attachment to Gilliam and what made the gaping hole in her heart."

His lips, so lush and moist, formed the words so perfectly. "So you expected the delay this morning."

"Yes. It's why I asked you to come in early."

"I'm ready," Radier said.

"Places, everyone," Aramis said. "Thane, count us in."

"You got it," the elf standing beside Radier said. "In five, four, three, two," then he pointed at Aramis.

In a blink of an eye, Aramis's expression changed from impassive amusement to wistful longing and deep heartache. "I can't explain it, Ebony, not even to myself. When I'm outside these mines, in the trees, on the mountainside, I feel whole. It breaks my heart because as much as I don't fit in here, this is my home, my family. I don't know. Just tell me to shut up and stop being mad."

I stared at him. I knew exactly what he meant. I felt the same way, especially since Regionals. His effortless transition and delivery convinced me he truly meant what he said.

"You're amazing," I swooned.

Aramis switched back to his normal self and laughed. "Cut. Thank you, Mabel, but I would prefer it if you said your line."

I hid my face. It could have been a lot worse. I could have blurted out how much I loved him. "I'm sorry."

"No worries. Thane?"

"Five, four, three, two."

"I can't explain it, Ebony, not even to myself. When I'm outside these mines, in the trees, on the mountainside, I feel whole. It breaks my heart because as much as I don't fit in here, this is my home, my family. I don't know. Just tell me to shut up and stop being mad."

My line, what was my line? Oh, right. "I'll not tell you you're mad, but I will tell you to shut up and make your move," I said, then pointed at the Mage-Stones board.

"Cut."

I had to get it right this next time or he would replace me with Emma.

"Much better. Just relax. It is like being at home with your brothers, talking."

Hardly. I breathed deep.

"Ready?" Aramis asked.

"Ready," I said and slowly let out my breath.

"Thane."

"Five, four, three, two."

"I can't explain it, Ebony, not even to myself. When I'm outside these mines, in the trees, on the mountainside, I feel whole. It breaks my heart because as much as I don't fit in here, this is my home, my family. I don't know. Just tell me to shut up and stop being mad."

I thought of the twins and their humor. "I'll not tell you you're mad, but I will tell you to shut up and make your move." I pointed at the Mage-Stones board the way Kenneth or Ross might as I said my lines.

Aramis smiled showing off his gorgeous dimples, which made me smile. I thought I'd made him laugh again but he didn't call "cut." He put down a white stone at the end of a long line of my black ones. They all flipped over to white. Well played, but then I hadn't set up the board and probably would have tried not to give him such a good opportunity.

"There. Are you satisfied? I'm just so restless. I want to climb trees. I want to see mountains, Ebony, mountains, so tall and majestic. I want to live in the trees that scale the mountains."

I stuck out my tongue as I studied the board. He had left himself open to an even bigger overturn than he had made. I put down my black stone and watched three rows turn from white to black. "I don't know what to tell you, Terrence. You belong in the mines, even if you don't feel you do. Who else is there to reach those high places in the caverns?"

Aramis made small advances on my black stones. "True. Just think of how many gems might have been missed if I weren't here. But I feel like I'm being crushed. At night I wake up because I can't breathe."

I fought to fend off his white stones and at the same time worked to set myself up for a massive takeover. "Does Mam know you're thinking of leaving?"

This acting reminded me of when I imagined the two of us fighting when I threw axes, except now he was my brother, not my lover, and in front of me, not in my imagination.

"No. I hoped you'd tell her for me." He looked up at me with a glint in his eyes, the way Max looked when he had done some mischief and wanted me to take the blame.

"Tell me what?" Frerin asked, coming into the room. She wore a golden ring around her beard.

I jumped out of my seat.

"Cut."

"Sorry, Mabel," Frerin said. "I didn't mean to scare you."

"Perfect," Aramis said. "Radier, look at the last take and tell me we can use it."

"Lunch is ready," Antinae said.

"Excellent," Aramis said. "We shall take two hours for lunch. Good work everyone." He gently touched my right shoulder. Warmth and a slight tingle went into my muscle. "If we can use the last take, you will not need to stay for the afternoon session.

I will be recording with Frerin. You are more than welcome to stay and watch if you like."

"Thanks. I think I will," I said. Anything to be around Aramis. I liked being here, behind the scenes, which was something else I never thought I'd get to do and now I was. I had no interest in returning to dust and doing nothing. Phillip and Emma didn't need me anyway.

"Good." The tingle stayed in my shoulder for a few moments after Aramis removed his hand and walked over to Radier. I flexed and rotated my shoulder before I put on my sling. It felt like I had a fraction more mobility now than when I first arrived.

Elven magic?

Could Aramis heal me?

I stared at Frerin through lunch as it began to sink in: my mam sat across from me. She did everything exactly as I did, the way she held her fork, the way she held her mug with her pinky finger hooked underneath for added support. She stared at me as much as I stared at her.

"Are you still friends with Emma?" she asked.

"How do you know about Emma?"

She lowered her gaze for a moment. "We were good friends with her parents."

Right.

"The two of you were nearly inseparable from the day you were born." She smiled. "I used to bring you with me when I'd visit. The two of you would hold hands as you napped together."

Everyone at the table had fallen silent to listen, even Aramis, who smiled at me. I blushed. How embarrassing to have my Aramis hear stories of me as an infant.

"Ah, yes, Emma and I are still friends." Though I didn't think we would be much longer. She had tried to poison me and take my Aramis.

After lunch, I watched Frerin and Aramis work but found observing Radier more interesting. He had a brilliantly craggy face with a lot of depth and character. I wished I'd brought some stone and carving tools to carve him. During a snack break, I worked up the courage to talk to him. "Excuse me, Mr. Radier, sir?"

"Mabel." He smiled.

"I wondered if I could… if you'd let me make a carving of you?"

He pressed his lips tight and I shrunk back expecting a gust of his notorious fury. Instead he chuckled. "I suppose you could, under one condition."

"What's that, sir?" I cringed.

"You help me. My eyes are starting to feel their age, and I need someone to watch the projections, help me catch unusual shadows, bad lighting, bad angles, if the crystal moves, and if faces are hidden."

I could be useful behind the scenes. Was this really happening? How did I get so lucky? "I'd love to."

At the end of the day, I walked with Frerin to the green room. I thought of the afternoon at the movie

theater with Max, and how we had been so desperate to know her. I had the chance now, and I couldn't
deny Max the same opportunity. "If I talked to Max,
and he wants to see you, do you want to see him? I
won't talk to the others. They've made it clear they
want nothing to do with you. But Max might."

She was quiet for a moment. She wiped her eyes.
Was she crying? "Thank you."

"HEY MAX, you'll never guess who is in town so
I'll tell you." I stumbled off my chair at the Prospector.

He put an arm around me and helped me stand
up. "Come on Mabel. It's closing time and Da is
waiting for you."

"Ugh. Da. I don't want to see him." The conversation I'd had with Da this morning seemed so long
ago but was still fresh in my mind. I had no desire to
go home, especially after such an amazing day. I had
no desire to face Da and hear him telling me he'd
found me a mate, or worse, that I was so useless and
undesirable no one in Gilliam wanted me.

"Sure, you do."

"No, I don't. Really. You haven't guessed who's
here. Right, I'll tell you." I dropped my voice to a
loud whisper. "Mam." I beamed at Max. "Yep. Here,
in Gilliam. But no one else knows so you can't tell
anyone."

"You're drunk." Together we bobbed and weaved our way out of the Prospector.

"I am, and she's here. And she wants to meet you. How come you're not drunk?"

"I am. I just hold it better than you do."

"Damn axe throwing. I am soooo glad I don't have to throw anymore. But you can't tell Mikey. You've got to promise."

"No problem. Easy now." Max helped me in through our front door.

"Mabel." Da stood by the door, arms crossed, his face as stony as ever.

"Don't worry, Da. I've been at the tavern all evening looking for a mate."

"And how did it go?" He asked.

"Very well, as you can see."

"We'll talk tomorrow. I want you to know I've talked to your brothers and they've agreed to help you."

"Oh, good." I despised my da for keeping Mam from me, for lying about her existence, about what she'd done. Even more than that, I hated him for making me feel useless and unwanted.

I stomped up to my room and slammed my door. I pulled out my carving of Aramis. I had done a fairly decent job. Many of the details were accurate, though I needed to make the dimples deeper. "Aramis," I whispered. "Aramis, my Aramis. You are real." And here. "What will I do if Da finds me a mate?"

I didn't want a mate.

Did I really believe that?

I opened up Dr. Thaddeus. "Think again, about what it is you really want in life. Take your time. Think about what makes you happy, think about when you are unhappy. Do any of those events or items connect with your first list of what you want? Write down what you really want."

I knew what I didn't want. I didn't want Da to find me a mate. I didn't want to be stuck in this house forever. I didn't want to feel worthless because my mining career was delayed or that I didn't look just right.

I didn't fit in here. And I didn't want to.

CHAPTER 19

"MABEL," MAX said softly, bouncing on my bed, shaking me awake.

I groaned and pulled the covers up over my head. "Go away." My head felt like the blown top of a volcano whose molten ash filled my mouth.

"Is it true, what you said last night about Mam?" Max sat next to me.

I stealthily laid my Aramis statue under my bed. "Frerin. Yes. Now go away."

"Does she really want to see me?"

I cleared my throat. "Get me some water and I'll tell you." Max handed me a glass. He must have brought it with him, the conniving bugger. I guzzled it and gave the empty glass back. "Yes, she does."

"Where did you see her?"

I rubbed my temples. "You know the movie being made in the mines? She's starring in it."

"How do you know?"

I sighed. "You have to promise not to tell anyone."

"You've got a lot of secrets lately."

My head hurt so much. Couldn't he go away? "Yes, well here's another one. Do you promise not to tell?"

"Of course."

"I'm in the movie." I lay back on my pillow and pulled my blankets around me.

Max ripped off my blankets. "You're what?"

I reached for the covers but Max held them just beyond my grasp. "Shush. Da will hear you. I auditioned and I've been given a small part."

"Why didn't you tell me?"

"I haven't told anyone."

Max lay next to me and put the covers over both of us. "Tell me about Mam. What happened? How did you meet her? What did she say? Were you ever going to tell me?"

I groaned. "You and Da are so impatient. I only met her yesterday." I told him about meeting Frerin and what she said about Da making her promise to have nothing to do with us under threat of banishment.

"Does Da know she's here?" Max asked.

"No. At least I don't think he does. He would have said or done something if he knew. Wouldn't he?"

"You're probably right. Unless that's why Da is suddenly pushing so hard for you to find a mate."

"You think? I don't know. I think it's because of the movie we saw her in. I bet because everyone knew Frerin's our mam, he thought it would be bad news for me because he thinks acting is so disgraceful. Her acting makes me undesirable. He's probably hoping I'll get a mate before her disgrace spreads to me."

Max said nothing for nearly a minute. "*The Gold-miner's Daughter* has been done for a few weeks. If Mam's profession reflected badly on you, we'd know by now. We would have known the day after Mam left. Da's decision is too abrupt. He must know Mam's here. Why else would he insist on finding you a mate on the same day you meet her?"

"How would he know?" I asked. "She snuck into town to avoid seeing anyone."

"Well, it seems like too much to be a coincidence. He knows something. Whatever it is, I'm sure he's only trying to look out for you."

"I wish he had more faith in me. I earned my place in the mines based on my own merit and the reputation of my family, not Frerin's. I'll find a mate the same way. She has nothing to do with me and my life."

"Look, Da's just being Da." Max shifted the covers over us. "He's doing what he thinks is best, even though it is old-fashioned. I don't think you'll have a problem finding a mate, I really don't. Don't concern yourself with Da. Do what you want to do and let him talk to us. If all of this really is because Mam is back, then he should have started to find you a mate months ago. And for the record, I only have a few friends who are interested in finding a mate, but they're not good enough for you."

"They're not good enough for me, or I'm not good enough for them?"

"Trust me," he said, poking me. "They are not good enough for you. They are fun lads, and they think they are ready to have a family, but they're not. If you were to end up with one of them, it would be nothing but trouble and you don't deserve that."

I smiled. "Thanks, Max."

"You're welcome. Don't forget, you've got eleven of us brothers looking out for your best interests. Da may be desperate to find you a mate, but we won't let you settle down with just anyone. As long as we have any say in it, we will make sure your mate deserves you. By the way, even if you picked the fellow, we'd all have to give our approval before any courting happened."

I laughed and pitied any fellow who found himself on the bad side of my brothers.

"Now, when do I get to meet Mam?"

"How about today?"

Max jumped out of bed and straightened his tunic and cap. "Do you think she'll want to see me this soon?"

"I do. Are you ready to see her?"

"I am."

That was good, because I wasn't sure I was ready to meet her, and I already had. "Okay. We are recording at the chief foreman's house. Come there at lunch time." I got out of bed. "The movie crew has a special catering team and they make the most amazing food."

"Excellent. Thanks." Max hugged me. "See you then."

I pulled a fresh tunic out of my dresser. "I have to get out of the house before Da comes to talk to me."

"No problem," Max said from the doorway. "I'll distract him for you."

FRERIN HAD the same twitchy smile I do when I don't want to show how happy or excited I am. As the morning wore on, she had a harder time holding off her smile and concentrating on her work.

"Cut," Aramis said for the sixth time. Radier stopped mumbling the spell that made the crystal record. I picked up the piece of limestone and my tools and worked on my carving of Radier.

"Frerin, what is the problem?" Aramis asked. "This is not like you."

"I'm sorry. My son, one of them, the youngest, he's coming to see me at lunch."

"How many more will be coming to distract

you?"

"I had twelve in total."

"Twelve?" Aramis asked, like he couldn't believe any family could be so big.

I guess he didn't know twelve dwarflings meant a small family.

"Yes, twelve, and they were turned against me or told I was dead. I consider myself lucky that two of them want to see me. So I'm sorry seeing my family for the first time in dozens of years delays your schedule. You knew the situation when you decided to record here. You should have thought of it before you asked me to come."

"You are right, I should have," Aramis said. "I thought you had three or four dwarflings, not twelve. Okay, okay, we are all professionals here. We shall start over after lunch, after you have had some time with your son. Everyone, we are breaking early for an extended lunch break. Come back in three hours." Aramis left the room taking the crew with him.

"Did I get you in trouble?" I asked.

"No, love. He's worried because it's his first time directing. He has plenty of time to make this movie and is already well ahead of schedule. He's been in enough movies to know recording almost always goes over time. When did you say Max was coming?"

"Any minute," I said. "Do you want me to leave when he gets here?"

"No. I've been away from you all so long, I want

to spend as much time with you as I can. You both were so young when I... I never... the two of you are the ones I never knew. I won't get to see the others, I don't deserve to see them, or you, but you're giving me my family back."

"Um," Max said from the doorway. He cleared his throat. "Excuse me, I'm early, is it all right?"

He hadn't finished talking before Frerin hugged him.

"Max, my Max. Let me look at you." She held him at arm's length and looked him up and down. "A fine young dwarf. A miner too, no doubt."

"Won't be long before I'm considered for promotion to rubies." Max grinned from ear to ear. "Welcome home."

"Come, sit down, tell me everything," she said.

The three of us sat on the sofa. "You are back for good, aren't you?" Max asked. "I mean, Da probably won't let you back into the house, but you can still live in Gilliam right?"

"No, honey. I'm afraid not."

Max inched away from her. "So you're here to disrupt everything and abandon us again? Don't we mean anything to you?"

"Of course you do. All of you do. Just because I can't stay, doesn't mean you can't come and visit me."

"Yes, it does. We're miners. We don't leave the mines, except maybe for the Dwarf Games, and those are never held where you live, are they?"

"No, they're not. Surely you could make an exception once every few years even, to come see me?"

"Why can't *you* make the exception and stay? Why couldn't you have made the exception, once every few years even, to come see us, or write us?"

"I couldn't," Frerin said.

"Right. The threat of banishment. Why are you wearing a different golden ring than the one you wore when you left? Do you have another family?"

"You are my only family, Max. I could never have another family. This ring is only for recording, a part of the costume for my character. I wear my golden ring when I'm not working."

I felt Max's pain and confusion; his need for Frerin to stay and be a mam; his frustration with her acceptance of her situation. I couldn't stay and watch them anymore. I decided to let Frerin and Max have some time alone and joined the others for lunch.

I was so confused. I was angry at Mam for leaving, for being so willing to stay away from her family. And yet she loved acting just as I did. When I was with her, I finally felt like I knew where I came from. We looked the same, we behaved the same, we liked the same things. And I fit in with the cast and crew of the movie so much more than I ever fit in with anyone in the mines. Even more than with my friends.

"How is your shoulder, with all the carving you're doing?" Radier asked.

"It's really the only thing I can do with my right arm," I said chewing on a mouthful of wild boar and apple sausage. "At least when I'm carving I feel like I'm still being productive."

"Is there no one who can heal it here?" Radier asked.

"I see a doctor every other week but there isn't much he can do. He said the best thing for it is to rest and let it heal itself."

"I might know someone who could heal you."

"Really?"

"Mmm." He lit his pipe and puffed out a few smoke rings. "Aramis's father. He's Lord of the Tree Elves. He has fantastic healing powers."

That explained perfectly why my shoulder tingled and felt better whenever Aramis touched it.

"If you were to come to Leitham, I may be able to convince him to come down and have a look."

"You know him?"

Radier leaned back. "As a matter of fact, he and I fought with Gillis to drive off the dragons from these very mountains."

"Does Aramis have those same healing powers? If he did, he could heal me and I could get on with my life." My life in the mines or my life in the movies? I didn't know, but at least I'd have a choice.

Radier chuckled. "I'm afraid not. Well, he does, but his powers are not nearly strong enough and he has chosen a different path so he is no longer able to develop them."

"Oh." Too bad. Maybe one day I would go to Leitham. It would be a chore trying to convince Da

I should go. If I told him I'd be fully healed then I could mine and be whole and find a mate, he might agree—if he and my brothers hadn't found me a mate before then, and if he didn't know Frerin lived there, or that it would be an elf who would heal me.

"May I ask you a question?" I asked.

"Of course," Radier said.

"What are you?"

"I am a wizard."

"Yes, I know. But what *are* you? You've fought with Gillis, which makes me think you're immortal like an elf, but you're not an elf because your ears aren't pointy. So then I think maybe you are a mortal, but you're not a dwarf or a goblin and you are most definitely not a troll. So what are you?"

"Ah. I am a little bit of everything, my dear," he said and winked.

The kind of cryptic response he was infamous for.

Aramis stood behind Radier and me and bent down between us, his neck and face inches from me. I tilted my head a fraction closer until his scent of deep forest oak and leaf surrounded me and I breathed him in.

"How is the recording looking?" Aramis asked. "Is there anything from this morning we can salvage?"

"It is looking fine. I am sure one or two more takes this afternoon and we will have this scene wrapped up.

"Good, good. And how are you enjoying your-self, Mabel?" Aramis laid a hand on my right shoulder.

I felt the tingling sensation again and it made me smile. I wanted to hold Aramis's hand on my shoulder until all the pain and damage and scar tissue had been eradicated, and a lot longer after that. "I'm having a great time, thanks."

And in all truth, I needed this break from mining, the dust, and listening to Emma prattle on endlessly about Zach. I could live like this full time, even after my shoulder healed. The more I thought about it, the more appealing the idea of traveling to Leitham sounded.

"NOT HIM," Max said, superbly distracting Da so I could sneak out for the fourth day in a row. I stopped at the front door to listen for a minute. I wanted to know who Max disapproved of today. "Don't be too desperate to find her a mate. He'll make her, and us, miserable. Who suggested him anyway?"

"Kenneth," Da said.

"Well there you go. Kenneth wasn't serious. He doesn't take anything seriously. He hates Travis. Who else is on your list?"

Thank the gods my brothers were on my side. My stomach growled as I left the house. At least as part of the movie crew I could grab some fresh pastries in the green room, or even better, go to the catering tables beside the set. They had breakfasts twice as big as the ones Da made, which were not small to begin with. The movie crew had such good food and I ate so much I thought I might actually gain some much-desired weight, though my clothes were still comfortable, if not a bit loose.

My stomach growled louder and I drooled at the thought of the pancakes the caterers made. I grabbed a pastry before I changed into my costume, and then hurried to have a real breakfast on set at the old crosscut. Today Jimmy and Emma were joining me. I needed a big breakfast to give me strength to listen to Emma, and to use my shoulder enough to act like a miner.

"Good morning, Mabel," Radier said when I arrived at the catering tables. "Your friends are coming in this morning aren't they?"

"Yes, they are." I heaped pancakes and syrup on my plate and savored a mouthful.

"Wonderful. You young ones are so delightful. It's why I agreed to work in this business, you know. After my adventure with the demon of the depths, well, I've never had the same need for danger. I'd rather have fun and enjoy a good laugh. Ah, and speaking of."

I turned around expecting to see a demon of the depths and I wasn't far off. Emma came in followed by Jimmy. Emma's beard now had two braids in it rather than her usual single braid. Either something had happened between her and Zach, or she had a plan to seduce Aramis. I didn't know which one I wanted less.

Emma walked toward me with a huge smile and arms outstretched. "Mabel. We've missed you."

I cautiously returned her hug. She hadn't been this happy to see me since the day I started at the mines. And that greeting was far more genuine than this one. "What happened to your beard? Zach hasn't dumped you again, has he?"

"Oh, no. We're fine. I decided my character should be unattached and looking for a mate. Bit of a mistake, though," she whispered. "Jimmy has been flirting with me from the moment he saw me this morning."

Nope. Hadn't missed her at all. I didn't care if Jimmy flirted with her or he didn't flirt with her, or if the entire male population of Gilliam flirted with her. I really didn't.

Emma helped herself to the food laid out. Even though she had every right to it, I resented her for making herself so comfortable. She'd said acting was disgraceful. She discouraged me from auditioning. She probably only auditioned because I had.

"Don't take so much," Jimmy scolded her. What a fool, falling for Emma. He could have her. "Are we allowed to eat this?"

"Help yourselves," Radier said, which made Jimmy jump.

"We have missed you," Jimmy said to me. "When

will you be done here so you can come back to mining?"

"I don't know."

He pulled me to the side, away from Emma who chatted with one of the crew members. "I hope it's soon. Phillip and I have been talking and we might see if I can switch with Emma."

I thought he wanted to switch with *me* so he could work with *her*. "Is everything all right?"

"Sure, well, no, not really. I don't mean to speak badly of anyone, but a certain someone is driving us crazy. Please don't say anything. It's really not that bad. We would just prefer to work with you instead, like when we did our masterworks. And the chief foreman's been getting after Phillip, something about missed emerald beds. Phillip doesn't want to do anything about them until you come back." Jimmy stopped talking and backed away from me when Emma approached.

I guess Jimmy didn't like Emma after all. What had made her think he did?

"There are no missed emerald beds," she said inserting herself between Jimmy and me.

"The chief foreman says there are," Jimmy said.

"How would he know?" Emma asked, hands on hips.

"Phillip told him, a few months ago," Jimmy said.

"No he didn't. If there were missed spots he would have told me and we would have excavated them by now."

"He's waiting for Mabel to get back so she can point them out since she's the one who discovered them."

Oh, Jimmy, stop. Why are you doing this to me? Wasn't it enough that you told Frankie about the sludge I was taking for my shoulder?

"Mabel? She couldn't find one to save her life. Have you forgotten how she told me to mine a spot not even close to the emerald bed? What, in the name of Gillis, makes Phillip think Mabel should be the one to find these missing beds, which don't exist?"

Jimmy may have betrayed me to my brothers, but at least he had done it because he was looking out for me. Emma, on the other hand... What had happened to my best friend to make her so vicious?

Jimmy opened his mouth to defend me but I stopped him. "Tell Phillip I have a day off from re- cording in three days and I can be there to help out then. And I hope you'll join us, Jimmy."

She could try and poison me, she could talk about fellows flirting with her all she wanted, but I would *not* allow her to insult my mining. These past few days without her constant chatter and backhanded compliments were too nice. I finally understood what Dr. Thaddeus meant when he said I needed to have enough faith in myself to not let anyone walk all over me. I needed to stand up for myself because no one else would. Exposing the emerald beds she missed would show Emma she had no right to insult me.

"Don't rush back just because Phillip wants you to," Emma said. "There is nothing to find. And even if there were, you wouldn't find it," Emma muttered as she walked away.

"If I go back to mining, I'd like it if you traded teams with Emma," I said, and Jimmy smiled.

Antinae and Aramis, papers in hand, strolled into the passage.

"Listen up everyone," Antinae said. "We will begin in five minutes. A few ground rules: when Aramis speaks, you listen and do exactly as he asks. When he says to stop, you stop. There is to be no talking while recording. And no food in the shot," he said, taking a plate from Emma as she tried to walk past him. "All right, places everyone."

Emma slunk up to Aramis. "Excuse me. Sorry to interrupt. I wanted to thank you for casting me in your movie."

"You are welcome," Aramis said without looking at her.

"Um," Emma twirled the end of a braid around her finger. "Where would you like me to stand?"

He glanced over the set. "Same place as in rehearsal."

I smiled apologetically to Aramis and dragged Emma to the wall with me. "Leave him alone. He's busy and he doesn't like interruptions."

"I only wanted to get my directions." She tugged at the two braids in her beard.

"When he wants you to do something, he'll tell

you," I said.

"You've worked with him for what, five days, and you know everything about him?" Emma grumbled. "That reminds me. Did you talk to him about me like I asked?"

Unbelievable. "No."

"Why not?"

Like I ever would. "It never came up."

"But you said you would."

"I said no such thing."

"What grit got into your britches?"

I couldn't take her anymore. I had to walk away before I said something I knew I'd regret. I turned on my heel and walked to the end of the passage. I couldn't remember Emma ever being so vile. I had the same feeling of my stomach twisting as when she faked her beard and blamed me, when she insulted my brothers saying no one wanted them, and when she told Ben and Zach I didn't know how to mine. I hadn't recognized the feeling then. It was the same as when I thought she intentionally poisoned me.

I walked back but kept Jimmy between me and Emma.

"Mabel, are you all right?" Jimmy whispered.

"I think so," I said.

"We're supposed to get into our places."

"Right." I flung off my sling, ready to pretend to mine. Emma gazed at Aramis, playing with her beard, tugging on her tunic, accentuating her stout figure.

"Emma," Zach said, stepping out of the shadows of the crew.

She let go of her beard. "What are you doing here?"

"I came to watch you. Your beard, it's in two braids. Have you changed your mind about us or are you cheating on me again?"

"Don't be so dramatic." Emma undid the two braids hastily returning it to a single braid.

"Take it outside," Aramis said. "We do not want any lovers' spats on set. And Emma, you are off the movie. Go sort out your personal life."

"But, Aramis!" Emma gasped. Zach grabbed her and pulled her out of the cavern.

I caught Aramis watching me. I had the feeling he'd sensed my discomfort with Emma and he'd kicked her off the movie for me. I nodded my gratitude but he'd already moved on. Still, he knew.

CHAPTER 20

I SIGHED as I entered the empty crosscut. Even after I lit all the lanterns, it was too dim. I had grown accustomed to the brightness of the lanterns used when recording. I'd spent two days dwelling on Emma's insults and I couldn't dismiss them as unintentional or harmless. They were typical of her and I had let her walk all over me and my family.

"You're here." Jimmy set his bag of tools beside mine. "I'm glad you're back."

"Only for today."

"Still, it will be fun to work together like we did in the toy workshop."

"It will." Though I would have preferred to spend the day working with Radier and Aramis, instead of getting coated in dust, working in the dark, with

Emma. I fretted as I sorted through my tools trying to enjoy the routine of preparing to mine. I shouldn't have let Emma's remarks bother me as much as I had. Maybe I was making a big deal out of nothing. Jimmy would know.

"Has Emma always been as cruel as the other day?" I asked.

He stopped sorting his tools. "Not as directly cruel. She's been more manipulative. Ever since your beard started growing. I don't know if she means anything by it. She is very competitive, and probably feels threatened by you."

"Threatened? By me?" I laughed. "Hardly." If that was all, then I might forgive Emma and her misguided jealousy.

"You shouldn't be so surprised."

Phillip entered and hugged me like he had my first day at the mines, and with the same genuineness. "You did come in. I'm so glad you're here. I told the chief foreman we would start exposing the missed emerald beds."

"Look who decided to show up to work." Emma said from the entrance. She strode in and threw her bag of tools on top of mine. Her beard had two braids in it. "You have some nerve."

I pulled my bag out from under hers, dumping out her axes in the process. "Excuse me?"

"Thanks to you, I've been kicked off the movie and Zach dumped me. He says he won't take me back, ever. So thank you very much for ruining my life. You're jealous of Aramis's interest in me, aren't you, Mabel? Like you would ever have a chance with someone like him."

Did she know? I had been so careful to hide my love for him.

"Emma." Jimmy and Phillip said at the same time.

"Excuse me for being honest and pulling Mabel out of her dream world."

"I'm sorry, Mabel," Phillip said.

I glanced at him. "Don't apologize for her." She didn't know, and she didn't love Aramis. If she did, she never would have talked about it. She said she was interested in him because she thought I was and she wanted me to let my love for him slip so no one would love me and I wouldn't be a threat to her.

"We should get to work on those missed emerald beds." Jimmy picked up an axe and handed it to me.

"The only emerald beds missed are whatever Mabel missed."

"No, Emma, you missed them." Phillip picked up his own axe.

"I did no such thing," Emma said. "Even if there were missed beds, Mabel wouldn't be the best one to locate them, would she? At best, she is well out of practice. She still has a bad shoulder, and let's not forget the way she tried to get me to dig in the wrong area. But fine, have it your way." Emma threw up her hands. "I think I'll just sit back and watch you try and find these supposed beds. It will be fun watching you make a fool of yourself."

How dare she? "Your brain must be addled from all your flirting," I roared. "You insisted the emeralds lay under the wrong stone. I had to trick you into digging in the right place so you could find your damned first-ever emerald." I cut off Emma before she could protest. "And there *are* missed emerald beds. *You* missed them. *I'm* the one who found them."

"Why are you being so mean?" Emma scrunched her face and I thought she might be about to cry those fake tears. "Why didn't you tell me I'd missed emerald beds?"

"Mabel didn't want to hurt your feelings," Phillip said. "Clearly she's more sensitive to your feelings than you have ever been to hers."

I would never let her use me or make me take the blame so she could feel better about herself again.

I took off my sling and marched to the nearest emerald bed waiting to be discovered. "This is where you were working, is it not?"

"Yes, but—"

I tapped my axe on the wall, the stone cracked easily. I pulled away the outer shell, ignoring the ache in my shoulder, until I had a first emerald. I pocketed it and massaged my muscles.

"Mabel, take it easy," Phillip said.

I ran my fingers over the wall of the shaft until I felt the rock change. "Don't you ever insult my mining ability again." I swung my axe. Pain ripped through me but I kept going until I'd exposed another emerald and added it to my pocket. I continued on to the third emerald bed. "You with your fake beard blaming me for your deception." I took out a big chunk of the stone and pocketed another nice emerald. "The worst of it though, you *poisoned* me, then denied it." I swung again for a fourth emerald. Pain seared and I had trouble holding on to my axe. By now I had reversed any healing I had achieved. I didn't care.

"I never—"

"The doctor said you put an old and rare ingredient into the medicine." I swung and barely made a chip in the rock. "He said you would have known much more common ingredients to use that wouldn't have caused nearly as much damage as what you gave me." The third attempt on the rock finally cracked open the fifth bed.

I turned on Emma. "I thought you were my friend, but you have done nothing but manipulate me, accuse me, and make me feel bad, useless, and completely inadequate." I had to stop then. I let my arm hang down and my shoulder felt marginally better. "There are two more, I can point them out to you."

"If you feel inadequate and inferior, it's because you are," Emma said. "You are weak, Mabel, and you will never make it as a top miner. You can blame me and your injury all you want for your failure, but you know the truth. No wonder your da is so desperate to find you a mate that he asked your brothers to help him. He is so desperate, he came to our house to find out if one of my brothers would court you. My brothers' beards haven't started growing yet but even they want someone better than you."

"Emma, get out," Phillip said. "You don't work with us anymore. The chief foreman is waiting to re-assign you."

Emma picked up her bag of tools. "Suit your-selves. Good luck working with Mabel. She will only slow you down."

"Leave."

"Don't listen to her," Jimmy said loud enough for Emma to hear as she left. "You're amazing, and strong, and you will make it as far in mining as you want to go."

I sat down and put on my sling. I shouldn't have let her goad me into damaging my shoulder. I never had to see her again. I had two very good true friends to work with and there were new emeralds to exca-vate.

"Thanks for standing up for me."

"Jimmy's right. Emma couldn't be more wrong about you. I'm sorry we let her go on as long as we did. Want to show us those other two beds?"

"Absolutely."

I pointed out the beds. Jimmy and Phillip tapped until the emeralds were exposed. They each took out the first emerald of each and gave them to me. "I can't take those. You excavated them."

"Don't be daft," Jimmy said. "You found them. It's only right you take them. Now go sit down until we have more exposed, then you can help."

"Yes sir."

They worked well together. When one tapped, the other cleared dust away. It didn't take long before they shouted and yowled as they had working on their masterworks. I hadn't realized how much I missed working with them. But I didn't miss mining.

After an hour of listening to them howl and yowl I could excavate. At first it went well; the emeralds were small and loose in their bedding. But soon enough I reached the most stubborn emerald I'd ever tried to remove. It didn't want to come loose. Every time I thought I had it, I'd pull on it and nothing happened. I grunted and groaned but it didn't move.

"Are you all right?" Phillip asked.

"Yeah, yeah, just have a tough one here," I said stepping back.

"Why don't you take a bit of a break? I'll work on it for a while."

"Good luck." I sighed and I watched Phillip chip at the stone surrounding the stubborn emerald, he pulled on it and dug some more. Several times he wiped the sweat off his brow before it finally came loose.

"Here you go." He had to hold it with both hands. "I don't think we've ever had one this big."

I took it from him and examined its almost perfect shape. It had only a few rough edges. I could have cried. This emerald represented everything I loved about mining—being the one to find and the first to hold the most beautiful gems in the world.

Jimmy stood beside me. "It is amazing. Can I hold it?"

I didn't want to give it up. I wanted to take it home. I lovingly placed it in his outstretched hands and it felt like I had given up a dwarfling.

After a few minutes of us all ogling the emerald, Phillip took it from Jimmy and placed it in a bucket. "There are more to be found."

We weren't ready to leave it behind.

"He is such a taskmaster." Jimmy winked and smiled.

I stared at the emerald for a while. It really was everything I loved about mining and it reminded me these moments were rare. My return to mining was delayed, but it was my future. Unfortunately, it was a future I didn't really want any more. I'd found happiness and maybe even a future outside of mining.

"Is Mabel Goldenaxe in here?" Antinae asked from the entrance to the crosscut. His high-pitched voice echoed in the passage interrupting Phillip and Jimmy's howling and yowling.

Happily, I looked away from the beautiful big emerald. "Right here."

"Thank the gods. It is a maze in here. Come with me."

"Is something wrong?"

"Aramis wants to do some re-takes."

"All right. I'll see you lads later." Dear gods, I hoped I hadn't upset Aramis. I never wanted to upset my Aramis. At the same time, this meant I could spend the rest of the day with him.

"Try and come to the Prospector when you're done," Jimmy said.

"Sure, I'll see you there." I grabbed my bag of tools and followed Antinae through the corridors to the green room, relieved to be free from the dim and dusty passage.

"He wants you in the purple tunic."

The purple tunic and matching trousers, boots and cap already hung in a change area. "I'll be ready in a couple of minutes." I closed the curtain.

"Just hurry it up," Antinae said from the drinks table, pouring himself a goblet of mead.

I grunted from the pain in my shoulder as I changed tunics.

"It took forever to find you. Aramis is waiting for us and he is not as patient as he appears."

It sounded to me the impatience belonged to Antinae, not Aramis. "Well then, let's go," I said, sliding back the curtain.

Antinae looked me up and down searching for something to criticize but he found nothing. He almost appeared disappointed, and yet I felt a hint of grudging approval in his silence and the slight tilt of his head. "Good, you have your bag and carvings with you."

I always had my bag of tools and carvings with me. I never left it anywhere, especially not the green room where so many dwarves and elves came and went without being watched. I might have before I heard Mam's story.

Without another word, Antinae marched me back up to the chief foreman's house.

We waited in the kitchen until Aramis and Frerin finished recording their scene. Used to the waiting by now, I sat out of the way of the lunch preparations, and took out my almost-complete carving of Radier. It needed a few finishing touches. While I didn't like to leave my carving tools unattended, they also gave me something to do in this hurry-up-and-wait game of recording, the one part of the business I wasn't a fan of. I hated sitting around doing nothing. At least in mining, if you weren't excavating you were chipping away at the rock to find the next emerald bed—except for me, lately. Today had been a prime example of more hurry up and wait. Hurry up and expose those emerald beds, then sit back and wait until I could help excavate.

With a few scratches to etch the laugh lines at the corners of Radier's eyes, I finished the carving. I blew on it and wiped away the last of the dust then polished it with my sleeve. I put the carving back into the front pocket of my bag and took out another piece of limestone.

Antinae dipped his finger into one of the pots and the cook smacked his hand with a ladle. He yelped and shook his hand. I smiled and decided he should be the subject of my next carving. I thought I might use his constant sneer but the look of subverted approval he gave me in the green room intrigued me more. I decided to leave the facial features and expressions, and started filing the bottom of the stone, shaping it into feet.

"Are they here yet?" Aramis called.

Antinae snapped his fingers at me and pointed for me to get into the back room. I packed my things, ready for more hurry up and wait.

"I'm here," I called, carrying my bag into the back room. Frerin sat by the fire place. Would I ever get used to seeing her? I didn't really have to; she was only going to abandon me again as soon as recording finished

"Good," Aramis said when he saw me. "I have looked over the edits of the scene we recorded and I am unhappy."

My whole body tensed. I had let my Aramis down.

"Something is not right in the scene, something is missing. Do you have the carving you did of Radier?"

I could relax and breathe again. I held it up. "I just finished it. What do you think, Radier? Does it look like you?"

Radier examined it top to bottom, side to side, around and around in his hands. "Dwarves have the most amazing talents. It most certainly does look like me."

"Wonderful, fantastic. I wish to use it in our scene, add some set decoration," Aramis said.

What an honor. "Of course you can."

"Excellent." He set my carving on the mantel-piece.

Frerin and I gasped at the same time.

"What?"

For someone who is best friends with a dwarf he sure didn't know much about dwarf culture. Had Sevrin taught him nothing?

I removed the carving from the mantelpiece. "Dwarves never, ever, put carvings over the fire. They are put in places of respect."

The table with the Mage-Stones game had a lowered flyleaf. I rearranged the table so I could raise the leaf that created an elevated shelf for carvings. I positioned the stone Radier on the shelf and angled it toward me, not directly facing the crystal.

"Fine. Good. Frerin, we shall record our scene one more time, then break for lunch. Mabel, do not go anywhere, we shall re-record our scene after lunch."

I could go back to the kitchen and carve some more but I felt more useful working with Radier. "May I help you again?" I asked him.

"Of course," he said.

I sat beside him and pulled the screen in front of me. The carving fit well into the set, though I didn't know any dwarven family who had a carving of a wizard in their home. Our kind only ever possessed carvings of dwarves. Somehow it still fit, probably because it was a movie about an elf raised by dwarves. A dwarven family odd enough to raise an elf just might have a carving of a wizard.

Aramis and Frerin recorded the scene perfectly in one take. I stayed with Radier and reviewed the edit two times to make sure everything looked right then joined the others for lunch.

My shoulder hurt too much when I tried to slip off my sling so I kept it on, which irritated me and slowed me down. I had become used to taking it off to eat. I wondered briefly if I should ask Frerin if she had anything to kill the pain, and what kind of medicine she might have made for me if I had been able to talk to her when I'd first injured myself. She hadn't been there and I didn't need to know. I would go to the doctor before going to the Prospector and get some proper medicine that wouldn't put my health at any greater risk.

"Finish up everyone, and get back to work," Aramis said after less than an hour.

Back on set he said to me, "I want you to do exactly what you did when we recorded our scene. All right?"

"No problem."

If I could get Aramis to touch my shoulder, I wouldn't need to go to the doctor. If his brief touch on my shoulder could provide even a little healing, how much more healing would I get if he held me and kissed me? I was imagining how I might get Aramis to kiss me when Frerin said her line, "Tell me what?" And I jumped.

"Cut." He took the seat beside Radier and studied the scene on the screen as they talked. Aramis frowned and shook his head. He pointed at the screen, rubbed his chin, then waved at Frerin. Radier said something, motioning toward the screen again.

Finally, Aramis came back and sat in his chair. Hands clasped, elbows resting on his knees, he leaned toward me. "I need you to shave your beard."

"You what?" Frerin and I asked at the same time.

"The two of you look too much alike. I need Mabel to look younger. She needs to get rid of the beard."

"How about if she trims it?" Frerin asked.

"It needs to go," Aramis said.

"You can't ask her to do that."

"What is the big deal? It is hair, it will grow back."

"After several months. Long after you're gone."

"As I said, it grows back. Mabel, I am afraid we elves do not know how to shave so I shall have to ask you to do it yourself."

"Stay right where you are, Mabel. Aramis, you're not listening to me. Hear me and understand, Mabel is a miner. It is her career, it is her life. Dwarves cannot mine without their beards. You take away her beard and she will not be able to mine for months. She will be an outcast."

Aramis sat back and considered me for a few minutes. "I'm sorry, Mabel, the beard goes or I must find someone to take your place. I would prefer not to since you are perfect for the role."

Aramis likes me. No way would I let anyone else take my place in this movie. Besides, a few months off from mining would be good for healing my shoulder. Except we were talking about my beard, which had taken so long to grow, and while it could be a lot longer, it was my *beard.*

I looked into Aramis's enchanting blue eyes. I really wouldn't refuse him anything. "All right. I'll shave it."

"Are you sure about this, Mabel?" Frerin asked.

No, but as it said in *102 Signs You're Interested: Female Dwarf Body Language of Love,* the first thing any female dwarf should do to attract the male of her dreams is make herself look the way he wants her to. Aramis would know I love him because I made this sacrifice for him.

"I think so," I said.

"Antinae," Aramis called. "Find Mabel what she needs to shave."

"Will do," he said and disappeared.

"Mabel, how will you explain this to your da?" Frerin asked.

I had no idea. "I'll tell him I lost a dare at the Prospector."

Antinae re-entered, snapped his fingers and waved for me to follow him.

If he snapped at me one more time...

Frerin came with me to the chief foreman's bathroom. A basin filled with water sat on the counter, soap, a brush, a razor, and a pair of scissors beside it.

"Take a moment and think before you do this. Is it really worth it?"

I looked in the mirror and ran my fingers through my beard, still thin but maybe a little better than it used to be with some new growth coming in. Perhaps if I shaved it right down it would grow back thicker, more evenly. I fingered my braids and thought of another potential upside to shaving.

I undid the braids. "Da has decided I cannot find a mate on my own. He asked my brothers to ask their friends if they'll be my mate. I think he wants to line fellows up and pick one for me. He intends to have a golden-ring ceremony as soon as possible. I can't really mine with my shoulder like this and no fellows are interested in me anyway. After I shave this, no one will want me and Da won't be able to find a mate for me. It will grow back eventually. By then my shoulder will be better and I can start fresh at finding a mate."

Frerin kept quiet while I brushed out the knots and dust from my beard. "When did he decide to find you a mate?"

"He told me the morning I met you." I picked up the scissors.

"Did he say why he is in such a rush?" She tried to take the scissors from me.

"He only said I didn't have as much time as I thought I did. I figure since I told him I had seen you in *The Goldminer's Daughter* he thinks it's only a matter of time before people hold your profession against me."

She hung her head for a moment. "Sort of. He knows I'm back."

I put down the scissors. "Excuse me?"

"The night I came into town, I stopped in to see him, to ask him to forgive me and let me see you all. Of course he said he wouldn't and threatened to take me before the council if I had any contact with you."

"You were in my house, while I slept, and you didn't come see me?"

"Your da threatened me. If he'd followed through, I would have no chance of seeing you, ever."

"Is that why you didn't hug me when we first met? Because of his threats?"

"I was sure he had turned you against me and that you wouldn't want me to hug you."

She didn't think of me as an abomination. She'd come to the house to see me.

"If I had known he'd already erased my name from all records, I would have walked right past him and gone up to you. I would have woken you up and hugged you and never let you go."

My future in mining was delayed anyway. Da was making my life more miserable by the day. It was time I made decisions for myself. I'd started with standing up to Emma, and now was my opportunity to make a statement.

I picked up the scissors, took a deep breath, held my beard taut and cut.

With each snip of the scissors and each handful

of hair that dropped I cried. I couldn't look at my beautiful beard, now a heap on the floor, or at my stubbly face in the mirror. I put down the scissors and picked up the razor. I pulled my skin tight and scraped. I cut myself a few times but I didn't stop until my face was as clean as a dwarfling's.

I dried my tears. My beard would grow back.

Frerin put an arm around me and walked me back to the set. Aramis smiled when he saw me, which made me feel a little bit better.

"Perfect. Now, let us do this scene one more time."

He put a hand on my shoulder and I felt the wonderful welcoming tingling. Sitting across from him, I contemplated his bare chin and I hoped he would like me because I guessed elves found bare chins attractive.

When we finished recording, my shoulder felt well enough that I didn't need to see Dr. Flint. I debated going to the Prospector and facing the ridicule of all the miners there or going straight home and facing Da. I chose to go to the Prospector and get it over with. At least there I'd have the support of my friends, I hoped.

Everyone gawked at me as I entered the tavern and looked for my friends.

Phillip and Jimmy waved me over to their table with Zach and Ben. They had ale waiting for me. Emma sat with her sister Rachel and a few of Rachel's friends at a table next to ours. Emma took one look at me and let out a howling laugh.

Jimmy glared at her.

"You're pathetic, Mabel. Did you shave so you would have a chance with an elf? Or are you trying to look younger to attract one of my brothers? They will never be desperate enough to court a beardless dwarf."

Well, good. That was the plan. And I liked that I stood out from everyone else.

"Hello lads." Emma slid over to us, sitting beside Jimmy. He didn't look at her. "I thought you might want some proper company over here."

Jimmy grunted.

"A real female, who looks her age."

"You know, Emma," I said. "I've never understood why you have tried so hard to make me look bad in front of everyone. I'm not competition for you. I never have been. You could attract any fellow in Gilliam if you wanted to. They all look at you. They never look at me. And you know it. Maybe you'd have better luck at keeping a fellow if you were nicer to others, especially those who are supposed to be your friends, instead of insulting them all the time. So why don't you worry about yourself? Why don't you do something to make yourself look good, without tearing everyone else down first?"

Emma turned to leave, then changed her mind and leaned toward me. "I wonder what your da will say when he finds out you're in a movie?"

CHAPTER 21

THE STALACTITES and stalagmites of the cafeteria were more beautiful today than usual. The light from the lanterns and the reflections from Radier's crystal made them sparkle and created a myriad of prisms around the cavern. It was a spectacle no dwarf had ever seen in here but one we could all admire.

I waited by the screen beside Radier for Aramis to finish giving instructions to the crew. When I wasn't distracted by the prisms, I worked on my carving of Antinae.

Frerin sat beside me. "What did your da say last night when he saw you?"

"He hasn't seen me yet. I've been avoiding him since he decided to find me a mate."

"Frerin, time," Aramis said.

"We'll talk soon." Frerin patted my arm.

Moments later, Radier adjusted the crystal in his staff. "Who are you carving now?"

"Antinae."

"She'll be pleased?"

Her? Oops. "I hadn't intended to show her."

"You should. She's definitely warming to you and this might convince her that coming here was a good idea."

"Places," Aramis said.

The last of the crew cleared the set.

Shouting came from the cafeteria entrance. It had taken all morning to set up. Had no one told the miners they couldn't use the cafeteria for lunch? Some of the crew left their posts to block the entrance. They needed to be careful or there could be a riot on their hands.

The chief foreman pushed through the crew. "What is going on here?"

"What does it look like?" Aramis said.

"I did not give you permission to record in here."

"Nevertheless, it is perfect for this scene. We will not be long. Say, an hour, two at most. You can have your cafeteria back and they can eat then."

He really could be a bit daft sometimes. You didn't ask dwarves, who had spent hours working in the mines, to wait for their meal, especially when they could smell the stew pot.

"You will vacate immediately," the chief foreman said.

"We will not. Go see Althea. She shall pay you for this inconvenience. Now if you will excuse me, I have a movie to make." Aramis walked back to Frerin and the other actors.

Miners shoved their way into the cafeteria, shaking their fists, but they didn't come at us; rather, they walked directly to the food service area.

"Mabel Louise Goldenaxe."

Everyone—all crew, all actors, all miners—fell to a dead silence. I turned slowly to face the entrance. Da blocked the doorway, hands on hips, his face ruby red.

Uh oh.

"What, in the name of all the gods have given us, do you think you are doing?" he roared. I swore one or two of the stalactites shook and were about to fall.

"It's just a bit of fun." My voice trembled like the stalactites. "Just until I can mine properly again."

"A bit of fun, is it, disgracing the family?" Da stormed into the cavern, charging at me. "Is this why you've been avoiding me?"

I glanced at the entrance thinking maybe I could run for it. Emma stood there, grinning from ear to ear. I should have known she would tell him.

"Kevin, keep your voice down," Mam said, her voice quiet. At least she wasn't trying to embarrass me.

"You." Da turned on Frerin. "I told you to stay away from us, especially Mabel."

"Give it up. Threaten all you want but I know

you have already erased me from all records."

"It's not her fault," I jumped in. "I already had a part in the movie before I met her."

Da ignored me. "You couldn't leave well enough alone, could you, Millie? You couldn't just ruin yourself. You had to come back and heap shame on my family one more time. I've worked too hard to bring the family name back to respectability. I will not let either of you ruin us again."

"Kevin, don't be so dramatic."

"It isn't disgraceful anymore," I said. "Lots of dwarves here have small parts."

Everyone who worked in the mines who had been in the movie, including Emma, turned their backs on us.

"Haven't I given you everything you ever wanted?" Da asked me, his voice quiet.

"Of course."

"Haven't I ever only looked out for your best interests?" he asked.

He was not innocent in all of this. "You mean the way you let me believe all my life that my mam was dead? Or how you're humiliating me by asking my brothers to find me a mate? How you're so desperate to be rid of me you'll make me mate with anyone, regardless of who he is or if I even like him?"

"How dare you disgrace me like this," he rumbled.

"It is just for fun, Da."

"Kevin," Mam interjected.

"Stay out of this, Millie. You've done enough damage."

"I made a mistake. A long time ago."

"Your *mistake* nearly cost us everything. Mabel, I will give you one chance to redeem yourself. Walk away from this right now, go back to mining, forget all about this nonsense, and her. Pray your future mate doesn't care you are a disgrace, and I will forgive you."

"She is *not* a disgrace, Kevin."

"I told you to stay out of it, Millie."

"Don't tear your family apart any more than it already is," Mam said. "Hate me, but don't hate Mabel."

"What will it be, Mabel?" Da asked.

I couldn't give up my family, but to stay, Da would forever think of me as a disgrace. Could I stay in Gilliam as a miner? I needed to heal. There would always be a place in my heart for mining but I wanted a break from it. What other employment could I take in Gilliam that didn't make me a disgrace to my family? I couldn't think of one vocation with enough respectability. I'd have to leave. If I couldn't stay, where would I go? Maybe I could go to Leitham to find Aramis's father and see if he would heal me.

I looked around the room, at the beautiful crystals and amethyst. I loved the mines. Could I really give up all of this?

Radier and Aramis stood to one side. I liked helping Radier. And Aramis, well, I would do anything for him. But give up my family and everything I've known? For him?

Not for him. For myself.

Of course, with all the personal drama going on now because of me, I was probably off the movie. Emma's drama had been far less when he sacked her. That meant I had no reason to continue acting, no reason not to go back to my family.

Except that Da didn't feel like family anymore. I would forever be a disgrace and a shame. Max stood in the corner, the only one looking at me. He shrugged. He had no answer for me. I looked to Frerin. What she had done, could I trust her?

"It's up to you," she whispered.

So much for her helping me with Da.

I looked back at Da. If disappointment was like tears, he would have been weeping. He looked at me as though he didn't recognize me anymore. I couldn't live with the disappointment in his eyes and I knew then that if I stayed, it would never change, no matter what he said. Even if I didn't trust her, I'd have to take my chances with Frerin. "I'm sorry, Da," I whispered. "I don't want to walk away from this."

"Fine," he said. "My doors are closed to you. You are no longer my daughter, and you will no longer carry the name Goldenaxe. Finish what you are doing then get out of Gilliam. If you dare to darken our streets again, I will have you thrown out."

He turned and strode away. Max had already left. What had I done? Had I really just turned my back on my family? For what? So I could be in a movie I'm probably no longer a part of? Where was I going to go? What was I going to do? I had no one now.

Frerin put her arm around me.

She wanted me. She didn't care if I mined or acted or did something else. She loved me. I'd go with her. If I decided I didn't like her, or couldn't trust her, I didn't have to stay. I could sort things out once I arrived in Leitham. "I want to go to Leitham with you."

"Of course. There is a large dwarven community there. We've become like an extended family. They will welcome you with open arms. I would love for you to stay with me." She rubbed my back and kissed the top of my head. "You're not a disgrace, pet, so don't let him make you think you are."

We stayed like this for a while. "Come on Mabel. Let's go get your things and get you moved in with me."

"All right," I said.

"Aramis, I'm sorry, but we'll have to do this later tonight," Frerin said, helping me up.

He sighed. "All right, everyone, pack up. Come back in five hours. You too, Frerin."

He must have regretted choosing to come here, especially casting me. I'd been nothing but trouble for him.

"I'm sorry, Aramis," I said. I could never apologize enough. He didn't have to forgive me, and I would totally understand if he sacked me, he had every right to, I just didn't want him to hate me.

To my surprise, there was no annoyance or dislike in his eyes, only sympathy.

Frerin and I left the cafeteria to the stares of every dwarf in the mines. At least Emma's smile had been wiped off her face. I guess she hadn't expected Da to react so severely. Though I didn't know why. She'd known why he'd banished Mam. How had she expected him to react?

"Don't worry about a thing," Frerin said as we left the mines. "There is plenty of room where I'm staying. And you'll love Leitham."

We turned onto the path to my house. My brothers blocked the walkway. On seeing us, they turned around and stood shoulder to shoulder, their backs to us.

"Frankie?" I asked.

They were as quiet and solid as immovable stone.

"I came to get my things," I said. "Then I'll leave."

Mikey came out of the house. "Da told us what you've been doing. You are no longer allowed on these premises." He joined the others though he continued to face me.

"Mikey, I want what's mine, nothing more."

"There is nothing here belonging to you," he said.

I wanted to scream and punch and kick them. We were family, we were supposed to look out for each other when no one else would, not turn on each other.

Fine, let them be stubborn idiots. I would not

stand for it. "You can't keep my first emeralds from me. You can keep everything else but you can't have those. They are mine and you know it. I can and will take you to the council if you don't give them to me."

"The only emeralds in this house belong to miners, and you are not a miner," Mikey said. "Now get out, and take your cloud of shame with you." His eyes were as cold as Da's.

"It's all right," Frerin said.

"No, it isn't. Those are my emeralds." I tried to go around my brothers but they expanded to block me. I tried to push through but they closed in so I couldn't.

"Mabel, come." Frerin pulled me away.

"You can't do this," I yelled as I walked away.

"We'll figure out a way to get your things," Frerin said when we were far enough from them.

Instead of turning off toward the edge of town, we walked back up the mountain and around past the entrance to the toy workshop. There were no inns here. This neighborhood belonged to the wealthiest of the non-mountain dwellers.

"Here's home, for now." She stopped outside a long bungalow.

"Did you live here before you met Da?" I asked.

"I'm renting it. I grew up in Mitchum and moved to Gilliam after meeting your da."

"Why did you go to Leitham instead of Mitchum?"

"The opportunities were there. And my family

sided with Kevin."

We entered the front room with the kitchen directly behind it, all in one large space. Three doors opened on the left. The first room was clearly Frerin's. The second door exposed an indoor washroom, a luxury I'd only experienced in Mitchum and the chief foreman's home. The final room held an ornately carved maple dresser, matching chair, and a bare mattress on a brass bed frame.

I stretched across the width of the mattress and my entire body fit onto it. If Da knew actors could afford these luxuries, would he take Frerin back? If Emma knew, she'd chase after Sevrin, at least until she wormed her way into a mountain dwelling.

"It isn't much, but it is comfortable," she said. "I'll get you some ale then get this room ready for you."

It isn't much? It was bigger, more luxurious than my home… or, well, the house I grew up in. What kind of place did she have in Leitham?

"It's all right, I can do it," I said getting off the oh-so-soft mattress.

Frerin brought in some bedding and together we made the bed.

We went to the front room and I poured us each an ale while she built up the fire. "Thank you for taking me in," I said.

"I am sorry, Mabel. I really thought he might have changed, relaxed a little, especially for his only daughter. He may be as stubborn as ever, but I am sure your brothers will come around."

"Do you think so? Max told me Mikey took me away from you when Da kicked you out."

"Max saw? Well. Yes, it was Mikey. But I'd like to think I had some influence on them growing up, and even if it has been a long time since I've been in their house, if they really are mine, one day they will see not everything is as rigid as Kevin thinks it is. They will see our world does change and they need to change with it."

"I hope they do." I sipped my ale. I put down my drink and wiped the foam from my upper lip. "So, Mam," it felt awkward to call her that, and I wasn't sure I would again, it just felt like the right thing to do after she took me in. "Is Millie your real name?"

She smiled. "Yes, though it has been a long time since anyone has called me that. When I started acting, nobody believed dwarves had such normal names so we customarily took a name of one of our ancestors. I chose Frerin Gillda."

"But Frerin is a boy's name."

"True," she said. "No one believed there were female dwarves either so I ended up playing a lot of male roles in those early days, though there are not many outside of the dwarven community who would have known Frerin is a male name."

We were silent for a while. "You'll love Leitham," Mam added.

It was the third time she'd said it. I hoped she was right and that she wasn't just saying it to persuade me that I'd made the right decision. It would take a lot more than me simply loving a place to convince me I had. I'd loved the mines, after all, and I'd just given them up. "I hope so. And I promise you, I won't just live off you. I'll find work as soon as I can. I have no idea what I'll do, but I'll find something. I won't be a burden."

"You're my daughter. You will never be a burden. You can take your time, explore, see all there is to see, then decide what you want to do. You can work in the movies, if you'd like. Or there is a large limestone quarry where you can get all the carving stone you could possibly want. I know there is a market for your carvings. Not many of the dwarves in Leitham carve. I'll ask Radier to write to Aramis's father and ask him if he can come to Leitham to fix your shoulder, too, which should broaden your options."

"Do you think he will?"

"I'm afraid I don't know him at all, so I can't say. But Radier can be persuasive when he wants to, and he's taken a liking to you. I doubt Aramis's father would have a chance to say no. I need to get back to do some more recording. Will you be all right by yourself?"

"If you have more ale, I'll be fine."

Mam smiled. "There is plenty in the kitchen."

I sat alone watching the fire long after she left. My brothers were idiots. They could keep me away from the house, they could even keep my first emeralds, but I wouldn't let them ruin this opportunity for me. When else would I get another chance to travel, explore, spend time with Aramis? Best of all, I would finally get to know Mam. I might return, eventually, if Da or my brothers changed.

"Mabel!" Max pounded on the door.

I ran to the door and let him in. "What are you doing here? Da will kick you out too if he catches you."

"That's why I have to make this quick." He dropped two large leather bags onto the floor by the door. "Your things, as much as I could salvage, including your first emeralds."

I threw my arms around him, sling and all, and hugged him as tight as I could. "Thank you, thank you, thank you."

"It isn't all there. Da collected your things and burned most of them. I had the emeralds and the carving of the elf before Da got home. I didn't save all your books, but some of them are there, and some of your clothes, and your axes, mining and throwing, including the ones from the tribute at The Bearded Prospector. I know you probably won't mine or throw axes anymore, but I hope they will at least give you good memories. And they're yours. It's the best I could do."

So that's where he'd gone. He hadn't abandoned me, he'd gone to salvage my things before Da got home. "This is more than I could have ever asked for."

"I have to go. I'll try and get them to change their

minds, but I can't promise anything. Write to me and let me know where I can reach you. Address the letters to me at the trading post. I'll go there as often as I can."

"I will." I started to cry. "Thank you for not hating me."

"I could never hate you. You're my baby sister. I have to go. Don't forget to write. I really am sorry."

"Me too." I kissed Max on the cheek. He did the same and gave me one more squeeze before disappearing out the door. I hoped he would be all right, and Da wouldn't know where he'd gone. I missed him already.

I carried my bags to my room and dumped them onto my bed. Max had managed to salvage quite a bit. All my emeralds were there: my firsts and all the others I had earned and saved. He had saved my hairbrush, the one he'd used on me after my injury—a trivial item that held such positive memories—a handful of tunics and trousers, the books I had copied from the library, and *Living Your Authentic Life*.

What would Dr. Thaddeus say about my predicament?

I curled up on my chair by the fire and opened the book. There was the first list of what I'd wanted out of life that Dr. Thaddeus had me write at the beginning of the book. Top of the list: *a mate*. I still wanted one, but not right now. Certainly not as immediately as Da thought I should have one. I looked forward to exploring careers. Of course I would look forward to it more if Da and my brothers weren't so cold to me. I had the opportunity of a lifetime ahead of me and I had no intention of wasting it, no matter what Da or my brothers thought I should have or want. I'd listed *getting promoted to the diamond mines* second. True, I loved mining, but mining is all I'd ever known. Now I wanted to see if any other career suited me, one that didn't involve working under a mountain. *Dwarflings* were the third and last on my list. I think I had written it because female dwarves are supposed to want dwarflings. But if I wanted to work in the diamond mines, I wouldn't have the time to have dwarflings. Now I could take them or leave them. Maybe if I ever found a mate, in Leitham or wherever I ended up, I would want a mate and dwarflings and to mine again. I couldn't imagine never mining again, but trying something else could be fun, for a while.

I flipped to where the third list should have been. The page was still blank. I didn't know what I wanted. Everything was gone. I had to start over, from nothing, and I had no idea where to begin. How could Dr. Thaddeus help me achieve the true desires of my heart if I didn't know what they were?

"Oh good, you're still up," Mam said, closing the door behind her.

I shut my book and covered it with my hand and arm. She may be friends with elves, but she didn't need to know I read books by elves. "Max came by earlier," I said. "He brought me some of my things.

He'd salvaged what he could before Da burned them."

"Oh, Mabel." Mam sighed.

"It's okay. At least one of my brothers hasn't disowned me." Funny how the two Da tried to protect the most from Mam were the most accepting of her and this whole situation.

"He'll help them see sense, eventually," Mam said. "Aramis is here to see you. He's in the back garden."

I stifled a grin, but inside my heart leapt up and down. My Aramis had come to see me. I walked as casually as I could to my room to drop off my book, quickly run my brush through my hair, and make sure my beard and braids were neat. Oops. I'd forgotten I had no beard. Thank the gods Aramis was an elf. Hopefully he wouldn't mind. Then I sauntered to the back door where I hesitated, inhaled a deep, calming breath, and stepped outside.

The house backed onto the steep slope of the mountain where a three-foot terrace had been cut to create a narrow garden the length of the house, bordered by a stone retaining wall.

Aramis sat on the wall, his hair shining in the twilight. "Good evening, Mabel." He hopped off the wall and leaned against it.

If there had been chairs, I would have offered him a seat, but there were none, only an axe-throwing post at one end of the terrace. If he didn't have a place to sit, he might leave, which was the last thing

I wanted. I could have offered him to go inside, but Mam was there, and he had chosen to be outside, so I hoped that meant he wanted to speak to me privately. I had a sudden flash. He had come to sack me from the movie. He hadn't before because he hadn't wanted to do it in public. "Hi."

"I wanted to see how you were, after what happened with your father," he said. There was no judgment in his voice. He was concerned, as a friend. And somehow, I had the feeling, he understood me and how I felt at that very moment; so alone, empty, lost, without the family that had been so important in my life. What happened to him? I wanted to know how he understood me just as Max had when we saw *The Goldminer's Daughter* together.

"I am sorry our presence has created such turmoil in your life," he said.

"I chose to audition. It's no one's fault but my own. You're going to kick me off the movie, aren't you?"

He furrowed his brow for a moment. "Not at all. What made you think I would?"

Oh thank the gods. "You sacked Emma, and after what happened today, I thought…"

"Ah. No." He looked away, as if he were embarrassed about sacking her. "It was an excuse to remove Emma. She was too much of a nuisance. I am sorry, I know she is your friend."

I tilted my head, looking up at him. "No, she's not. She was, but we haven't been for a while." It felt

strange saying the words out loud. I'd thought them
for some time, questioning the friendship I had with
Emma, but saying we were no longer friends made it
so final, and in my heart I knew it to be true.

"What happened?"

"She poisoned me, and she told my da I'm in the
movie."

"Ouch. Not exactly the behavior of a friend."

"No." It was so comfortable talking with Aramis.
I had no need for him to fix my problems, or give me
advice. Somewhere in the last few weeks, or maybe
only minutes, we had become friends. He was no
longer Aramis the actor I was infatuated with, he was
Aramis, my friend, whom I loved.

"I know today has been the worst day you have
ever had," he said.

"One of them, yes." The day I blew out my shoulder at Regionals wasn't too far off.

"But I am pleased you will be coming to Leitham
with us. I think you will love it."

"Do you?" I joined him at the wall.

"I do."

"I mean, do *you* love Leitham?" I looked into his
beautiful blue eyes.

"I do." He held my gaze. "It has everything anyone could ever want. So many opportunities. It is a
wonderful place to start over, if that is what you wish
to do."

"Did you choose to start over?"

Sadness tinged his eyes. It reminded me of the

time Mikey told me why he quit throwing axes. "I did."

I held his hand, my tiny one in his, and gave a little squeeze. "Will you tell me about it some time?"

"If you like." He tucked a stray strand of hair behind my ear. "I am definitely pleased you will be coming to Leitham." He bent down and kissed my cheek, his lips soft, his breath warm and moist on my skin.

CHAPTER 22

THE KISS. The *kiss*. Small, short, one a friend would give another. Still. He *kissed* me.

I touched my cheek where Aramis had kissed me two days earlier, and bit my bottom lip. The best part of all of this, he wanted me in Leitham.

I packed the last of my things into the bag Max had brought me. "That's everything," I said to Mam. I'd caught her smiling non-stop the last few days. I hated leaving my friends without saying goodbye, but they must have agreed with my da, believing the worst of me, that I would align myself with a thief. I hadn't seen any of them since Da disowned me.

I tossed my bag into her wagon. Time to forget my friends and family and focus on my new adventure. Together we threw the animal-skin cover over top.

"Mabel, wait." Jimmy ran up the drive.

Oh sure, now my friends come, or one friend, anyway. The others probably made him come to say a token goodbye once they heard I was leaving. "Mam, this is Jimmy."

"Nice to meet you," she said. "I'll check to make sure we've got everything." Mam disappeared inside.

"I've been looking everywhere for you. Your brothers wouldn't tell me where you were. I finally found the elf and he told me where to find you."

Why would Jimmy be looking for me?

"Aramis?" I asked.

"No, the other one."

"Antinae?"

"Yeah. Him."

"Her," I said.

"He's a she? Oops."

"I didn't know for the longest time either."

"Well, *she* told me where to find you."

I didn't have time for this. Every moment I stayed here I felt like I was cracking under the weight of the pain and my failures. If I didn't leave soon I would shatter and never recover. "What do you want, Jimmy?"

"Don't go, Mabel." He reached for me.

What? Don't do this to me, Jimmy. I turned away from him, tying down the cover as best I could with one arm. "I have to."

"No, you don't."

"You heard what my da said. My family doesn't want me here. They'll kick me out of Gilliam if I don't go on my own. And even if they let me stay, I wouldn't have anywhere to live."

"Forget your da and your brothers. You can live with me."

I pulled the ties tight. "Your family wouldn't want me living with them."

"They would, but I'm not talking about living with my family. I talked to one of my uncles. He's on the Gilliam real-estate board and he has a small place he can sell me."

Sweet Jimmy. I can't believe I spent so much time being upset with him for trying to help me after Regionals. If I could do it over again, I would. He was clearly my only true friend. He was the only one who came to look for me. He was the only one who tried to find a way for me to stay, even though he hadn't thought through the dire consequences for himself if I did.

I shifted one of our bags that poked up too far as I walked around to the other side of the wagon. I pulled the skin tight and kept tying. "It's very kind of you, but I won't bring you shame."

Jimmy followed me. "Stop. Look at me." He held my left hand. He had wonderfully strong hands, his fingers were perfectly calloused brushing against the back of my hand, and he had the beautiful smell of a deep mountain mine. "Don't you know?" He looked into my eyes. "You don't know. I thought... Mabel,

I love you."

Jimmy? That wasn't possible. Sure, he'd carried my bag for me, complimented me, and he was always there for me. But he'd always been that way. He'd also told Mikey and Frankie about the sludge I'd been taking to kill my shoulder pain. He'd done it because he was my friend. A good friend, not like Emma. When had it changed from friendship to something more?

Was that why he'd been so desperate for me to forgive him? To like him? How could he love me when I had been too selfish and self-absorbed to notice? I had done nothing to encourage him. We'd just been friends. That's all.

"I'm not a mountain dweller," he said. "The house is only a small cottage and might be all I can ever offer you, but I'm a hard worker, and a decent miner. You know I am. I will always love you. I will give you everything you could ever want, and more. Your da can threaten all he wants, but if you'll be my mate, then I'll be your family and he's powerless."

I could. I could stay with him. I didn't need a mountain dwelling. I'd have a home and a fellow who loved me. But mining. Even if the chief foreman allowed me into the mines, my shoulder still needed to be healed, and I shivered at the idea of spending all my days under the mountain.

He caressed my stubbly cheek. He didn't mind that I didn't have a beard or that it would take months for it to grow back. He'd said it. He thought I was perfect the way I was. Wasn't that what I'd always wanted from a fellow? For him to tell me he loved me even if my beard was scraggly, I wasn't stout enough, and my voice was too high? Jimmy had said all of it to me.

"Please stay, Mabel. You can mine as long as you want, and we can have as many dwarflings as you want."

And then there were those. I couldn't mate and not have dwarflings. It would break his heart. "I don't think I want any," I said quietly.

"You've always wanted… It's all you and Emma ever talked about."

"I know, but, I don't, or I don't think I do. Not yet, maybe. Or not ever. I don't know."

"It's your shoulder. We don't have to have dwarflings right away. We can wait until you're healed. Whatever you want."

"I won't heal here. There is a possibility I can get the right healing in Leitham. But it's more than that. Since Regionals, I've hated working in the mountain. I love being outside, the trees, and the birds. And I love working on the movie with Radier. I get to carve when things are slow. It isn't boring. Mining is so tedious. I know it's horrible for me to say that. I know I'm a disgrace to all miners. I may come back, some day, when my shame has lessened." I grasped his hands. "You're my best friend. I am so sorry. If things were different, if it were a few months ago, before Regionals, before…" Movies.

"It can be that way again. Don't go, Mabel. Or go, get healed, and come back to me. I don't care about dwarflings, or if you never mine again. I love *you*, Mabel. I just want to be with you. Please."

Did he really love me that much? "I don't—"

"What do you want? Anything. You name it, I will give it to you."

"I don't know, Jimmy. I just know that I won't find it here."

"You don't know that, Mabel."

"I know that if I stay, I'll have no friends. I know that I don't like mining, but it is the only career I'm allowed to have. I know that everything I do doesn't meet what is expected of me. I don't know who I am or what I really want. I know I will never figure that out while I'm constantly trying to fit myself into someone else's idea of who I am."

"Let me figure it out with you," Jimmy said.

"Your friendship. Your faith in me. Your love. It means the world to me, Jimmy. It does. But if I stay, I'd be asking too much of you. I can't do that to you." I could feel whatever emotional shell that was holding me together crack. "Come with me. Come now, or follow us. Meet me in Leitham." Even if we didn't make it as a couple, we would always be friends. I wouldn't be so alone.

"I can't," he said. "My life is here. *Our* life is *here*."

I couldn't stay and bring him shame. If he loved me he would come with me, or find me in Leitham.

He loved who I was, not who I am.

"Mine isn't. Not anymore. I am so sorry." I climbed onto the driver's seat before Jimmy could stop me. "Mam, I'm ready,"

Moments later, Mam sat beside me, reigns in hand. "Are you sure?"

I hesitated a moment. My emotional shell had stopped breaking. "I am."

Mam snapped the reins and the horses stepped forward. As we turned off the drive onto the main road, I looked back to wave goodbye to Jimmy only to see him undoing the braids in his beard.

I faced forward, my strength, my resolve growing. Everything would be all right once I got to Leitham. I'd know my mam. I'd be healed. I'd figure out what I was really meant to do, who I really was.

I grinned. I couldn't wait!

Did you enjoy Mabel the Lovelorn Dwarf?

Mabel's advenutres have just begun!

Visit the link below for three exclusive stories of Mabel's quest for love and the desires of her heart, special offers, news on release dates, and more, FREE, just for signing up!

Visit now: www.dwarvenamazon.com

About the Author

Sherry Peters attended the Odyssey Writing Workshop and holds an M.A. in Writing Popular Fiction from Seton Hill University. When she isn't writing, she loves to have adventures of her own including spending a year working in Northern Ireland. *Mabel the Lovelorn Dwarf* is her first novel. For more information on Sherry, visit her website at www.dwarvenamazon.com.

CPSIA information can be obtained at www.ICGtesting.com
Printed in the USA
LVOW13s0608090714

393433LV00002B/15/P